WORMWOOD

WORMWOOD

Trauma and
Snacks
at the End
of Days

NICKOLAS PAULLUS

NICKAARONPAUL

Revelations

Revelations: 10-11

The third angel sounded his trumpet, and a great star, blazing like a torch, fell from the sky on a third of the rivers and on the springs of water. The name of the star is Wormwood…

-St John (The Elder)

$$+\,+$$

"Surely, this must be the end."

The words could have easily been Andy's own.

Andy stood behind a worn mahogany bar, a grip on a glass like he wished he had a grip on himself. He swirled the ice, watched the water slosh like an angry sea with nowhere to go but back in on itself. He watched the cherry, severed and red. Did it pulse, as it lay somewhere between floating and sinking?

A man stood, a statue in front of Andy. He stared at Andy's hands, ravenous. Ever nimble, Andy's fingers went through the motions. He peeled the orange, misted the glass, and the air, with its oil.

He then lifted the glass, looked but didn't see. On the other side, a full bar stared at him. Andy, however, only saw himself, bent in the curvature of the glass.

"You done?" the man asked, eyes fixed on the old fashioned.

Andy looked at the drink, and felt its weight.

"Ya. I'm done," he said.

He downed the drink and walked from behind the bar, out the front door.

He didn't think he walked far, but he couldn't have walked further. City blocks defy dimension. They curve in on themselves, paths with no end, especially after a night of drinking.

On nights like these, roads never wind up where they are supposed to. They seem motivated to lead people where they want them to go (which is almost always where the people don't want to be lead).

Andy didn't trust where his own feet would lead him, so he resigned himself to let the road guide him.

On this night, however, the streets didn't have much control over where Andy was going. They wanted it. They would have lead him past old heartbreaks. They would have lead him to where he could buy little baggies of white powder. Heck, maybe they would have led him to a bridge. But again, the *streets* weren't leading Andy anywhere.

Andy found himself lost.

Well, he didn't find himself much of anywhere. He was the kind of lost only drunks find themselves in. Lost to time and space, lost to themselves. Lost in a way that only cops, hungry animals and God can sniff out.

He thought he was near 5th Street. South 5th or North 5th didn't make much difference right now, because knowing even that much meant he just wasn't lost enough.

Damn it. When you want to lose yourself, any inkling of where you are means you're not far enough gone. A baker's dozen cocktails and he still sort of slightly recognized landmarks. *FUCK.*

He just wanted to get away. From himself. From what happened, from what hadn't happened, and no doubt what was about to happen. He pushed even the thought of the thoughts from his mind.

"Fucking shit," he muttered to himself.

Andy *was* mired in some serious shit. So mired, in fact, that he forgot that the Universe dreams a glorious garden's growth in even the dankest of turds.

The dankest, drunkest of turds.

Andy was drunk, of that much he had no doubt. He wasn't sure of much, if he was honest. Maybe four things in all:

He was sure that he was sad.
He was sure that he was hurt.
He was sure that he was lost.
He was sure that he was drunk.

A mantra, Andy enumerated these Four Not-So-Noble Truths for blocks and blocks. It gave him a little pep in his step, despite the toxicity of the sentiment.

His high was halted, however, by in the involuntary stopping of his steps. Well, it felt involuntary on behalf of body, but something deep down had clearly volunteered him.

He stood still, silent. Waited.

Waited for, what? *Is that...? Was that... a song?*

The melody drifted on the wind, danced among the light poles.

Andy was now sure of five things.

Andy was sure he heard the most beautiful song he could imagine in that moment.

The melody was hopeful, heavy. Vulnerable. The singing of the sort that is a gift lovingly crafted. A sure song, a sultry song, a spirited song.

It was so close, yet so far. Just enough out of reach to be enticing.

Andy thought he heard "night" and "reveal," perhaps even "portent," but much of the rest was muffled on the maze from mouth to ear.

He still couldn't see the singer, but Andy felt them. Felt the sway, the love, the vibrations, as the voice would come back, time and again, with a resonant "Vermouth."

"Vermouth Vermouth *VERMOUTH.*"

A heartsong, with Andy's name tattooed on its chest.

"Vermut Vermut *VERMUT*."

Truly, no sweeter words could be uttered.

"Wermud Wermud WERMUD."

There's a point in all intoxication where the intoxicant starts to lead itself. Drunkenness seeks drink, high reaches higher. As if God reassembles itself, in the act of like seeking like. A distillation, where alcohol is trying to alchemize itself.

"Wormwood Wormwood *WORMWOOD*."

The song stopped. Silence.

Andy turned a corner. There stood an old fountain, a shapeless mass of swoops and swirls, chipped and worn. Perhaps enough water to bathe a lonely bird. Upon it lay a bouquet of flowers, discounted, a spray painted $5 clearance bouquet from the grocery store.

A man, dressed in neither red nor brown, stood beside the fountain. He wasn't dirty, but he wasn't quite clean, at once dapper and dingy. He was tall, stretched in fact, and even his thin mustache seemed to be lanky.

And there was a bottle too, neither red nor brown, that swung back and forth in his hands.

Unmistakable, Andy's mind whispered, as if the man could hear his thoughts.

"Ho! Vermouth, you say?" Andy bowed, perhaps a bit too proper.

"Is that what I said?" asked the man.

"Well, its part of what you said. I couldn't hear the rest really. But I liked it! You've got an amazing talent." *Flattery*.

"Much thanks," the man bowed. "And OK, yes, yes, that's what I was singing. You see," he motioned to the sky, "on this night of nights, I was singing a hymn to him! A hymn to him! Singing a Holy Song to the Holy Star Wormwood, asking for gentleness on this eve of Apocalypse."

"OK," was all Andy could muster, as he continued to creep forward, one step at a time.

"My friend! Haven't you heard? Haven't you read? It's

been said! In the Bible no less! That the fallen star Wormwood will mark the Apocalypse, bittering the waters! Wormwood. Wermud. *Vermut.* Oh my sweet red vermouth, I knew you were fallen from heaven the moment I laid lips on you!"

The man held the bottle close, swaddled in his dust.

"Oh whoa, crazy." *Like, really crazy,* Andy thought. "No, I've never heard that! That's a cool story for sure though!" Andy strained to feign interest in the ramblings of the clearly kooky man.

His arm reached out for the bottle, despite his normal propensity for decorum when it came to weird drunk preachers on the street.

"Cheers?" he squeaked as he grabbed the bottle out of the man's hand.

"Wait a second boy! Didn't you hear me? I said Apocalypse. End of Days. The World torn asunder! Is that the flavor you're looking for?"

"I'm already there."

Andy struggled with the cork. It popped open with a formidable hiss, and the noise glanced off the marble fountain. The air stilled, and Andy took a more than sizable swig.

"Cheers," whispered the man.

Vermouth

There was a flash of light, a wall of trumpets. Andy didn't know what brimstone smelled like, but he was pretty sure this was it. Acrid and sharp, like burnt hair, with notes of clove and currant berries.

Lightning cracked the sky, and the clouds parted. Down descended a blazing star, at once human and celestial. It, no *he*, was red; a warm luminous light from the inside out. Or from the outside in. For he was the skies and the skies were he.

The glowing man was vaguely threatening, and Andy was vaguely worried the impact would not so vaguely incinerate him. Despite this, he couldn't keep his eyes from the falling star as it neared and came into focus.

It was absolutely, unequivocally, the same guy he had just grabbed the bottle from (who was now conveniently missing). Same suit, same creepy mustache. Just now with a glow, as he floated down towards the ground below.

He alighted gently on the fountain in front of Andy.

"And so what? Does this make *you* Vermouth? Wormwood embodied, or some angelic shit like that?"

"It is so!" hollered the man to a fanfare of trumpets.

"So you're trying to tell me, you were heralding your *own* coming?" asked Andy.

"Hey now! Its precedent to announce your own coming!

Jesus himself, famously proclaimed his very own coming! So yes! I am coming! In fact, I have come!"

"Ugh," Andy felt dirty, "And what, pray tell, have you come for?" Andy asked, not sure if he wanted to know.

"For you Andrew! Oh sad bartender guy, wandering the alleys in the middle of the night! I have come to relieve you of your pain! The Great Shift is at hand! The Time of End, and the End of Time! The Apocalypse is *NOW. NOW. NOW!*"

Andy had to admit, the echo was effective.

"The Apocalypse? Like lava, locusts, and blood running down the streets? The Apocalypse like demons and angels fighting for the heart of the world?" It all sounded rather exhausting to Andy.

"I'm not so sure it'll look like that. And not the heart of the world, likely just your heart," Vermouth said.

"So you're here to help me drink away my pain, as the world descends into endless night?"

"Not quite. A little bit, yes. But no, no! Not quite. In truth, I'm really just a messenger, here to announce the Second Coming!" he said triumphantly.

"One coming was enough thank you," Andy countered.

"Not my Second Coming Andy! *Your* second coming."

"Come again?"

"Exactly," snickered Vermouth.

"Wait, so its *my* rebirth."

"Or re-death, its hard to say right now. I don't honestly know what's going to happen."

"So you come here, pronounce the end of days and then claim to not know anything? Can't you tell me anything?" Andy shook his head. "Some angel..."

"First, I'm a star, not an Angel, thank you very much. Stinky lot, those Angels, especially when you get their feathers wet. Second, I truly don't have much more for you. I'm just here to announce the End, not to elaborate on it. I mean, frankly, *NO ONE* can know how your End ends! That's for *you* to find out."

"My End? Like there is more than one Apocalypse?" Andy's mind spun at the thought.

"It's Apocalypse, every moment, of everyday. Just, for someone different at each and every second. Hell and Rapture are dancing in perpetuity. You've just been lucky until now because it wasn't your turn. But now your tick has tocked, my friend. And no use trying to beg and get out of it. Everybody has to go through it! This moment sort of defines the human experience."

"OK, sure. I guess I can accept that. I've watched the news. I get that everyone has their own little hell. But certainly, there's got to be something you can tell me! Tell me there's an Apocalypse coming, and you don't even tell me how or when! Stress a guy out why don't ya."

"How? Hmm I wonder *how*," the star was lost in thought.

"Well, I think it's kinda interesting that I came to you as a bottle of alcohol. That's gotta mean something, right? Maybe it just means you're a drunk. That's totally in the realm of possibility. But, I just know I've never been an actual, literal, bottle of Vermouth before. A big green Wormwood bush on fire, sure, I could see that! But not a bottle of booze," Vermouth caressed his curves as he talked.

"And I didn't say I don't know when. I know exactly when your Apocalypse is going to happen. Give or take a couple days."

Silent, Andy stared at Vermouth.

"OK, fine." Vermouth lifted the grocery store bouquet from the fountain, "When the last petal, from the last flower, in this grocery store clearance bouquet store falls. That, Andy, is when you fall."

Am I the beauty, or am I the beast? thought Andy.

"No one's ever bought me flowers, so I don't even know how long one of those bouquets will last," Andy stifled a sob.

"Five to seven days, depending on if you use this little packet of crystals that comes with it," Wormwood flicked the bouquet's little drug bag as if he'd done it once or twice.

"Well come on now! That's easy! Dump her in!" *No brainer!*

"Now hold on a second. Seven days of pre-Apocalyptic visitations? Angels and Demons wooing your soul for a whole week is bound to be pretty exhausting."

Andy paused. He felt tired. He was always tired. Maybe he should just skip to the climax, get the dang thing over with.

"I'll follow your lead."

"Good call kid. Five days it is," he said, tossing the little baggie over his shoulder.

Vermouth set the flowers on the fountain, and disappeared in a blaze. And as the blaze faded, Andy was left, alone in the dark.

+The 1st Day+

Andy woke up to the sound of birds. Lots of birds. Too many birds.

A bevy of bushtits scrounged the ground around him. Upon waking, this was more than enough to make him freak the fuck out.

"Gahhhh!" he screamed, as he shook his wet noodle arms at the birds. The tips of the wet noodles, his fingers, looked a little too much like earthworms and one of the birds pecked at him.

"Ack!" He hid his arms under his body.

Half asleep. Half dreaming. But half awake? Not sure yet...

The street came into focus, the bouquet of flowers sat on the fountain.

Oh Jesus, was I going to drunkenly bring her flowers, he thought. *No, those flowers were given to you,* he heard, from a little deeper within.

Andy sat up and surveyed his surroundings. He was pretty sure he was on South 5th Street. That was at least a reasonable guess. And if Andy's intuition served him right, there was a bad ass little espresso bar, two blocks in one of the four possible directions. Which, was hard to say.

He had honed his coffee shop radar to a science. An art. When pressed, he could precisely pinpoint a pour-over despite any multitude of nefarious smells. He, the scent hound, and the cortado his opossum.

Sniff.

Sniff.

Sniff.

Gott'er.

Andy would have loved to run, but his legs disagreed. They were sore, they were stiff.

He knew his brain was in desperate need of aid, however, so he began to walk. With each step, his synapses tried to reassemble all the things. But the things, whatever they were, were all so broken, and there were just so many of them.

He still wasn't quite sure what happened last night. He remembered drinking Vermouth with that vagabond. That was certain (and certainly a misstep).

He also remembered seeing the craziest shooting star. Bright, maybe blinding. So much so, it hurt his eyes.

Not just his eyes, he hurt everywhere. Outside and in.

In front of the coffee shop were those tenacious bushtits again. The little birds were cute, and oh so fluffy. They were all joy and feathers, and hopped to and fro, eating whatever microscopic vittles the concrete afforded.

But, they seemed a bit out of place. *More at home in a meadow or in a bush*, thought Andy. Country birds, not city birds.

Still, they brought a spark of life to the muted grays of the city-scape.

Despite this inherent adorability, however, Andy again screamed when he saw them. Not fearful, but totally involuntary. And quite loud. The girl at the table by the window found it quite scary, jumped and nearly overturned her latte.

"Go away!" Andy yelled at the birds, as he gripped the door handle.

Andy stepped into the most glorious smell he could imagine.

He woke that morning with a nose full of spray paint, burrito wrappers and bushtit turds, so the smell of the grinder was an actual Godsend.

"Howdy," Baristo said from behind the counter. *They* self identified as a Baristo. Often. It was important to them, and Andy respected that, even if they were the only Baristo Andy had ever met.

Baristo chatted amicably enough with the lady they were making a latte for. They asked good questions, showed genuine interest in plot development, and laughed at the requisite parts. A darn good customer service representative.

Andy couldn't help, however, noticing their eyes returning to Andy, time and again. And it didn't feel like in a good way. *Nobody could find me attractive this morning*, thought Andy. So that wasn't it.

"That's awesome. I'm so glad to hear that ma'am. Congratulations."

The woman said something Andy couldn't make out, and turned towards the door.

"Tell your son I say hi!" said Baristo.

As the woman walked past Andy, he felt himself propelled forward, not entirely by his own volition.

"How you doing my friend?" asked Baristo, edged with more than a little concern.

"I feel like shit. Probably look like shit too, based on your all too obvious appraisal," Baristo didn't disagree. "But I know exactly what I need, and that's why I came to you dear friend. A cappuccino please. I need fluffy clouds. Pillows of foam! Aerate that milk baby. Aerate my heart."

Baristo turned to the grinder.

Andy took a moment to look over Baristo, who was always impeccably dressed, "Also, I love that tree-bark hoodie, it totally makes you look jungle as shit. Very cool."

"Thanks babe, I love it. It really ties together that Baristo chic. Tres Organique," Baristo struck a mean pose as they deftly steamed the milk.

The foam was dancing just right, and Baristo poured it over the shot, carving out a swan or a leaf, or perhaps a swan sleeping under a leaf.

All that was left of the milk was what was stuck to the inside of pitcher. Baristo ran their finger along the inside, and sucked the foamed off their finger.

"And one for the help," said Baristo with a sultry smile. "Would you like one of our amaranth bars this morning? Its an oh so fancy Rice Krispy Treat."

"Absolutely. Easy sell," Andy said, as he handed over a reasonable pile of wadded singles.

"It was really good to see you," they added. "Enjoy your drinkie-poo babe!"

"I already am," Andy said, as the foam touched his lip.

Cappuccino

The lights faded as Baristo pulled up their cool woody-brown hoodie. As the hood reached their head, Andy couldn't help but notice all of Baristo's facial hair was growing at what seemed like a breakneck pace.

In fact, all their hair was growing that way. Little tufts of fur poofed out of the arms of the comically tight hipster hoodie.

Wiry, brown. Primitive, in the literal sense.

And it all came back, like a wave. The simian smiled at Andy's comprehension.

"And this would make you Cappuccino I suppose," he noted the brown cloak. "Brother Cappuccino? Sister Cappuccino?" It was hard to feign confidence with a cute, yet unnerving, ape in front of him.

"I would prefer Sibling Cappuccino, if you don't mind."

"Sibling, totally. But Holy Hell! Sibling! That means, that wasn't a dream last night," Andy shook his head. "Or wait, is this *still* a dream? And I'm only half awoken. Half awakened. Half awook?"

Is this, really, the end of days? Andy thought.

"So you're here to what, fight for my soul or something?" Andy didn't know what came next.

The Monkey held up their hands, "Hey now, nobody is fighting here. Or there are no hostilities on *my* part, at least.

No, everyone just gets to share their piece. And you get to decide your fate from there. We're just here to provide a little context. Sort of like cosmic narrators for your transformation. Give voice to the trauma, give form to your fall."

"Yeah, but why are you a monkey?" Andy couldn't help but ask the obvious.

"Come on now! Capuchin Monks? Capuchin Monkeys? Cappuccino?" Andy stared blankly. "And to think, I thought I was being super clever!" they pouted.

There's nothing sadder than a frowning monkey, thought Andy.

"I mean, I *want* to get it. I just didn't know that Capuchins were monks. I thought they were just cute little, *eep,* monkeys," Andy couldn't help but squeal as he looked at the monkey monk's cute little monkey monk face.

"Oh ya, monkeys named after monks. Coffee drinks named after monks. Or was the coffee named after the monkeys? Hard to say. They *claim* it's just a color thing, since you know, we are all *brown,*" the Monkey spat the word out.

"Not *just* brown though. Its divine resemblance! Analogy baby. Metaphysical metaphors abound on this plane! Everything is connected," the Monkey Monk waved its lanky arms mystically, if that's a way arms can be waved.

"Let's go all the way back, to the original primate. The progenitor to my species. The original Capooch, if you will. He is who am I representing today in this meeting, actually. I am merely your latte liaison."

"That'd be Father Capuchin?"

"Pretty much. Great dude from Assissi, he went by the name Francis. *Loved* animals, like in a very real way. Could talk a wolf down from eating a sheep, so deep was his love," the Monkey's eyes shined.

"It was real. It was profound. It was powerful. People came from near and far to have him bless their ducks and marry their goats. It's why he is the patron saint of animals. The horse whispering Angel, a God of the garden!"

"Oh I know who you're talking about now! The little metal statue guy! I always see him in old lady's yards with the birds perched on his shoulder!"

"The one and only! Francis was also the Patron saint of ecological responsibility."

"Makes sense. Birds are absolutely ecological," Andy nodded.

"And *all* of Italy," added Monkey.

"I guess the Pope of Pizza would have to be environmentally inclined, ya know?"

The Monkeys face grew serious. "And stowaways."

"Um, OK. I guess so?" Andy was unsure. "But whatever, they totally need one! I always thought it'd be super scary to hide inside a barrel. And it's good to have someone looking over you when scurvy is a really real possibility."

"But that's oddly specific though, right? A Holy Man to look after the very small demographic of people? Specifically, people who travel across water, that don't want to pay for the fare. How curious that they deserve their own guardian."

"Right. Like I said, that sounds terrifying. Well deserving," Andy reiterated.

"Everything deserves its own Divinity, Andy. And God, being super duper all powerful, did just that," the Monkey's spread their arms wide. "We are talking old school animism here. Everything has an equal piece of the world soul! Spirits of every ilk, my dude! We're talking paperclip Gods. Navy Angels. Glass Blowing goddesses. We got daemons representing every type of butterfly and moth you could imagine. Astroturf Spookies, Textbook Monks, and Alley-Cat spirits. I could go on and on, because it goes on and on. Existence is *fully* full to the brim, my friend," Monkey didn't seemed burdened by the weight of it. Maybe even enlivened by it.

"But *your* universe, it seems, is dominated by taste. You're a tongue forward sort of fella if I do say so," they winked at Andy. "And so, from what I can tell, you shall be tempted by all manners of food and beverage spirits in the days to come. It sounds kinda yummy, honestly! Especially when compared to like, St John's Apocalypse. Who the fuck wants beasts, and seals, and curses, when you can have Baklava?" Monkey licked their lips.

"So every time I eat, I'm going to have some transcendental experience! Sweet! That doesn't sound half bad, minus the whole leading to the end of days thing," the weight of oblivion was not lost upon Andy, but it did sound delicious.

"Understand this Andy, it may be peaceful, informative and delicious for a bit. I promise you though, the hell raisers *will* come forth. They love building suspense, but they will show their faces, mark my words," Andy marked them, truly he highlighted them. Lest he forget what end of days was likely to mean.

"I appreciate you, really I do," confided Andy. "It's been super informative, but I'm a little worried you haven't given me enough."

"Not enough?" Monkey asked through gritted teeth.

"Not enough, I don't know, Good Angel guidance? Like, you've taught me a lot about demonology and stowaways and Monks. Don't get me wrong, it's been great. But shouldn't you, like, guide me on how I am supposed to become the ultimate bastion of goodness or something? Maybe teach me how to conquer demons in the days to come? How will I best cope with the trials and tribulations of the next few days?"

"Oh Jesus, forgive me! I totally got carried away and pissed all my time away! I um, don't really have time for uh, well, much of a lecture on morality. Plus, you're really your own man. So it's not really for me to say."

Andy's eyes pleaded for more.

"Um, hmm. Hmm? Oh wait," Monkey rubbed their temples, "Francis is giving me a message for you. I think I have it. Yes. Yes, I'll tell him right away sir. Very good sir. Thank you sir."

Andy would do his darnedest to cling to every last syllable.

"He said, 'Be nice to animals.'"

+ +

Baristo lowered their hood, and the scene came back into focus. Houseplant, pour-over, woodblock print, nose ring, nose ring, nose ring.

Ooooh, cute toe ring.

Andy hadn't forgotten the Holy scene once it faded before his eyes. The brain, however, will naturally gravitate away from likely hallucinations, towards cute foot accessories, in order to maintain a modicum of sanity.

Andy looked at his cappuccino, dazed and allowed his feet to once again steer him onwards.

May fate and espresso guide me where they may.

Andy stepped outside and nearly upended a scrounging bushtit with the swinging door.

"Fucking bird!" Andy yelled at a more than audible level. That same woman at the window was likely to suffer from whiplash when the day was done.

Andy studied the bushtit, heart filled with as much compassion as he could muster.

And Andy saw the bushtit, it would seem, for the very first time. Saw its tiny little bushtit body hopping around on tiny little bushtit legs. He heard its little bushtit voice, knew its little bushtits dreams.

As Andy reached out to the bird in his mind, nay with his heart, he was sure the bushtit reached back.

"Fucking bird," he whispered, as he threw the seedy amaranth bar on the ground and walked down the block.

Andy was much more aware of the neighborhood now. It's not that he knew where he was. Not exactly. But he had driven on parallel streets! He'd been on proximal corners *more* than enough times! More than enough times, to be pretty sort of a little bit sure. Right?

5th street. For sure. Or maybe 4th now. Either way, right round those parts.

He knew if he kept this way (or perhaps that way), he would run into a street (which street?) he actually recognized.

Andy pulled out his phone, intent on pulling up a map. With 30 notifications and a miraculous full charge on his battery, however, Andy quickly forgot all about wayfinding.

He walked head down. Scrolled, read. Read, scrolled.

Of the 22 missed texts, exactly 13 were pictures of snails from his coworker Brian. Andy and Brian planned to make a bunch of t-shirts of snails playing recess games with the text "Slow Children at Play."

One particular slug Brian sent (not a snail, but hardly faster despite having lost the giant rock it was carrying on its back) looked like it would be particularly adept at tether ball with its ever so vertical eyes.

Andy looked up. He still didn't recognize the neighborhood. *Maybe I was further north than I thought I was,* he thought, as he walked past a building that seemed vaguely *not* unfamiliar.

Andy returned to his phone, and noticed two missing texts from *her.* He opened an extremely boring political survey, sent to him by a robot, instead of her text.

He was genuinely scared, especially considering he couldn't help but see "I'm worried" was how her message to him began.

She's worried? Andy thought to himself. *She could be worried about anything! She could be worried that I've been lying, which I have been. Or worried I'm going to quit my job, which I think I did. Or worried that I drink too much, which I do. But maybe she's just worried about her mom's dog and my existential dread isn't even on her fucking radar.* Didn't matter, Andy was not prepared to deal with *any* of her worries.

Andy realized he had answered "None of your fucking business," to all of the questions of the survey, and decided now was a good time to lift his head back up.

He wasn't sure where he wanted to be, but he was certain this wasn't it. Bleak apartments, cracked sidewalks. Not quite suburbia, but equally pallid and sad. Nothing remarkable, except a little blond girl on a bench with a bag of movie theater popcorn.

Weird, he thought, although he wasn't quite sure why he thought someone eating on a bench was odd.

Andy walked on, now distracted from his many doom-ridden existence by videos of a high flying Labrador named Louie. Andy had always considered himself a talent at the hibachi table, never one to miss a flying shrimp as it flew at him. Louie though, now Louie had a legit talent for catching food in mid-air. Owner would toss a snack, and Louie would tumble and twist his treat into submission.

Andy studied Louie's technique, intent as he walked down innumerable blocks.

It amazed Andy how many videos of dogs catching snacks there were on the internet. An entire treasure trove of training material, freely available whenever he needed it.

Social media is a beautiful thing, he thought.

Andy's reverie was broken, when in his periphery he saw something more than a little unnerving. Andy passed a bench, in front of an old decrepit apartment. There was a girl on the bench, with a bag of popcorn.

Same girl. Same bench. Same, but emptier, bag of pop-corn. He'd walked more than a couple blocks, and was certain he hadn't made any turns.

Huh, he wasn't sure what to think.

Andy turned to face the girl. She looked at him, her face not unfamiliar. She looked at her bag, then right back at him.

"Want some?" she said, her head tilted towards the bag.

Andy felt like he wasn't ready to do this all over again. He felt tired. He felt hurt. He felt like he should probably deal with his messages on his phone. He felt like he should probably figure out where he was.

Most of all, though, Andy felt hungry.

"Boy do I," he said.

She tossed a few pieces, rapid fire, at Andy. Her aim was terrible, although a lot of that could be chalked up to popcorn's not so aerodynamic nature.

Despite that, however, Andy caught each and every one.

Louie the Labrador would have been proud.

Popcorn

Andy looked up and smiled. The girl grinned at him, very much in admiration of his snack catching prowess.

As if in acceptance of Andy's unspoken challenge, she began to throw more and more popcorn his direction.

The kernels, however, never made it to Andy's mouth. Stopped by some invisible force, they began to orbit around the girl. Broad ellipticals, a popcornian ring formed around her tiny body.

As she threw more and more popcorn (much more than a bag of its size would presumably hold), the orbit of the kernels began to take shape. The undulating mass of corn became a giant face. Ever changing, details blurred into each other. It was at once a single face, and all faces that had ever been. He saw his own face for a split second, as well as a myriad of others, as the kernels shifted and changed.

The face stopped growing, but kept changing. Its eyes fixed on Andy.

Here it comes, thought Andy, *Demon face talks about the evils of butter alternatives.*

"DID YOU KNOW," boomed the voice "THAT EVERY SNOWFLAKE IS COMPLETELY UNIQUE AND DIFFER-ENT?"

Not what I thought it was going to say, thought Andy.

Shook, Andy hesitated to respond, "....yes?"

"Yes? Yes!? Know this, foolish mortal! Snowflakes are late-comers in the lineage of most unique-est of things!" screamed the face. "Snowflakes are mere fetuses of freshness! At best, newborns of novelty!"

If the popcorn could pop again, it probably would have, "Do you think fragile little *SNOWFLAKES* were there at the beginning of time? Of course not. They weren't even invited! But we sure were!"

"Popcorn was there at the beginning of time?" Andy asked, incredulous.

"Of course! We were there at the beginning, and we are *here* at the end," the face paused, for effect. "We are chaos embodied, so we belong at the Alpha and Omega. For Creation is infinity and infinity is creation! Novelty is the one truth we can hold onto, in an ever changing cosmos. Each and every experience is utterly unique. There are no second chances, no repeats, no do overs. It all happens once and only once."

The popcorn seemed to admire itself, eyes turning inwards, "And what better beautiful body to exemplify that infinity than some fresh popped corn. We are singular, all tiny tears of eternity, and then we are transformed! Birthed of circumstance, of happenstance, we can be nothing but ourselves. Completely unique expressions based on heat, internal moisture, a multiplicity of factors. And so, there is no other like us! Each of us, eternity embodied in a seed. Infinite potential, infinite permutations!" Andy felt validated in his affection for the movie theater lobby.

"Whoa," he said.

"Whoa indeed! I see your black shirt! I see your black pants! I know you! You imagine 'chaos' in the cosmos. You think mere randomness brought you to this point. You believe that shit just happens. But that is not what chaos *means* my friend. You imagine anarchy loosed on the cosmos, but it is only anarchy if you ignore cause and effect. You assume randomness because there is no consistency. You deny the truth that change *is* the constant," at this, the face changed shapes yet again, this time the eyes less menacing.

"Look at your own life, you little Andy Christ, you. You were a seed. It would seem, just like all the other kernels. But given your relative proximity to the flame of life, the "climactic" conditions of the world around you, and then the amount of agitation in your pan, you popped as only you could. You are misshapen, yes, but beautifully so. Shaped as only you could be shaped. Chaos lives in you because you are without parallel," the face was smug.

"Ah I appreciate that. That's super sweet," Andy blushed, "but what does that do for me exactly? It sounds like even though everything is different, it's just fucking dominoes. Sounds a hell of a lot like destiny. Which means I don't have any say in what happens. Everything happens *to* me. So if that's the case, why even bother with this whole charade of choice? If I'm destined for the Devil, that's just the way it is."

"You're right. But honestly, the universe doesn't care what you are Andy. Creation revels in its infinite forms. It *likes* the weird shit. The universe sees angel and demon as just a couple kernels in a big ass bowl of deliciousness."

The face continued, "And bringing awareness to all of this isn't meant to help you make decisions. It's meant to help you be OK with the decisions that were made without your consent. It's meant to alleviate the pain of things happening *to* you. We are all products of what came before, and we can't stop what is happening to you. *But,* understanding cause and affect can help you begin to cope with being a victim of it," there was compassion in the white Styrofoam eyes.

"So I'm supposed to be cool with my lot in life, that's the lesson. Just take what I'm given, because I am just a product of time and space. Accept Apocalypse because it was mean to be. That way I can love myself, for the unique little snowflake I am," Andy's frustration got the better of him and he recognized his mistake too late.

"Excuse me?" boomed the face as it grew before Andy's eyes.

"Sorry! Sorry! I meant, so I'm a unique little kernel. Great. Each experience is unique, chaos wills it so. Neat. But what if instead of a beautiful fluffy white existence, I'm just one of those unpopped kernels burned to the bottom of the pot? Then what?"

Andy's sadness crept back as his anger deflated.

"Andy, dear boy," said the face, "I thought you would have known by now. The crispy unpopped kernels are the most delicious in the whole pot."

++

With black hole precision, the floating popcorn reinserted itself into the bag. Andy returned to himself, shaking off the planetary popcorn like it were commonplace.

"Thank you friend," Andy told the blond haired girl as he walked away. Andy stopped, and turned around. He was going to ask her what, who, how, but instead said, "Actually, would you mind giving me a couple handfuls for the road?"

"No proooblem," said the girl with a familiarity that bothered Andy. She handed him the rest of the bag, then stood up and walked through a comically tall wrought iron fence.

Andy turned back to the street, and placed a tiny pile of popcorn beneath a nearby streetlight. *Fuckin' birds,* he thought.

He then began heading North (South?), in hopes of getting a better understanding of his current whereabouts. He saw what should have been building numbers, studied what were likely street signs, but they all looked like they were written backwards, upside down and inside out. They gave him vertigo, if words could do that, so he stopped trying.

Andy walked another half block or so, crossed a not quite deserted street. Well it was not deserted because there were cars, not because there were people. Evidence of humans, but with the girl gone, all but empty of living things.

So empty, that a movement in the corner of his eye made

him jump and squeak. There, just out of stone's throw, he saw a bushel of bushtits feast on a popcorn pile.

So I'm not loopy, I AM looping.

He took a hard left onto the perpendicular road, dropped a pile of popcorn and started walking East (West?).

It looked boring. Residential, although without any residents. Even though he knew it would help orient him, Andy didn't even want to walk down such a ho-hum road.

He looked again down the block, just hoping. For what, he didn't know. And as if in answer his prayers, this time Andy noticed that there was, in fact, a restaurant one block down that had a sparkling new *OPEN* sign.

Andy didn't run, because Andy was not a runner. He had never been a runner. He didn't believe in it. He thought it made him seem like some flighty antelope, and he was weak enough that he didn't need to encourage predators to chase him.

No, Andy generally slunk, sticking to shadows if he could. But if he had ever come close to running, it was now.

Each step sent a shock wave through his body. *Jesus I'm out of shape*, he thought. Although upon inspecting his fancy dress shoes, he could have just as easily blamed the pain on them.

Andy thought back to all that he had consumed in the last 24 hours. A handful of popcorn, a cappuccino, and more than a couple liters of alcohol. He didn't remember anything else. At all. He felt a hunger that felt more than a little ravenous. He promised himself he would eat *anything*.

As he got closer, he slowed. He sighed. "Lucy's."

Why does it have to be a diner though? He thought to himself. Andy didn't *do* diners.

In fact, Andy hadn't been in a diner in years and years. Andy liked to pretend it was on principle, a matter of quality. It was actually, however, that Andy couldn't stand the smell of sausage *with* pancakes. He loved the idea of them together, considered them a masterpiece of pairings in theory. And he liked them separate, for sure. But he had a real deal visceral reaction when he smelled them being cooked at the same time.

Could it be the chemical reaction of denatured myoglobin molecules combining with the steam of lukewarm syrup underneath the warming lamps? Or was it just inherently gross, more spiritual than chemical? It didn't matter either way, because Andy just did not do diners.

So Andy walked on (he was done with running) and counted his steps, until he came right back to the pile of popcorn.

And there's the fuckin' birds. Back again, he sat at the bench across the street.

Running was a terrible idea, he thought to himself. It had made the black hole in his stomach all the more gaping. *Black hole belly, black hole neighborhood.* Andy felt his whole life being sucked into the singularity.

Come on Andy. You're supposed to be learning self-control, or something, right?

Maybe he could do the diner. Fuck it, yes. He would do the diner.

He stood up, and paced himself this time. He mused about bad coffee and cinnamon rolls, daydreamed about floppy bacon and runny eggs.

As he neared the restaurant, however, he noticed the open sign looked decidedly less new. And it wasn't neon, but worn paper.

He looked at the words painted on the window.

"Queen of Shiba."

Ethiopian food. Ethiopian food? Ethiopian food!

No offense "Lucy," but talk about an upgrade. Andy was ecstatic.

Andy walked into a bustling Ethiopian restaurant. How

quick he forgot what it was like to be around lots of people, and he felt a bit of anxiety at the sight.

Big groups of Ethiopian families took up the tables in the middle. The smaller tables, at the sides and back, were filled with everyone else you could imagine. Crews of hipsters, monks and nuns, businessmen pouring over portfolios. It was packed.

Andy saw the waitress and motioned to the only table available, a mid-sized round table in the corner.

"Cool if I take this one?" he asked her.

"Fine fine," she said as she loaded a family of four's table with a veritable rainbow of food and beverage.

Gurgle! Hiss! Snarl! Andy's tummy nearly jumped out of his mouth.

Andy loved Ethiopian food. He would always go with Angie, order not quite the whole menu, and drink coffee until the stars were well awake.

Angie, he thought, *I haven't even allowed myself to think her name.*

Angie, he thought, *I wonder what she wants to talk about.*

Angie, he thought, I *wonder what she's doing.*

Angie, he thought.

"Just you?" asked the waitress.

"Yep, just me today," Andy replied.

"OK fine. Know what you want to order?" asked the waitress, not quite paying attention as her eyes were diverted to a family who just walked in the door.

"Oh damn yeah," he said, not even looking at the menu. "Doro Wot, plus *all* the veggie stuff. In fact, give me *WOTever* you got."

"Yes. I see what you did there."

"Did you like it?"

"Not particularly."

"And can I get some coffee too?" asked the un-phased Andy.

"You got it," the waitress said as she made eye contact with a gray suited business couple in the corner, who clearly wanted more injera.

Fuck yesssss, Andy thought to himself.

Andy picked up his phone, tried to distract himself from his hunger.

OK, he thought, *I can do this*.

Andy opened her first message: "I'm worried about you babe. I know you're going through a lot. I'm sorry it's so fucking hard right now. I just want to make sure you're OK. I'm trying to make room for you, and I hope you have room for me."

Of course there's room for you, he thought. Andy was frustrated, but he wasn't surprised. Andy retreated a lot when he was sad, and he was expert at pushing people away. And he drank a lot. And smoked a lot. More than enough to suggest he might not want her to be around.

Her second message was, "Matt made strawberry shortcake today at work. I'll save you some bites, and we can talk."

Aghhh. Talk? Why did she want to talk to him? That felt loaded. Scary loaded.

Andy was also, perfectly fine not talking about what was going on.

Definitely not disassociating and creating fantasy landscapes to escape into.

Andy brooded for some time. Andy brooded, because brooding transcends time. When penguins brood, they stand on an unchanging plane of bleak whiteness for 65 beyond freezing days. They brood so they can time travel through their frozen hell of a landscape.

Andy became the penguin. He brooded, and in his brooding, despite having "just ordered," Andy found the food on his table. Blessed, like a baby penguin. He hadn't noticed its arrival, but he was thankful nonetheless.

Andy noticed his coffee wasn't steaming. Andy realized

his food and drink had probably been in front of him for a while.

I'm too good at brooding, he thought.

The waitress caught his eye across the room, and with horror Andy realized she was coming back to ask how it tasted.

"How is everything?" she asked, not exactly caring, but still making Andy feel ashamed.

"Oh its gr..." Andy shoveled a handful of lentils and injera into his mouth.

Injera

Andy's mouth was too full to go further. So instead, Andy just smiled, lentils punctuating his teeth.

She has the cutest eyes, Andy thought. *Adorable, in fact.*

She held a beautiful clay pot, the most beautiful coffee vessel Andy could imagine. She tipped it back and forth as she studied Andy.

She smiled, and as she held her gaze, she started to pour what looked like atrociously hot coffee all over her face.

It came from the pot like a torrent, a veritable deluge of brown flood waters.

And when the boiling coffee waterfall receded, the waitress was transformed.

A Queen, maybe a Goddess, stood before him.

Jeweled sandals stood in the pool of coffee before him. His eyes moved up her body, but not in a creepy way. He was just interested in, enamored by, her drip. Gold, on gold, on lace. Her dress, her hips, her chest all adorned in riches beyond Andy's wildest dreams.

Royal and regal, and yet when Andy's eyes reached her face, he was not greeted by a stern queen. Instead, a face far cuter than he could have imagined met his gaze.

A foxy face, ears pointed just enough. Her snout was strong, punctuated by the cutest little black nose. She turned slightly, and her big furry tail wagged in the darkness. He recognized her at once.

"I bow to you, oh Queen of Shiba" Andy winked, "Inu."

"Andy, dear boy, how is your food?" asked the Queen with an air of formality contradictory to her fuzzy little form.

"My food? It's lovely. How could it not be, it came from you! Thank you my liege. Wait, am I your liege? Or are you my liege?" Andy wasn't quite sure.

"Dear boy, you are only subject to *yourself*. Painfully so, it would seem," said the Queen with eyes full of pity. Those eyes were particularly pitiful, given the stuffed animal nature of the Queen's face.

"What do you mean, m'dame?" Was she a dame though? Or a lass? A lady for sure.

"Look at you Andy. You're sitting on a round stool, at a round table, eating a round piece of bread, covered in round little piles of about 8 different foods. A feast. And yet, you do it alone. Would a visitation from a royal a bit more *Arthurian* make the point better?" the Queen jested.

"Alone, you're right. But, I don't have anyone. Well, didn't have anyone. I mean I do have someone, but I was just alone. I was just really hungry, OK?" Andy struggled with the justification.

"No need to explain yourself Andy. *You* made this place happen, after all. You walked past a diner, one of the best places to be alone in the cosmos. And instead you managed to end up here. And as someone who is well versed in *here*, I will tell you it is a very lonely place for a single person to be," said the Queen as she looked around pensively, the tables now full of fellow royals in all manner of bling.

"You're not trying to suggest that you are lonely, right? You're a Queen! *The* Queen in fact. Rich beyond measure, wisdom overflowing, surrounded by your adoring subjects," Andy couldn't imagine a less empty room, as he watched the guests' eyes gravitate towards the Queen.

"Of course I'm lonely, Andy. I'm a Queen with no King," her eyes hinted at her desires, but her pointed nose betrayed any attempts at seduction.

"At first, of course, I chose this life. I was empowered! I didn't shave my legs, dabbled in shoplifting early on: a picture perfect rebel youth. But then it got old, being Miss Independent. I got cold in bed at night. I always hunted alone, and realized, despite my servants and confidants, I had no *pack*," she sniffled.

"A snow dog with no pack, what a sad little Shiba I was. And then, I met that dog, Solomon. He was a good man. Well, good as far as Kings go. Still razing cities, still using slaves to build his temple... but he treated *me* well, ya know? And he gave me my son," she motioned to a boy behind the counter, who weighed spices by the kilo.

"Why didn't you stay with Solomon then, if he was your pack?" Andy asked.

"I chose self-interest. I had gone there to make that money, son. I was a trader, and was too busy thinking about growing my own Queendom. Too busy thinking about securing the bag, whether it be of spices, resin, trinkets. Whatever. And maybe," she mumbled, "planning a long-game heist of the Ark of the Covenant from him."

"How did you intend to steal something of such *magnitude*?" asked Andy, who couldn't imagine moving a giant boat all the way from Jerusalem down to the sea.

"I didn't say I stole it. I said I was planning something along those lines. It was actually my son who did the deed," she winked at her son, and he winked back. "He snuck off with it, in the middle of the night. Smart boy even managed to leave a replica in its place," she beamed.

Andy had a newfound respect for the son. Ship forgery was no small feat.

"And so our Queendom, our culture flourished. I had everything I could ask for. Food, money, and power. I had power most of all. And it wasn't worth a damn," she let that sit for a moment. "I ask you, Andy: You have no Kingdom. No riches. No power, it would seem. Why, then, do you choose to be alone?" she asked solemnly. *Solomonly?*

"If I don't let them in, I can't hurt them. And they can't hurt me," Andy knew the excuse was pathetic.

"That excuse is older than I am, and I'm nearly 3000 years old. Hurt is the least of your worries. Andy, do you know the 10th Commandment?"

"The powers not delegated to the United States by the Constitution, nor prohibited by it to the States, are reserved the States respectively, or to the people?"

"Wrong list. No I mean the very last Commandment housed in our great Ark."

I didn't realize the 10 Commandments were a Noah thing, thought Andy.

"You shall not *covet*. For some reason, people always thinks it means don't lust for your neighbors wife. Ya, don't do that for sure. But that's a gross underestimation of a Holy Commandment," she was visibly angry about it.

"Covetousness is attachment. It's a yearning, some deep seeded desire to hold and control something outside yourself. You covet time. You covet space. You covet control, which I promise dear Andy, you do not have. These things you covet, and so you create walls. You create boundaries with your desire, to maintain these things that aren't even yours! And the more you long to hold to something, the more likely it is to slip through your fingers. The people around you, they see you holding onto everything except them. This time is trying for you Andy, and you think that in order to get a grip, you need to have your paws free. But I promise you Andy, you will do better with your paw in another's."

Andy was silent.

"I too built walls. Solomon thought he knew how to build walls, but I am the true master mason when it comes to keeping people out. I'm alone even here," she motioned around the room, "I chose an eternity of solitude, for saffron and myrrh. No one comes to visit me, no one comes to check on me, no one comes to rub my belly. My son is married, and *Solomon* definitely isn't talking to me. I haven't heard from him in Millennia. The only ones who call on me are the living, but they pray to *me*, asking *me* for things. What good are they to me? Most can't even conjure a good cup of coffee," she said, eyes flooded with tears.

"But at least you've got your boat," Andy said as he scratched the Queen behind her ears.

She cried and she cried, tears rising up to her neck. As the waters reached her mouth, she said "What good is a boat, with no one with me at the oars?"

With her snout just barely above the sea of tears, she whispered, "Wait... what boat?"

++

"Mmmm delicious," Andy said to the waitress who had already turned to serve coffee to the neighboring table.

Andy wanted to eat like there was no tomorrow. Well, he wanted to eat like there were only a few more tomorrows left. He was, however, worried he would be revisited by the cute little doggie with each and every bite. *Does it work like that?*

So instead, he stared, longingly, at the remaining injera and savored whatever remnants were stuck in his teeth.

Andy left a wad of dollars on the table, thanked the waitress and stood up. He looked at the table in the middle, a family of eight laughed, joked, spat insults back and forth. He smiled as he remembered that there were people in his life that he wanted to let in. People he wanted to be with.

Outside the restaurant, he decided to take another perpendicular. He checked the road sign, just in case, but was met with ever shifting runes. *Well it was worth a shot,* Andy thought.

He looked down the road and noticed a good old fashioned bar. Not a good bar to get an old fashioned, but a good old fashioned bar nonetheless.

Just one drink, he thought to himself as he hesitated to walk in.

He felt his heart squeeze and squish, like a blood pressure machine that decided it would work better in someone's chest instead of on their arm. It squeezed and just kept squeezing, and he got light headed.

I don't want to be alone, he thought.

Andy studied his phone.

Dante always wants a drink, Andy thought to himself, so he pulled out his phone and called "Dirty Dante."

Dante answered in a whisper, "Bro. I told you to *never* call me. You know I hate the sound of my own voice."

"But I'm the one that has to hear your voice!"

"Exactly! I don't want to put you through that torture! But fine whatever, what's up?"

"Want to get a beer? I'm at..." Andy looked up at the sign, "Tiddy's Tavern?"

"Ah fuck yeah! I'm always down for some Tiddy's. I'll be there in like 10 minutes."

Andy sat on the stoop out front. He really did love strawberry shortcake. And he really did love Angie. The fear weighed heavier than Armageddon, but was it worth it for some strawberries and cream?

It's always worth it for strawberries and cream, Andy thought self-assuredly. He texted Angie, "Deal. Hit me up when you're off work."

Fuck why'd I do that, why'd I do that, why'd I do that.

Andy wasn't sure how many "why'd I do that's" he'd mustered when he felt a gentle tap on his shoulder. He looked up at Dante, the hairiest man he'd ever known.

Dante's hair and beard had stopped competing for supremacy long ago, and now blended into a beautiful cylinder of hair that surrounded Dante's sizable torso.

"Hey bud," Dante said as he helped Andy to his feet. "You kind of look like shit."

"Thanks man. You too, as always," Andy said bowing.

"Shall we beer?"

"We shall," said Andy as they walked into Tiddy's. The bar was nearly empty, yet the ambient noise made it feel like the joint was packed. White noise echoed, via not quite muted TVs and hunting video game that announced "a buck for a buck."

It all gave Andy the warm and fuzzies. It was a familiar sort of place.

Dante sat at a high top, hollering distance from the bar. Dante had really intense eyes, and bartenders always thought he was either trying to fight them or screw them. So Dante, knowingly, chose the path of least resistance and always sat at tables. The waitress came over, and said, "All domestics are on Happy Hour. No seltzers. No ciders. No German stuff."

"Boo!" said Dante. "Well screw your Happy Hour, I want a Kolsch anyways."

"Ooooh. Ditto," said Andy.

"Be right back," she said as she wandered behind the bar to pour her own beers.

"So what's new man?" asked Dante. "It's been a minute since caught up for sure."

"New? Well I'm worried I'm fucking it up with Angie. So there's that."

"*New* Andy. I said new!" Dante teased.

"Um, I walked out of the bar, like 30 minutes into my shift last night. Then proceeded to get hammered. And now it would seem the world is coming to an end. Literally and figuratively."

"*New* Andy! I said new!" Dante laughed.

"I just can't do it man. Any of it. There's just too much to handle. I feel like, to function, I have pretend to be happy, but for my heart, I have to let myself be sad. These pendulum swings of grief and celebration are brutal. I feel like Angie and I are either having the best or worst days of our lives, every single day. And I know that's all me! I feel like I'm trying to live every day, only to want to die every night by the end of it. It hurts."

"Duality is brutal bro," Dante smacked his lips as the heady beers were placed on the table.

"Well here's to Heaven," said Dante raising his glass.

"And here's to Hell," said Andy as he clinked glasses.

Kolsch

Dante didn't change, not entirely. In fact, from a certain vantage point you would be convinced it was just Dante. He moved, quite buoyant, through a vortex of kolsch that had engulfed the entire bar. There were bubbles, so many bubbles. They spun and danced around Dante, and he around them.

As Dante rotated ominously in the beer, though, Andy could see that Dante was exactly one half not himself. The left half's eye was no longer vibrant, but hollow. The skin, a negative space. Where right-hand Dante's lovely locks tumbled like golden rays, left-hand Dante had curls of anti-gold. Not silver, but more the antithesis of the radiant warmth, grown not in the treasure chest of the Mother's womb but in the cold emptiness of space. He could feel the not-silver hair suck his energy, as it pulled all hope and love into its nexus.

All was consumed by it. All that is, except right-hand Dante's glorious golden glow.

There was terror, there was beauty, and yet there was balance. Beauty. Like an energetic black and white cookie.

"I dig your polarity," said Andy.

"Oh, wow! Thank you! No one has ever complimented me before. Thank you, wow, jeez! I had a whole intro but, wow. Thank you for saying that," the hyper-cosmic being blushed. Andy marveled that something so cosmic, could be so demure.

"Oh I'm sorry, I didn't mean to ruin your entrance. By all means," said Andy with a bow.

The two sides of Dante glowed (and anti-glowed), and he spoke in dual tones, "Humans have this notion. It's a tiny notion, so silly, and yet they believe it so deeply. Humans believe they can be one, or they can be the other. Often it's expressed as gender, or race. Politic or morality. I am this, or I am that. You believe *deeply* in your either/or-ness. So much so that you end up tearing yourself apart. All loneliness can be attributed to this separateness."

"Bummer."

"This estrangement is strange, no? Everything in this cosmos works in tandem with its opposite. Always and forever. That whole yin yang thing. And yet people insist on tearing something apart, and for what? *IDENTITY*," he spit.

"Now, look at me, the almighty Kolsch. I am beautiful, no? I am oh so delicious, am I not?"

"No, you are not. You are not *not*. I mean, yes! You are lovely," offered Andy.

"Those of singular mind, they shout 'You must be lager, or you must be ale!' But my process is lager, my process is ale. My body is lager, my body is ale. And yet they insist I cannot be! Entirety made me as I am, and I am both, and yet they say I cannot be!"

"They demand I choose a side! They demand I profess my alliances. 'Are you Koln or Cologne? Are you French or are you German?' And again, I must affirm that *I AM BOTH!*" He was proud, his glow and anti-flow danced in tandem.

"OK, so you are both."

"We *both* are both! I know your mind, feel your thoughts ping and then pong from light to dark. Is this trauma, or is this salvation? Privy to the End of Days, am I Christ Reborn, or you know, the other guy? Do I bring hurt or healing? And will I be hurt, or healed? It begs the question time and time again! But the answer always has been, and always will be the same: Both."

"I am savior and scourge of my own personal Apocalypse?"

"You are savior and scourge of your own personal Apocalypse. All these demons, all these angels, do not forget Andy, that they are yours. Half-truths just lead to other half-truths, so why not allow yourself to put those pieces back together? This is your beginning, and this is your end. You are allowed to mourn and celebrate, to feel both pain and pleasure. You are allowed to be the blame, and the resolution. This moment is entirely yours, so may you own it entirely."

It felt like a curse and a blessing.

And it was both.

He felt the two truths mingle inside himself. They merged, coalesced and as they did he watched the two halves of Dante melt back into each other. The vortex stilled, and the beer, went flat.

+ +

Andy didn't remember drinking too many beers. The thing about drinking too many beers though, is that each beer past a certain point erases memory of both itself, and any proximal beers.

No, Andy didn't *remember* drinking too many beers, but everything else was trying to remind him.

Hint number one. He was horizontal, and the sun was still up.

Hint number two. The couch was not entirely unfamiliar, and the room was vaguely not unrecognizable. And yet still, he was lost.

Hint number three. He was hungry in that hollow sort of way. Andy loved food and food loved Andy, but *Drunk* Andy was easily distracted and forgot to eat. Always.

Hint number four. Andy could smell the soured Kolsch in the toilet, from the couch. *Gross.*

Andy didn't want any more hints. He just wanted to avoid gifting the toilet any more beer, lest it end up like Andy. Drunk.

More than even water, Andy needed food.

So he got up and walked into the kitchen.

The kitchen was like any other in the city. The cabinets, not made from, but made to look like old wood. The kind that smelled like mildly digested forest when they got wet.

There was a sink with a detachable head that wouldn't detach. There was that weird tiny corner cabinet that could only hold olive oil and a baby waffle iron.

And there was a fridge that could have been any other fridge in the known universe. A fridge that could have held just about anything imaginable. Too much produce, all in their sad floppy stage? Just mayo, olives and hotsauce? Perhaps a whole keg of Kolsch? It was too hard to say.

Andy opened the impressively well-suctioned fridge door, with a sickening slurp. The fridge indeed, only had three items.

Bread. Peanut Butter. Jelly.

This was a dinner that Andy could get behind. Delicious, nostalgic, and foolproof. A little unnerving because the peanut butter was in the fridge. But a drunk super-food, for sure.

Andy didn't sweat a person's impending arrival at this random apartment. And Andy didn't worry that there were only a slice and a butt end in the bread bag. Andy just worried about applying a meticulous shmear of peanut butter and a substantial slathering jelly.

Andy cut the crusts off, because sometimes Andy just liked to be a fancy boy.

As Andy was about to take a bite, though, Andy did start to worry. He worried about life and death, Heaven and Hell. He worried about love and hate, and then he just worried about worrying. He worried about having to carry both, to carry all.

He worried about specters of trauma. He worried about if he even had the capability to internalize *any* of these lessons, in any sort of meaningful way.

He stared across the room at the blank TV screen. He imagined his carnage splattered on the evening news. His Armageddon, his End of Days, on full display for the world to see.

He worried about the people around him, what the end

of the world meant for them. He worried people wouldn't be-lieve him, worried more that people would. He worried and worried as he stared at his reflection in the TV screen.

In the end, Andy decided that only one thing didn't worry him. Peanut Butter and Jelly. So he took a bite.

Jelly and Peanut Butter

Andy studied himself in the TV reflection as he chewed. It was Andy, but the picture didn't quite match his lived reality.

Andy sat on a red couch, with a sickly light brown wall that loomed behind him. Andy's reflection however, sat on a brown couch with a red wall.

Andy noticed every minute difference, a black dog statuette replaced a white cat. A cactus on the coffee table in substitution for a succulent. Minute, but noticeable differences.

These subtleties, however, gave way to something much more glaring that Andy had missed. The entire scene was upside down. The reflection's feet were on the ceiling, yet still the two locked eyes.

Bizarro Andy chewed when Andy chewed, moved when Andy moved. A reflection, but as seen through a marble.

"So this one's already got me a little confused," Andy pondered aloud, "Why would Peanut Butter and Jelly be upside down? If anything, Peanut Butter and Jelly suggests all that is right side up in the world. Surely PB&J must represent divine order in the cosmos."

"Whoa whoa whoa! You have clearly mistaken me for someone I most certainly am not. Peanut Butter and Jelly? Gross! As if! PB&J is a bore. A snooze fest. Good ole PB&J, reliable to a fault. You know exactly what to expect from ole PB&J! Where's the excitement? Where's the pizzazz? The joie-de-vivre?"

Andy was worried. If he hadn't just eaten a peanut butter and jelly sandwich, then maybe he really was losing it. He looked at his reflection, a little afraid of what was coming next.

"Jelly and Peanut Butter, at your service," the lookalike said with a bow.

"Uh..."

"Orientation matters, Andy. Perspective matters. There is a tangible, palpable difference between jelly on the tongue and jelly on the palette. They are unique experiences. Please, do me the courtesy. Flip your sandwich and tell me it's not a different thing all together," implored J&PB.

Andy flipped the sandwich, and took a bite. He had to admit, it just hit different. The nuttiness was more prominent, the consistency and the chew were completely different.

Poof! Another, more recognizable reflection appeared, right side up in front of Andy next to the inverted one.

"It is I! Presenting, the one, the only, Peanut..."

"I've got this covered Peebs, thanks though," said J&PB, with a snap of his fingers.

Another *Poof* and Andy was again alone with the upside down sandwich man.

"The world you know is ending Andy. Has ended. It is changed. And not just changed Andy. Most of it is about to be flipped on its head. Its time you became more nimble with your perspective!" Andy felt dizzy. "Not that you have a choice about it! The world is *not* as it was, and sometimes the only way to get a grip is with a new angle," said all-knowing J&PB.

"What's a different angle on Apocalypse? That it's a good thing? That I should welcome Angels and Demons as they usher in my End? Is that a more metered, a more respectable perspective?" said Andy bitingly.

"Maybe. Your life was in need of dynamic change. You were floundering. You were already in a place where you didn't know up from down. Maybe you didn't know what was what, because up *was* down, and down *was* up." As J&PB said this, the reflection rotated. Evidence of the topsyness and the turvyness of Andy's situation.

"Well ya, everything was... OK, everything *is* all fucked up. And maybe I've known all that for quite a while. Knew that my priorities weren't quite straight."

Andy thought for a moment, "Not quite straight. I guess I see what you're saying about orientation. I wonder though, is wholesale annihilation necessary to right my wrongs? How about a slight rotation, rather than a head over heels approach?" said Andy.

"This aint as simple as a simple tilt of the head Andy. Sometimes standing on your head is just about all you can do."

"Easy for a magic talking upside down sandwich man to say."

"I thought you'd have caught on by now, Andy. I'm not the one who is upside down."

++

The Peanut Butter and... the Jelly and Peanut Butter Sandwich had slowed the spin, for sure. Andy, however, still felt more than a little disconnected from his body.

He felt heavier, and the sandwich had glued his mouth together. Andy felt claustrophobic.

Andy needed water.

Andy grabbed his phone and looked at the time, as he walked towards the sink. It was damn near Shortcake o'clock. He needed to sober up, or at the very least smell a *little* more sobered up.

Andy stood at the sink, stuck his head under the faucet, and chugged.

Water

Fairies danced, sang, and frolicked in the droplets as they cascaded over the stainless steel sink.

They were beautiful, clad in nothing light, flowers and good feelings. Love and tranquility, some honest to God piece of mind, exuded from their wings.

He couldn't take his eyes off them.

One of the tiny fairies flew up to Andy's face. It looked like a rose, smelled like a baby, and danced like a spark. It danced around Andy's head, showered him in pixie dust. It sang a song in a tongue known only to the oldest of Gods.

"Water. Oh water. I bet you have some really amazing, deep knowledge to impart. I'm ready for it," Andy was hopeful.

"Absolutely," sang the fairy in the most melodious of voices. The sound made Andy's hair stand on end, his knees weak, and his breath stop.

Andy stood expectantly, mouth agape in anticipation. His heart sang a song of welcome, his spirit inched closer to The Truth. He knew, at last, he would be welcomed into the Spirit's eternal embrace.

"Drink more water."

Andy waited a beat.

"Drink more water?

"Yes, drink more water."

"That's it?"

"That's it."

The fairies giggled. They flew about as water sprayed from the faucet. Spectral jewels were sent in all directions.

As they laughed, their luminous little bodies dimmed like candles at wick's end.

And all that was left was a stainless steel sink, covered in glitter.

++

Andy felt better. He still worried about Armageddon, but at least he felt... what?

At least he felt hydrated.

And that was more than he could say about himself for the last couple days (weeks? months?), if he was honest. *Drink more water. Drink more water.*

Andy collected his belongings. That meant his phone, and his shoes, and sometimes he wasn't sure those even *belonged.*

He retied his tie, even though he didn't remember that he had been wearing a tie. Even though he felt like shit, he didn't have to look it.

He looked at the door, tried to amp himself up for whatever lay on the other side. He had no idea where he was. He might have to, *gag,* stand in an elevator with another person. Or worse yet, he might have to walk down the stairs.

He gripped the knob and turned.

Andy watched from a distance as his eyeballs turned inside out, and his supple skin stretched from here to infinity. Light became a wave became a particle became a wave. And then a tsunami of color, awash in a sea of rainbows. In the periphery of his inside-out eyeballs, he was sure he saw pink helmeted night-crawlers, with tiny pick axes.

"Wormhole," he thought, as he watched the specter of

some hyper-cosmic Bushtit scare them beyond the event horizon.

He was flung back into his body with the force of a fart let out after a first date.

Andy stood there, feeling awkward. Angie just stared at him. He still gripped the knob, although not the same knob he had just held.

"I said come in," she said with enough oomph to help him remember his legs were his own.

He strode through the door, then walked across the room.

It was her apartment, as he had always known it. Too much art, and just enough comfy cushions. It was the first truly recognizable place he'd seen all day.

Angie *did* have too much art, but only because Andy was often distracted from conversation by all the spectacles.

It was one of the things he loved about her from the start. Before he knew he might maybe sort of love her, he loved her artsy-fartsiness.

He loved her passion for ruining new clothes with acrylic and oil. Loved her ability to convey an emotion in an image. Loved her tendency to melt reality and fantasy together in a blur of strokes.

She painted because she didn't know how not to. She had nurtured in herself what Andy had hidden from, for much of his adult life. Honest self-reflection, told through movement of her hands. Therapy through artistic expression. It was one of the many reasons she was so much better adjusted than Andy.

"I really like that one, with the octopus and the cherry blossoms," Andy motioned with his hand, and moved closer towards the couch and Angie.

"You say that every time you see it," she laughed.

"Can you blame me? Its fucking adorable," he laughed, then paused as if he remembered his place. "How are you doing?"

"Honestly? I'm tired as hell," Angie responded, the sleepiness dripped from her words. Andy looked in her eyes and saw the weight of the last few days, the last few weeks, the last few lifetimes.

"Me too. I hope you're not tired of me," he inserted with only a *hint* of self-loathing.

"Stop it. I invited you here, didn't I? I want you here. And I want to make sure *you* are OK," she said.

"Am I OK? Well I'm right in between Heaven and Hell. So I guess that makes me OK? Just barely. I mean I might be losing it. Or maybe the world is *actually* coming to an end. Not that the two are terribly different."

"That's shitty, but I feel that way pretty much all the time, if that makes you feel any better," she said, reaching for a white takeout box.

"It doesn't. And I mean, that's not what I mean. Well it is what I mean. I don't know what I mean. I mean, I really think something bad is happening, or happened, or maybe will happen?" Andy felt lost in time.

"I'm just, I guess I'm just trying not to freak out. But I'm kind of freaking out, and I bet I'm freaking you out."

"You're not," she said, and he knew she meant it.

"Does *this* freak you out?" she asked, as she slid a bite of strawberry soaked cake towards his mouth.

"You have no idea," Andy admitted as he took the bite.

Strawberry Shortcake

Angie's long black hair whipped and whirled in a vortex, a shampoo commercial as strawberries danced in the background. Her hair swirled, until it began to wrap around itself, all knots and twists. The strands weaved, and as they wove they took the shape of two half-tied braids. The rest of her was naked. Terrifyingly, beautifully naked.

Andy was lost in the curves of her body when he felt some part of himself pulled from his body. The levity of his spirit, shed the cumbersome skin-sack with an audible *slurp*.

Andy watched as his body walked in front of him, as if it were compelled to movement away from where his soul floated. The body reached out to touch the woman's braids. The gravity with which they seemed to pull his body left Andy feeling a little uneasy.

Andy's body sat behind not-Angie and continued to braid where the magic wind had left off. It was then that Andy noticed his body's clothes were not his own.

Andy's body was wearing an absolute boatload of beads. Beaded belt, beaded headband, beaded choker, beaded sash, beaded moccasins, beaded beads. Fractal beads, crystalline, each containing tiny universes within. The beads glowed, they glew, they had a glow about them that was otherworldly. A glow that reminded Andy equally of the Earth's core and a Supernova, alight from within and without. There was a warmth and a chill, both a beginning and an end, in the light they emanated.

"I'm here to tell you a story," Shortie-cake began. "You are a storyteller, and storytellers need to hear stories most of all," her voice was cool.

Spirit Andy wanted to get comfortable for the story, because who doesn't love relaxing for a good story?

How though, he thought, *does a disembodied spook get comfortable? Pull up a cloud? Fluff some ectoplasm? Conjure an ottoman's ghost?* Upon investigation, however, Andy realized that he could float in the ether, like it was some overly saline solution. He leaned back, and bobbed like a cork in the sea of eternity.

"This story begins before the beginning. Before time, before history, before her-story. In a void filled by Creator and Creation. Great Spirit had created the animals, the Earth, and had given life to first Man," she motioned to Andy's body, "and First Woman," she added with a raised eyebrow. "But much remained unmade. Perhaps it was this ineffable lack which led First Man and First Woman to fight," Andy noticed First Man shift nervously in his seat as he braided First Woman's hair.

"The Cherokee, the guardians of this story, seem to have forgotten what the fight was about. Maybe they couldn't agree on Spruce or Pinewood to build their home. Maybe it was that First Man suggested First Woman clean up after him. Or perhaps," her eyes looked back towards Andy's body, "Firstman forgot his bow in the lodge one too many times. Whatever the cause, eventually the fighting proved too much for First Woman and she left."

"While First Man slept, First Woman walked towards the rising sun. She was so angry, she didn't dare turn back, lest she forget her anger. She walked and walked, and by the time First Man awoke, she was well beyond his reach. First Man could feel that he had lost her, probably for good. But he chased her anyways, knowing he most *certainly* wouldn't get her back by sitting where he sat."

"First Man was heartbroken," she continued. "His sadness was bottomless. Even Father Sun, perched high in Mother Sky, could feel First Man's pain. Father Sun spoke down to First Man, asked if he carried his anger with him, for it would only slow him down. First Man said he had shed his anger, and wished only to rejoin with First Woman. Father Sun, taking pity on the lonely man, shined his rays upon the path First Woman was walking. The Earth opened, and from the dirt grew a great Huckleberry bush. Robust, and attractive certainly, but First Woman just kept walking."

Andy imagined how angry he would have to be to pass up a free meal. *Nope, couldn't do it*, he concluded.

Shortie-cake continued, "The Sun again shined down on the fertile Earth, asking for Her to bring forth gifts to entice First Woman yet again. This time, a bramble of large juicy blackberries erupted from the ground. Despite the sweetness to entice, and despite the thorns to hinder, First Woman again did not stop. She did, however, smell the berries and the aroma made her heart, and so her feet, skip a beat. She wondered if she was angry enough to keep walking, but still she did not stop."

"Finally, their hearts weeping for First Man, Sun and Earth conspired together. They brought forth a great patch of Strawberries in front of First Woman. The smell filled every crevice of her soul, and she stopped and knelt next to the plant. As she took a bite, she saw her and First Man's blood mingled in the heart-like shape of the fruit. She thought of his skin, of his hair, his heart. And so she gorged herself on the berries, and hoped they would somehow bring him back to her."

"First Man came upon her in the clearing, surrounded by white flowers and red fruit. She turned when she heard his footsteps. She laid in the flowers and with the first shared strawberry, they were never again parted."

"Oooh and let me guess," said Andy with a lick of his lips, "She was ripe, and red, and juicy, so he laid in *her* flowers. And so all the supermarkets brimmed with strawberries, birthed of their love and those tiny little seeds."

"First, gross. Don't lick your lips. Second, those aren't actually seeds. They're like tiny ovaries. And third, yes. That is kind of what happened."

"Ha! One day of metaphorical thinking and I'm *real* good at cutting to the chase."

"I promise, no chase has been cut. That definitely was not the *point* I was trying to make."

"Right. So this story wasn't about berries and multiplication..." the words hung and Andy's wheels turned.

"It's about the power of gifts to fix broken relationships!" Andy yelled, triumphant.

A grasshopper trilled from beneath the still white flowers.

"It's about forgiveness?"

Chirp.

"Perseverance?"

Chirp.

"Patience?"

"Correct in their merit, handy metaphors to be sure. Those are every day lesson though, and we are looking for an End of Days lessons. Heavy shit!" She hissed, "It's about divine intervention."

"Ewww," Andy liked berries and patience better.

"Yes, First Man was repentant. Yes, he was steadfast. There's no way in Hell, however, that he was *ever* going to catch her," she seemed to flex as she said this. "She was with the Moon and he was with the Sun. First man was convinced, with his own power, he could move the Earth and shift her heart. But she was *gone*," her eyes were cold, and First Man looked dejected.

"But then the big ole hot one in the sky, chucks some berries at her and preserves the lineage of men?" she tickled First Man's ears and he straightened up. "One of the great tribal legacies, cemented by the Sun throwing some fruit and fixing the world. A not so subtle whispering of angels."

Andy shrugged.

"Often it feels like you're making headway, but the spirits are keenly aware that you aren't making *shit* for progress. Divine intervention is a leg up, where you never knew you were lagging in the first place. It's a chance to start over, to make amends. To fix what you broke."

Sweet, Andy thought to himself.

"So now what?" he asked plainly.

"Divine intervention isn't always nectar and ambrosia. I wish it was going to be strawberry fields for you Andy, but be prepared for some very strange flying fruit."

Andy's body tensed. Well, Andy's spirit, but he also noticed his body, First Man, tense as well. First Woman embraced First Man, and as she kissed him, he lay down amongst the white flowers.

Andy watched the vines consume his body, and First Man began to scream. And the screams were made mute by a mouthful of sweet sweet strawberries.

✚✚

Andy felt like he had cliff dived back into his body. Seamless, fluid, but scary as all get out.

He grabbed the fork and forced another strawberry soaked bite into his mouth to avoid the silence.

Maybe a little too eager with that bite, thought Andy as Angie eyed him like *he* was the dessert.

He weighed if he wanted to have sex with her. Were Seven Heavens of Pleasure worth Seven Hells of Pain? He studied her body, looked at her lips. Scanned his inroads. Calculated velocities. His libido jockeyed for position with his common sense.

Andy's body lurched, his jaw snap open. The words, "thanks for the shortcake," flew from his mouth. He ghost walked through the next few words.

His entire body embraced his shoes, like a hug he didn't know he needed. With a jolt, they led him out the front door, and his whispers of "love you" and "see you later" were consumed by the sound of the door as it swung closed.

It wasn't that he teleported out of the apartment, like he had when he came in. It was more his head and heart went comatose as his body hurried him out the exit, lost time parallel to teleportation.

He recognized the street, but that didn't matter much. Andy's mind was a game of air hockey. His thoughts back and forth, breakneck, with the occasional rough point scored by either sadness or anger. Andy was blinded by it.

He tried to gain some composure, tried to reason with himself that he hadn't just acted like a complete and utter fool.

As Andy's anxiety peaked, he thought the only logical thought. *I just need pot.*

When his mind wasn't his own, marijuana, or even musing about marijuana, brought serenity.

His mind stilled, and the air stilled.

I just need pot, he reminded himself.

A bushtit trilled in the distance, and Andy allowed his brain to drift back to its teenage years. Nothing compares to an adolescent nose's ability to pinpoint Mary's musk. It's why high school stoners don't even try to hide it. They know that every freshman for a quarter mile could smell the Devil's Chard buried 6 feet under.

Andy imagined that theater girl he sat next to in Geometry, Debbie Dundiddit. Her bouquet of baby powder and dirt weed had haunted his dreams for the 25 years since. All he had to do was imagine her yellow (see: not blond) hair and her two sizes too big Joy Division shirt and...

Poof, a cloud of pot smoke appeared like a dropped bottle of baby powder. A cloud that obscured much of the street in front of Andy. Andy felt he could cut the smoke with a butter knife and his limbs a-quiver with anticipation dreamed of spreading that smoke on a blueberry bagel.

He swam through the smoke, knowing his night was about to level the fuck up.

Through the haze, Andy saw an opening, a place to come up for air. He walked forward, towards the clearing in the fog. He expected a hacky sack circle, based on the surplus of smoke.

And there it was. The very same fountain sat, a sentinel in wait. Andy made eye contact with the vase at the far end of the marble. Made eye contact *actually*, the Gerber daisies turned to meet Andy's gaze. They *saw* Andy.

And Andy saw them. Saw the flowers, a bit more floppy, especially the frilly little green ones that were victim to the heaviest layer of spray paint.

As he followed the curve of one of the more droopy flowers, Andy saw a downright dirty human sprawled over the fountain. Dirty with dirt, saturated in soil, but also smelly, visible pee-ew lines and all. Andy half expected the fountain to spring to life, to free itself from the grips of his stink.

Andy imagined Angie's sweet sweet shortcake. His mind pinged over to work, ponged to his abdominal pain, and swung back round to a bushtit that circled overhead.

In short, Andy's mind was scattered, like dandelion seeds to the wind. The only thing that could bring him back down was some ganja. *Just a wee little joint to re-calibrate.*

Andy approached the giant dust bunny of a man, prepared to shoot the shit and puff along.

Upon inspection, however, high, low, and in between, there was no joint.

He saw the haze beyond the fountain, remembered the smell. Still, there was no actual smoke in the immediate bubble of the fountain. The air was crisp, clear, like laundry on a clothesline.

Andy's intuition, however, begged to differ, sure he was not mistaken.

Andy approached the man.

"Whoa, whoa, stop" the man spit out with extra saliva. "What you gettin' so close to me for? And sniffin' like a gawdam beagle?" He seemed more than a little peeved, which was reasonable considering Andy's nose was mighty close to him.

"Sorry to bother you, I was just sure someone was smoking over here! I wanted to come show my support, profess some solidarity. Where's the pot hiding abouts?" Andy immediately regretted his choice of words.

"Git off it! Don't the feckin' police aint got nothin' better to do than hound me bouts my smell?" the man muttered to himself.

"My dear sir, I am no NARC!" Andy's words sounded a little more NARC-y than he had hoped. He decided to try a different approach. "What if I told you the world was coming to an end?"

"I'd say about feckin' time!"

"Really! Last night, a star, embodied, told me that in five days the world as we know it will come to an end. So now I'm stuck in purgatory, forced to walk until the End of Days with only ghosts to keep me company." The man's eyes widened.

"Sorry," Andy let out an audible sigh.

Andy was ready to give up. Was Armageddon so bad? It might be restful in the afterwards, if nothing else.

Andy wanted to curl into a ball, so Andy curled into a ball. He made sure, however, to keep a safe distance from the vase. Eternal rest was good and all, but no need to speed up the process. He also kept an equally safe distance from the dirty fellow.

Andy closed his eyes to sleep, but he was grossly aware of two eyes fixed firmly on the top of his head.

Sleeping on the street two nights in a row should be avoided anyways, Andy thought as he pushed himself back up to the seated position.

As he rose, he found himself eye to eye with the man.

"Dat's Purgatory alright! You said it! I been sayin' its purgatory for long as I can 'member! Same feckin' faces, same feckin' places. The most borin' afterlife I could imagine!"

Afterlife? Was this guy trying to imply that Andy was already dead? Because he most certainly didn't feel dead. In fact, despite the logical parts of his brain telling him otherwise, this all felt painfully real. Painful and real. Really painful even.

"I been tryin' to escape fer just about an eternity! You

don't happenta remember how ya got here, do ya?" the man asked, as he snuck a comically giant brownie into Andy's hand.

"Honestly?" Andy laughed, "It started alot like this," and he took a bite.

Pot Brownie

The man's face, which was still about four inches away from Andy's face, didn't change. Andy expected a puff of smoke, a jungle of pot leaves. Andy had visions of dreadlocks and rishis. Maybe some primal ganja serpent was about to rear its head to meet his eyes.

But none of those things materialized. In fact, the only thing that changed was the expression on the man's face. Where he had been hopeful, now only loss leaked through. The twinkle in his eyes, the ornery angle of his brow, everything was now washed in a very particular shade of gray. It was like the life had leaked out of him, and he was showing himself as the ghost he truly was.

"Purgatory," he began, "is the in between. It aint heaven, it aint hell. It aint living, and it most certainly aint dying. Its the waiting, for at least one of those things to come."

Andy was certain this wasn't what he was promised when he ate a pot brownie. He was also a bit surprised the man was somehow *more* coherent now.

"Some'd call it limbo," continued the man. "I like that word, limbo. Its a precarious sort of word. Its the kind of word that might fall over if it leans too far back. It aint stable, y'see. No no, limbo, it aint stable. Its tryin' to resolve itself. Its trying to force a decision one way or the other."

"You mean the whole Christ, Anti-Christ thing, right?" offered Andy.

"Why you so fixated on being God and Devil? What bout being happy or being sad? You either hate yer life or you love it, and that's the decision you're expected t'make."

"You either want it continue, or ya don't. You either want it to end, or you don't. You act like you're ambivalent to the whole thing. Resigned to yer fate, whatever it may be. You aint swimming one way or the other. Your body aint just in limbo, yer heart's in limbo too."

"That's gotta be an option! I feel like that's got to be the middle path," Andy was always looking for the middle path.

"Middle path? Aint no path at all! It's a razor's edge!" the man spat. "Ya teeter. Ya totter. And depression aint no good on a teeter-totter."

Andy frowned as the man continued.

"Y'know why assassins smoked hash?"

Andy tried to answer.

"Twasn't to put them in some berserk rage."

Andy was disappointed.

"Twasn't to give 'em miraculous psychic powers."

Strike two.

"Tweren't even to make them more suggestible to dark deeds."

Andy was glad for strike three.

"Nope. Twas to help them find a wee bit of levity in the heart of self-hatred, to find peace in the midst of dark times. Twas to remind them that Heaven was still somewhere, just not where they were. Twas a balm to help them come to terms with the lived reality of Hell. Twas a gateway into the limbo of the in between. That's war for ya, righteous evil. Pain for the sake of pleasure."

Andy swallowed hard, and tasted the pot at the back of his palette, "So I'm just stuck in between."

"Not fer long Andy. Like I said, that's the thing bout

limbo. It's always trying to resolve itself. And might be that you're gonna fall. Probably that you're gonna fall."

Andy was not feeling particularly flexible, and his balance was more than a little shot. It seemed like every time he felt upright, he was actually damn near parallel to the ground.

Andy watched as the man walked towards a broom, held by two cloaked figures. The Brownie man passed under the stick, and beckoned Andy from the other side.

As Andy approached, the figures lowered the broom closer and closer to the ground.

He bent over, coaxed by whispers of "how low can you go? How low can you go?"

Lower Andy went, and lower still. Until finally, Andy fell.

+The 2nd Day+

Andy didn't sleep.

It wasn't the existential dread. It wasn't the resonant sound of *doom doom doom* in his chest. It wasn't regret, fear, doubt, or guilt.

It was the cute little movies that kept playing under his eyelids.

Andy's mind was a formidable thing when he was stoned. In the confines of his consciousness, Andy imagined wacky scenarios with ducks and plungers. He watched wolves grow fins and turn into killer whales.

He even deduced the cure for carpel tunnel was most likely to be found in an actual really deep tunnel, somewhere. He resolved that he would go mining when he had the chance. He would cure the maladies of *all* the beleaguered receptionists if he could.

This was good and all. Super Entertaining, but by the end of the brownie's duration, Andy hadn't slept one wink.

The haze surrounding him started to glow, and Andy resigned himself to a fate of sleepless loopiness.

The bushtits were at their most voluminous. They chirped aloud to maximize their fluff, all in effort to fend off the last remnants of a quite cold evening.

The brownie had hardened Andy to the cold. As his high

faded, however, it not only scared off all his precious dream-ducks, but made him more than cold enough to stand up.

Coffee.

If only he knew which way the coffee shop was. The dank haze of the night before had shifted to thick coastal fog at some point. And it was impenetrable, even to a bloodhound like Andy.

Andy tightened his pea-coat around himself, as he skulked through alleys. *Foggy mornings really are the best time to skulk,* Andy thought. Only then did he remember he didn't own a pea coat.

No matter. Andy let the thought roll off him as he walked through the streets. His memory lead him, which in the midst of a pot hangover, meant he was going the long way.

He was glad for the long walk though. It would help his bones work off the cold, and maybe allow him some time to come to terms with his descent into the bowels of Hell.

Hell doesn't look like LA, Andy reflected. *More like Seattle.*

Angie waltzed through his head, and Andy felt the Hell-fire flow seethe in his veins.

Why was I so weird last night? Besides the whole the world is coming to an end thing, of course.

You can't BESIDES the End of the World, the gentler half of him offered, ever generous.

Andy walked slower, tried on the weight of Armageddon. It was sad, for sure. He felt heavy, and angry and lost. And he hurt. Spiritually. Emotionally. Physically.

A bushtit trilled at his feet, did a little dance, a caring act of distraction.

I'll cope later, Andy thought as he suppressed feeling his feelings. As if in agreement, the bird flew up into the air. It ran, full force, into a glass coffee door.

Ah little guy! Andy reached out to the bird, but it shook its head and flew off. Andy was left alone, and with nowhere else to turn, he opened the coffee shop door.

There was no one in line, but five toe tapping patrons waited for their drinks. The tension was palpable as Andy walked to the front counter.

"London Fog," said Baristo.

"I know, right? Weird weather out there," Andy observed.

"Wasn't talking to you," Baristo growled back.

"London Fog!" Baristo yelled it this time.

A most remarkable man, wearing a fresh little three-piece tweed suit stood up. He walked to the counter, grabbed the drink, and headed for the door. Andy nodded at him and his outfit in approval.

Andy began, "So anyways, can I get..."

"London Fog!" yelled the Baristo.

No one moved.

"London Fog!" they tried again.

"You already made that," Andy offered, as the room groaned with impatience.

"I did? Shit, I'm sorry. It's this morning! Everything's just a little foggy."

"I see that. Anyways, can I..."

"You wouldn't want a London Fog, would you bro?" the Baristo batted their eyelashes.

"Otherwise, I'm just gonna toss it," Baristo held the paper cup over the trash can.

Andy sighed, "Sure. Fine. Definitely don't waste it. Fog me up!"

London Fog

The scene rewinded. The scene rewound. The scene went backwards, and Andy watched the dapper man walk backwards from the door. He walked backwards not up to, but behind the counter. The Baristo stepped to the side.

The man who took Baristo's place, though, had the same face, if decidedly fresher duds.

Andy counted. Counting the argyle pocket square, the well-dressed Baristo's suit contained forty, nay fifty shades of gray. This was remarkable mostly because Andy was able to notice that spectrum of grays on display. He was astounded how different one shade of black/white was from its neighboring hue of white/black.

Horns blared somewhere close behind Andy's left eardrum, and he jumped.

"Presenting the esteemed Earl of Grey!" yelled one of the other customers.

"That's Lord Grey to you!" Grey volleyed back.

"I hate being called Earl," he confided in Andy. "I hear Hurl Earl enough growing up to make me want to shriek!"

"Oh please don't do that," said Andy.

"Don't do what?" asked the Lord.

"Shriek," said Andy.

"Now why would I do that?" he asked, eyes innocent.

"Because you just..."

"My word!" interrupted the Lord. "Look at the fog out-side! It must have just drifted in off the river."

"Bro! It's been foggy for hours now! Um, Sire." The sire, in hopes that it would counteract the "bro."

"Has it now?" the Lord trailed off.

"Weren't you here to tell me something?" asked Andy.

"I'm most certain I already have, my good man!" the Lord boasted.

"You haven't told me a damn thing." Andy's impatience was showing.

"Oh my! Fine. I'll tell the story again! No need to get your knickers knockered." Andy looked down to make sure his knickers were not, in fact, knockered.

"Now I'm sure you've heard," began the Lord, "of Earl Grey tea."

"Yes..." Andy didn't like where this was going.

"Now I don't know if you'll believe it, but I am the very same! I, humble Lord Charles Grey, am the very Earl it refers to!"

Pained, Andy said, "You don't say!"

"Yes! And the fates look down upon you today m'lad! I'm going to tell you how the most delectable tea in the kingdom has procured its illustrious name!"

"Lucky me," mumbled Andy.

"Once upon a time, there was a lovely Mandarin man. Now forgive me, but I do forget the chap's name. Never you mind, but this chap gave me the lovely tea after... well, I don't even know what I did! But he gave me the tea, and now the tea is me! Or I mean to say my name is the tea."

Andy didn't know what to say. So he didn't.

The Lord began again, "Once upon a time, there was a lovely Mandarin man. Now forgive me, but I do forget the chap's name," Andy's voice caught in his throat. "Never you mind, but this chap knew Englishmen like no Englishman I've ever met! He was a master blender, and blended a tea to suit my complexion, the local climatological considerations, and even the PH of my saliva!"

Andy waited.

"So Once upon a time, there was a..."
"Lovely Mandarin man!" the room blurted.

"Heavens me, no! Why would you say that? Quite offensive really! No, it was some British chap from Westminster. Named Jackson."

The room groaned.

"He had a real good knack for tea, that one! Down Picadilly way, if I remember correctly," Andy could see the Earl wandering London's streets in his own mind. The Lord even moved his pointer and middle fingers about like little legs.

"Do you even *KNOW* why the tea is named after you?"

"I do! No, yes, I do! I think. It is a bit foggy now that you mention it."

"Yeah, I get that," Andy couldn't help feeling let down.

"Does it really matter though?" the Lord asked no one. "The tea bears my name and I bear my tea. The why doesn't seem to quite matter much, now that I think about it."

"But you brought it up!" rebelled Andy.

"There doesn't have to be a reason," the Lord mused, ever distant.

"The past is nebulous. Especially cloudy when we imagine the past is a means to ascertain *WHY* something happened. No, there are simply too many factors to consider. Multitudes have conspired to bring this moment to fruition, and to lay the blame squarely on one factor is an exercise in futility," his stare was distant.

"Blame? Are we still talking about tea?" asked Andy.

"Sometimes it's OK to let things be unknown. The mystery enlivens the past. And I don't think it necessarily helps us cope, knowing the why. In fact, sometimes it's better NOT to know."

Coming from a haughty English noble that said things like "Mandarin Man," Andy was sure he agreed.

Sometimes it's better not to know, Andy thought, as the fog wrapped round him.

++

Andy embraced the lingering bits of his drink as he walked out into the dismal day. An extra sip didn't send him back into the Lord's chambers, and Andy was relieved for that.

As Andy walked, zombie-like silhouettes ambled about in the far reaches of the fog. He admired the somber tones, and muted sirens in the distance. Being a sad guy, feeling doomed to be doomed, just felt more valid when the sun was obscured by mist. End of Days was so much more valid with spookies walking about.

Andy didn't wander aimlessly, but the aim became less and less clear the longer Andy walked. He imagined he was looking for something. Something tangible, but everything was washed in the haze. Hazy hazy haze.

A haze that worried Andy more and more with each step.

The shadows became ghoulish, with ambiguous intent. The more Andy thought about it, the more his common sense reminded him, *sometimes it's better not knowing. Just keep walking.*

So Andy walked with his head down, and watched his feet as their tiny circle of influence cleared the haze.

He walked like he was trying to find the bathroom in a dark hallway, late at night on vacation. Hesitant steps. Modest steps. He wasn't sure if he had walked four blocks, or four feet, but he felt confident that this was the fastest he was willing to move, lest he have to look up and come to terms with spooky shadows left and right.

A bushtit careened over his shoulder, and Andy jumped.

If this London Fog is Hell, then surely Jack the Ripper is idling around here somewhere.

Andy's feet glanced a park bench. *Who knows what manner of demon is lurking nearby?*

Andy felt for the bench, in hopes to sit for a moment. Collect himself. He thought he had better take stock before he chanced upon any more spiritual encounters.

What are you afraid of? Andy thought.

"What *ARE* you afraid of?" repeated a voice from further down the bench.

"JESUS CHRIST!"

"Oh, he's not so scary. And I doubt he's wandering about right now. I think he prefers deserts," said the tiny voice.

"Eh, I wouldn't be surprised," Andy countered.

"I'm surprised you can get anywhere at all, looking at your feet like that," the girl's eyes were piercing and cut right through the fog.

Andy admitted, "Well, I don't exactly have a destination in mind. I'm just sort of out here. And what about you, what's a little girl do…"

Andy's voice caught in his throat. As he spoke, the fog had cleared and Andy saw a dead bird directly in front of the girl. A meticulous geometric pattern of orange, yellow and white candies surrounded the cute, fluffy, and rigid bushtit.

"Fucking bird," he muttered.

"And candy corn," the girl said matter-of-fact, as she followed Andy's gaze.

"Candy corn?"

"Yep."

Andy couldn't take his eyes off the morbid little mandala. He didn't think the girl was the type to ritually sacrifice songbirds, but his mind was at odds with the scene. He stared blankly, and imagined bird-masked kindergarten cabals that trapped sparrows to appease some primeval deity.

He jumped as he felt the girl's hand in his own. When she took her hand away, Andy could feel that she had left something in its place.

"Care to say a few words?" she asked.

"A few words."

"Very funny," she stared at Andy, neither laughing nor blinking.

"Uh, right. For the bird," Andy felt he was being put on the spot. He didn't know the bird that well, didn't feel like it was appropriate to speak out of turn. Andy felt that clammy, oppressive air of public speech closing in on him.

In the absence of any presence of mind, Andy's mouth spoke for him.

"Better you than me," his mouth whispered.

Andy immediately regretted that, in the presence of the dead, even if was just a "fucking bird." His mouth tried to swallow itself, tongue and all, but to no avail. So it settled for the next best thing, and swallowed a candy corn whole.

Candy Corn

The dark was oppressive. The kind where even the shadows have shadows. And it was instantaneous. One moment the world was awake with luminous fog, the next was the black that preceded time itself.

One by one, the candy corn at Andy's feet were filled with a radiance akin to the flames they so clearly resembled. The oranges and yellows grew vibrant, little furnaces within their luminescence. From the depths of these flames, Andy's eyes caught visions of flowers being born and withering away. They were marigolds, cascading like a garden center sales racks.

The marigolds birthed more marigolds, and the flaming candies joined them in spirited dance. They moved this way and that, framed the girl on the bench and masked her in shadows. She stepped forward into the warm swirling tones, as a soloist steps into a spotlight.

Her face was skeletal, framed by a crown of candy corn and marigolds. At first, Andy thought he saw a Dia De Los Muertos style Catrina before him. Stylized bones highlighted by deepening layers of black and white makeup. As she moved forward, though, Andy realized that she was *actually* skeletal.

Bleached bones and empty sockets. And yet, the girl was somehow both macabre and adorable. Perhaps it was the flowers or maybe it was the comical candy corn fangs in her mouth. Either way, the girl was the least repulsive dead thing Andy could imagine. Dead still, but endearing.

When she spoke, Andy felt as if the entire spirit realm was channeled through her vocal chords. It was a haunting sound, or more so, a haunted sound. Her voice had voices, and they were all speaking at once. It was disjointed, hollow, and Andy's bones seemed to understand before his head.

"Death is celebratory," the little skull child began. "The end is a love song to the beginning." The words seemed heavy, and didn't want to travel much further than Andy's ears.

"So often in the face of Death, people shy away. They turn back towards life. Proper mourning, however, is looking Death straight in the eyes. It is a recognition of the power of loss. The remembrance that healing is not *moving on*. It is the *Dead* that move on, the *Dead* that return to the circles and cycles of the soul. It is the *survivors* who are to be mourned, because it is the *survivors* who must remain."

Andy couldn't speak. Andy wouldn't speak.

"You think, perhaps, that this is sad. Absolutely. It is heart breaking, the power of loss. Impermanence is suffering, is it not? Knowing that Death is absolute, knowing that the End is final, is not something to shine a light upon. No, Death is meant to be mourned. Sadness is meant to be embraced. Mourning is the proper celebration of Death."

"Loss is requisite. Ends are necessary," she continued. "Certainly, life can only be understood fully in the face of death. We mustn't sidestep the power of the End or lessen its magnitude. Death is not good. That would be another misstep. No, Death is not good, but Death is true. Everything has an End, and the Dead ask you to look into their eyes, not to avert your gaze towards Life. Loss leaves an empty space which will never again be filled, and that is to be given the gravity it deserves."

The words resonated, so Andy felt for the empty space inside himself. The emptiness that surrounded him, the visceral dark, however, overwhelmed any chance at self-reflection at that moment.

"In the face of the world ending," the eye sockets blazed with the fires of a thousand candy corns, "you think you should find peace. You think you should find meaning, hope, and understanding. You will not find these things, and if you do, you will find them empty. No, in the face of the End, all you will find is Darkness."

Andy tried to speak. He really did try.

"There may be light after the darkness, Andy. But that doesn't mean the darkness ever leaves. Healing is like stars, tiny points of light amidst cosmic despair. Loss is eternal, pain is eternal, sadness is eternal. Mourn what was had, mourn what was lost. Mourn, because loss is half of the process. Mourn, because for Life to be, Death has to be."

"So, it's OK to be sad?" Andy managed to squeak.

"No Andy. It is *necessary* to be sad."

Andy watched the luminous kernels extinguish themselves, one by one, through tear filled eyes.

++

Andy cried and he walked. He walked and he cried.

Being given permission to be sad was all Andy needed. He hadn't given himself time to process. He was propelled forward by circumstance, and only now was he able to begin to find the words for what he was feeling.

Andy felt betrayed.

Why betrayed? He asked himself.

He knew he had plans, expectations, and desires. There were plot holes, moments that needed to be fleshed out and he felt like any hope of existential resolution was a lie. Meaning collapsed at the feet of decay.

So he cried and walked. He walked and he cried.

He thought, *this is what people feel like at the moment of death. Only, I have to endure for four more days!* As he thought this, a darker part whispered the truth, *you never HAVE to endure. You choose this, but you could make another choice.*

The thought of self-induced oblivion really sent him over the edge. His tears were cartoonish. Huge tears cascaded off his ski jump nose with world record velocity. One tear, however, caught the crease of his cheek just right. It sped down his lip, and stopped, only to tickle Andy's lip. Andy licked his lip, and drank his own sadness.

Salt Water

The sound of the sea rose in Andy's ear, like only the sound of the sea can. It swelled and swayed, crashed and retreated. It danced across Andy's world, commanded attention like nothing else.

Andy felt small, smaller still, as he watched the waters engulf the Earth, which was far below him. It did this, not like the battering ram of a tsunami, but more like the slow fill of a bathtub. A gentle sort of ablution.

A flood yes, but a flood of the 97.6-98.4 degrees Fahrenheit variety. Biological and primordial waters, to be sure. The kind that salamandersome things climb up out of.

Andy saw airy little fairies, as they danced off in the distance. They beckoned the swells, charmed the waves as they peaked and troughed. They were spunky, and alighted so much like a sparkler, that Andy assumed they must have been pixies.

As they flew closer, he noticed they were pixies with adorable little sailors' outfits. *Nautical Pixies,* Andy thought. *Nixies? Is that how that works?*

A particularly effervescent Nixie flew up to Andy.

Andy prepared himself for a particularly petite voice to tell him about the importance of emotional and physical release, all in mouse-sized sailing jargon.

The "voice" that greeted Andy, however, spoke no words.

The wave engulfed Andy, setting him afloat in an embrace that could only be likened to a mother. He rocked, and he swayed in the tide of its love. It held him closer than close, up to the very limit of separateness.

Returned to the womb, Andy did as one does. Andy cried.

++

Andy was unsure how long he cried. Well, "had been crying for" is more accurate since he had not stopped. Nor had he stopped walking, for that matter. He was pretty sure he couldn't walk too far, though, even if he tried.

Behind his tears, he found himself a bit more aware of his surroundings.

He saw that the street was aglow in an otherworldly light. A dive bar on Mars sort of glow. The beautiful kind of lighting that only exists where primordial mist and neon light come together.

He didn't care where he was, he'd take a warm bowl of just about anything right now.

"Noooooo," he wailed as the sign came into focus.

Mary's All Night. A diner.

He ran past the doors, allowed the fog to swallow his sobs. He realized he couldn't see a single moving vehicle, so he didn't have to be careful where or how he ran. So he ran like a crying kid runs home from school. If he had a backpack, it would have fallen off as he ran, as his arms fluttered behind him.

It felt good to cry, but terrible to run. It hurt. Still, Andy ran until he couldn't run anymore, which wasn't terribly far. With no landmarks, Andy assumed he had run about 3 blocks.

Still got it, Andy thought, chest puffed, as he looked back at his wind tunnel through the fog.

The catharsis he felt from his cry and his runner's high were so strong that Andy didn't remember what he had even been crying about. *Everything,* he supposed.

The glow of the sign was much the same, a rotisserie chicken on a wharf kind of feel.

Andy rubbed his eyes, certain the tears were smearing the words on the sign. The words, though, were actually just smearing themselves. They resembled the English alphabet being squished between the Cyrillic and Arabic alphabets. Both familiar and foreign, Andy was sure he could pronounce the word but knew he'd do it wrong.

He walked through the front door, to such a comforting aroma, his muscles gave out at the first available chair. This happened to be a very tiny chair, right next to the entrance. Andy sat down in it and immediately felt like a giant in a kindergarten class.

I can't be doing this right, thought Andy.

"My friend, let me!" said a heavily accented man who wore an extremely novel hat, and an equally ordinary black fast food uniform. Tassels, shiny bells, fantastical embroidery, and a polyester polo shirt.

He lifted Andy by his armpits, turned him around, and did all but kick Andy's knees out from under him. Andy was now in some sort of kneel of devotion, with the tiny chaired tucked in some indefinable spot in his nether regions.

"Traditional Sartocian stool. Is very good for digestions" the man said, again in an accent that Andy couldn't quite place. "Here is menu, this is only today."

"Thank you," Andy managed to spit out, despite being hypnotized by the menu.

Weird words, weird pictures. Andy didn't know what anything was. Not. A. Clue.

It's beautiful, Andy nearly wept.

Andy had a deep affection for any and all ethnic food. He reveled in a culture and history transformed into num nums. He felt it the most authentic way to partake in a loving embrace with an entire people, without being an absolute creep.

Lately, though, the novelty was all but missing. He hadn't been *excited* by food in oh so long. Lebanese food? *Neat.* Korean food. *Yay?* Tajik teahouse? *Fine.*

So when faced with this indecipherable mess, Andy was downright giddy.

When the man returned, Andy didn't wait for him to speak first.

"What should I order? I'm cold," Andy cut to the chase.

"Sartocia is very cold in the all the time. Bachik herders always need strong soup for walking long ways. Is perfect for tending to many sheepses. I bring you this, OK?"

Ok, perfect, thank you, Andy thought, instead of said, since the man had already burst through the swinging kitchen doors.

Andy really was beside himself. He had just had a good cry. So now, in order to come to terms with his sadness, he needed soup. It was the natural order of things, liquid out liquid in.

Andy supposed, Sartocian stew would fit the bill.

Sartocia. Sartocia? Andy was well versed in geography. He always kept an atlas sitting on the tank of his toilet. He ogled Pakistan while he pooped, took in Tanzania when he turded.

He could not, however, for the life of him, figure out where Sartocia was. He thought maybe it was close to Azerbaijan. *Maybe it's an old name for Kurdish Turkey? Isn't Bachik the Greek name for the Basque lands? What are the hinterlands between Vietnam and China called? And what did the colonials call Nubia, anyways?*

Andy was broken from his globetrotting reverie by the

slam of a soup bowl on the table. The man put a spoon directly into Andy's hand.

"Hey, I was wondering..." Andy began.

"No. You eat soup hot and only when hot, and is now hot."

"O...K..." Andy dipped the spoon in the soup, not breaking eye contact with the man.

There's something familiar about that hat, Andy thought. He watched the man's lips turn up into a smile, as Andy spooned the soup into his mouth.

Sartocian Bachik Soup

The color bled from the scene like a slaughtered cow. As the color wept, oh so violently, it was replaced with, again, zombied hues of black and gray. *What a dismal* day, Andy thought.

Other than the spectrum, the scene remained the same. Andy took in the fancy tea kettle, the pictures of toothless grins and load bearing donkeys.

"You turned black and white," Andy stated the obvious.

"Maybe it is you that are black white," responded the Greyman.

Andy considered this for a moment.

"No, no I kid. It was me," said the man.

"I'm not the best person to fuck with right now, to be honest," responded Andy, almost pleading. Andy's grip on reality was tenuous enough without some mystical being messing with his perception.

"Sorry to say, but your skin, it does looks like ashes, no?" said the man in a nonjudgmental tone.

"Can you blame me?" Andy felt his mood kindling, his anger and confusion growing.

"No wait," Andy remembered himself. "Before we get mired in philosophy and all that, can I ask a question?"

Andy couldn't let it slip away. "Where exactly is Sartocia?

It's a very tip of the tongue, memory of a memory sort of thing."

"I don't know," the Greyman averted his gaze.

"You don't know?" Andy was aghast.

"No, but I know a lot. I know Sartocia was beautiful place. Apricots, lots of laughings. Spring time folks dances. Happy sheepses in the tall grasses. You get picture," Andy smiled at the image.

"It knew suffering as all good places still do. Stilled births, cheated husbands, and bad poetries. It was very very ordinary. And then came the war. Invasion from within and without. Family was torn into twos. Fathers forgetted sons, neighbors forgetted neighbors, and peace forgetted peace."

He was solemn, "Of course at first, the internationals condemn. They condemn and they condemn and they condemn. They call for peace talk, diplomatics, sanctionings and aid. Sartocia was a world's problem, so there was a uniting against the pain and the suffering of mine peoples. But then there was Afghanistan. Or was it Bosnia? Rwanda maybe. No matter which, the world found new focus. New condemn. And the world forget Sartocia and so did I."

"But HOW?"

"I don't know. I am patron saint of Sartocia, and so you think I would know what happens! But sometimes people just forget."

Still reeling, Andy implored, "People just forget? A whole nation, a whole culture is just lost to 'I dunno?'"

"All thing is forgotten. History makes illusion of memory. Illusion of rememberance. But history is so that a humans *CAN* forget. Real moments, tangible moments, and ordinaries peoples are always forgotted. It is the essence of time. Infinity is big, yes? But still too small to hold all of sadness of even this one momentous moments."

"But surely someone must remember? Surely someone cared enough to pay attention!"

"People cared. People do care. That does not matter for long terms. Attention is a slipperies, and there is critical mass to amnesias. Things just fall away from public eyes. The Sartocian genocide was an real Armaggedons. It was very evil moment that should have been pivotal moments in humans understanding of suffering. It should have been a good instructions. But there have been an infinities of Armaggedonses, a googling-plex of terrible shit. Each *SHOULD* have impact the way lives are lived. Each and every though, is lost in the time of sands. Sands of times. When suffering is out there, when suffering isn't your own, how do yous hold it all?"

"It's too heavy," and Andy felt that weight.

"Yes, too heavy. So people, they lets it go. Even we Gods. Your suffering is real, your pain is as deep and vast as all oceans and sea. But Andy, you too will be forgotted."

I too will be forgotted.

Andy watched the man fade away. Or was it Andy that faded away?

+ +

Andy faced that vast and infinite sea. He watched it wash against the shores of oblivion, saw his face, a mere ripple in the eternity that was a bowl of soup.

It was very delicious. The soup, not the suffering. The suffering left him empty, despite a sloshing belly full of liquid. Not other people's suffering, not even the suffering of an entire nation, could keep Andy from focusing on on his woes.

Sure people could forget kingdoms. That made sense. History was vast, incomprehensibly so.

But not Andy! Surely people would take notice of the hellfire, trumpeting Angels, and inevitable vaporization of their beloved Andy.

You too will be forgotted. And deep down, Andy knew it was true.

In fact, Andy was pretty sure the waiter had forgotten about Andy already. He busied himself with another table, as he detailed a very intricate tea ceremony involving a bunch of tiny plates, cubes of brown sugar, and a really really long candle.

So Andy left a pile of crumpled dollars on the table, and walked out the front door.

The haze outside still hazed, stilled Andy's desire to see just a little bit ahead of himself. But still, Andy tried. He tried to imagine a next move, a logical step following the realization that he was just about due to fade into oblivion. He imagined writing a tome or constructing a megalith. But building things that transcend time, takes time. And Andy didn't have enough time for much of anything.

What did Andy have time for?

Forgiveness? No, that would definitely take too long.

Selflessness? Absolutely not, he was too wrapped in himself.

Andy realized, if anything, he had time for drink. Andy always had time for drink.

You too will be forgotted? Well they can't forget me if I forget them first!

Andy texted Dante, "Tiddy's?"

The response came right back, as if it were pre-loaded. "Tiddy's."

Andy didn't care which way he was supposed to walk to get to the bar. He just knew if he took a left turn, every second block, he would arrive safely at some point. Quantum wandering.

And he did. He didn't pay attention, he was too busy wallowing, but he showed up just as Dante was walked up to the front door.

"Madame..." said Dante as he held the door open for Andy.

"Oh my, what a gentleman," Andy said as he eyed Dante's package.

Dante carried a parcel of sorts, wrapped in old yellowed newspaper. So old, in fact, that Andy was surprised Dante was able to wrap it at all. It should have disintegrated in his hands. It was more filo dough than wrapping paper.

Great, and now I'm craving baklava. Bloody unlikely in a place like this, Andy's head whined.

"I got us two banana liqueurs," smiled Dante as he walked back from the bar.

Andy lost himself in the marvel that Dante was quite

good at pronouncing both u's *and* the e in liqueur. Then he came back to himself, to the dark realization that the baklava was a dream. He was *not* about to meet the god of honey, pistachio and delicate pastry. Instead, he was destined for a demon of fake banana boozy corn syrup. He felt grimy just thinking about it.

Dante opened the package in front of Andy, only to reveal to bottle of banana liqueur.

"A little redundant, don't you think?" asked Andy.

"Don't act like you don't love it bro. And this is the good shit. 1986 vintage."

The waitress arrived with rocks glasses full of liqueur. No mere shots. Dante grabbed both and emptied them into the plastic plant behind him. He popped open the musty bottle and poured not a couple fingers, but a whole fistful into Andy's glass.

Andy was skeptical, but he hazarded a sniff. His body shuddered, and his heart stuttered.

"Who am I kidding, Dante? You're fuckin' right. I do love me a good liq-u-e-u-r," Andy slurred as he took a nip.

Banana Flavor

The darkness was complete. Suffocating.

And then, the lights in the room pulsed to life and brought the room with them.

Andy wondered if a jungle rave awaited him, the way the energy in the room shifted.

The lights, however, were all wrong. They were soft and warm. The perfect light to read some historical fiction by. Maybe drink some hot cocoa or smoke a cigar perhaps.

The already low lights dimmed, just a bit, an invitation to pay attention. Andy was hushed and waited for what came next.

Dante stepped forward into a lonely spotlight, dressed like Dante would no doubt dress on the beach. The shorts were very short. The Hawaiian shirt was sheer like paper, and oh so delicate. His hat was made from fronds, his feet were calloused by the hot sand.

Despite the riotous outfit, the quiet in the room was all consuming.

Dante had sunglasses on, which fit his face like they had never left. Andy eschewed sunglasses himself, thinking his dark inner life didn't need any more shade. But they looked good on Dante.

Dante slid the frames down his nose, and looked over

the top of the rims, somehow professorial despite being really quite laid back.

He began, "My name is Banana Flavor and I'm here to talk about the past."

Andy was stilled. The room was rapt.

"You imagine your past and your present diverge. And yet you travel through time each and every moment you think about the past. What if you allowed your very essence to embody that past? I promise you ladies and gentle*man*, this is well within your reach."

Andy noticed that he was the lone gentle*man* in an audience of many, many, middle aged women. On all sides he was surrounded by well curled hair, apricot chap-stick and responsibly sourced hand bags.

"Look at me," the silence was cut like cheese, as the women took him all in. "I may look like some derelict lab created flavor." The ladies chided Dante, whispered their sweet nothings.

"But I am actually a quite good approximation of a near extinct species of banana. I am the very essence of your grandma's grandma's banana," that made Andy vaguely uncomfortable. "That banana died off decades ago, in a blight. But not before I was synthesized. The banana died, and yet I lived. So through the magic of chemistry, you can still taste this." Dante motioned and Andy groaned.

"So yes, I *am* time capsule. I *am* a time traveler. And not to alarm you, but I have the ability to bring you with me, into the past," the ladies gasped.

Dante paused. "Would it surprise you, ladies and gentle*man*, if I told you that I have already done said bringing?" This time Andy gasped.

"Nostalgia. Nostalgia is more than an illusory thing. It's tactile. Take you, Andy," a spotlight spotted Andy. "I happen to have your first memory of Banana Flavor written on this card right here," the women in the audience eyed Andy. Andy shriveled.

"It says, and you can correct me if I'm wrong, but that your initial run in with banana flavor was disgust. Abject horror in fact. Not uncommon, with a flavor like this," more gross motions.

"Despite this, however, you ate an entire sleeve of banana taffy. You then," he consulted the card, "proceeded to lay on the beach towel in 110 degree Phoenix weather for a couple hours. You then did approximately 136 sit-ups so you could impress all the ladies with your abs and your bronze."

Andy flushed under the women's hot gaze, but he couldn't help but laugh.

"Then you went into your cousin's house, laid directly in front of the 52 degree A/C, and proceeded to watch two hours of soft core porn as your bodily functions began race. From the extremes or the taffy, its hard to say" Dante winked and the room swooned.

"Bahaha true, true! Holy shit what a day. I remember my aunt made me ramen after she found my rigid on the floor," the woman nearest Andy bit her lip. "She thought the MSG water would be good for my belly, then insisted I not chew any of the noodles, because she said chewing was likely to fatigue my already stressed adrenals." Andy's aunt was absolutely not a nurse.

The Bananaman interjected, "And so you see, ladies and gentleman, the mighty power of memory. You relive every detail, are taken deep into the heart of the moment. You are transported."

"Yeah. And? What for?" asked Andy.

"You imagine the past is just that: the past," Andy was sure it was. Let bygones be bygone and all that. "But it belongs here just as much as the present. It's a salve to the present, and it's a prologue to the future. It's beautiful. Enlightened types always seem to think that the Now cannot include the past. That you must be *here,* always *here.* But why not bring there, here?"

"What power can the past have over a moment as momentous as the End of Days?" Asked Andy. A little bit of nostalgia seemed insignificant in the face of Armageddon.

"Do not doubt the power of disassociation, Andy," the Bananaman said. "I promise you this: what's about to come, your mind is going to want to be as far from here as possible."

Andy gulped, "Why, what's about to happen?"

"The Apocalypse of course."

"Don't give me that shit!" Andy's patience was beyond thin. "Why is everything got to be so goddamn enigmatic? You'd think a supreme deity would be supremely detail oriented! Fuck your cryptic this, fuck your esoteric that! Just tell me what to expect, other than a few days of my lunch talking back to me!"

"Fine. It's gonna hurt. I can tell you that much. They'll probably skin me alive for saying that much, but it's going to hurt Andy. Physically. That's why having someplace to flee might not be such a bad idea."

"I always assumed hellfire would hurt, but what can I expect? Sizzling skin? Flaying? Disembowelment?"

"Eh... probably something like this." Dante's eyes were hollow.

Andy watched in horror as the Bananaman was peeled before his eyes.

✚✚

Oh it hurt all right. It hurt as much as an afternoon of super saccharine banana grain alcohol could hurt. Which is to say, a lot.

Andy layed on the couch and stared at the ceiling. Well, laid on the couch because layed isn't a thing.

It was a gross ceiling. Some might call it a popcorn ceiling, but Andy always thought of the style as cottage cheese ceiling. Lumpy, curdy, and decidedly wet. Andy stared at the ceiling in horror, expecting it to drip on him at any moment.

Andy tried desperately to think about the future, or what was left of it. Through the mire of his pounding head, he managed to pull together just a few thoughts. *The world is ending. It is going to hurt. Angels and Demons are super eccentric, but fairly instructive. And they don't have too many moral imperatives! They're honestly not bad company.*

But what about everyone else? Andy thought. The divine aspects were fine and all, but Andy wondered if he should invite any other humans into the reality of what was happening to him.

Of course, he wondered if he should confide in Angie. She already thought his grasp of reality was tenuous, so maybe not.

Should he wax poetic to Dante? If anyone would believe Andy about eschatological foodstuffs, its Dante.

And what about Andy's mom?

Shit. Mom.

Andy hadn't talked to his mom in weeks. Weeks and weeks actually. The last time he had talked to her, he had scream-cried at her because she was wanted to throw away a bunch of his childhood memories to make room for more craft making supplies.

I should call her.

Andy picked up his phone, hesitated a moment, and found and dialed "Mum Dearest" in his contact list.

The phone rang once, if not even.

"Andy! Jesus, I've been calling you for days and you haven't answered and I was beginning to really get stressed. I even called Angie and she said you were out of it. And for *her* to say you're being weird means you're being really freakin' weird."

"Wait, you've been calling me? I haven't had any missed calls." Andy realized he hadn't had *any* calls in the last couple days.

"It never rings, it just goes straight to voicemail. But whatever. Are you OK? I'm seriously worried about you. Angie said you aren't working."

"Honestly," Andy hated being honest with his mom, "it's all been a complete shit show. Angie and I are on the rocks, mostly because I suck. And work sucks, probably also because I suck. So I quit. Well I didn't quit exactly, I just stopped going. And there's this thing..." Andy wasn't sure how to tell his mom that it was all coming to an end, without making her think he was suicidal.

"Oh God is she pregnant?"

"No mom, she's not pregnant. I've just been, well, I've been having these visions. And I mean this truly. This isn't a joke. I think the world is coming to an end."

"End of the World again, huh Andy? You used to keep yourself up at night worrying about the atomic bomb you know. And gangs. Boy were you afraid of gangs. You know, I know that you hate when I say this, but I think you need to be on antidepressants," Andy groaned. "They've helped me a ton and I think that you've been having a really hard time lately. What with your grandpa dying and all."

Andy hadn't thought about his grandpa. In all his thoughts of death, dying, and the undead, the most important corpse he knew hadn't even crossed his mind.

Andy's grandpa had been his best friend, his way-finder, his confidant. A true gem of a human being. And, as with all good things, he had been taken from Andy without so much as a goodbye. Just the swift kick in the groin that is a heart attack.

Such bullshit. The person with the best heart I've ever known has a Goddamned heart attack. Stupid bullshit irony.

"I don't need meds mom. This is the real deal. You fucking *claim* you believe in angels! For God's sake your car has a 'Don't Drive Faster than Your Guardian Angel Can Fly' bumper sticker. Why is it that when I am the one having a mystical experience, I need pharmaceuticals, but when a middle aged housewife on TLC says it, it's fucking gospel?"

"I don't know how to talk to you when you're like this," his mom replied ever so gently.

"Then don't fucking talk to me!" Andy slammed the phone down. Andy missed land lines. Slamming a cell phone into a couch cushion while pressing "End" didn't have the same punch as smashing the giant plastic receiver down on a giant plastic base.

Why did I think she'd be any help? Andy thought.

More and more, Andy felt the impression that there wasn't anyone that could help him.

Actually, maybe there is someone that could help me.

Andy sat up and stared at his, yet again, unfamiliar surroundings. It wasn't the same apartment as yesterday. That was certain. It was a decrepit, creepy little apartment. Old carpet, somewhere between puke green and burnt orange, if that was possible.

The lighting was dingy, coming from two floor lamps that looked like they were from a thrift store reject dumpster. They cast eerie shadows, warped facsimiles of the goofy spirits he would no doubt meet any moment.

The kitchen seemed just as miserable from afar, but he did see a brand spankin' new juicer on the counter. *That's a little out of place,* he thought.

As he walked towards the kitchen, he saw movement out of the corner of his eye. He wound his arm back, as if to slap whatever approached. At the window, a bushtit tap tap tapped at the glass pane. Andy walked over, and opened the window a crack.

The bird hopped inside, with a pained sort of gait.

"I'd call you a fucking bird, but it seems inappropriate. A low blow," Andy looked concerned. "What happened little guy?"

The bushtit hazarded a chirp, but failed about halfway through.

"Oh dude, no good! Is this from when you hit the glass earlier?" Andy ran over to the sink and palmed a handful of water. He walked back over to the bushtit and the bird took a couple sips, bowing its head in between each, in what Andy assumed was thanks and reverence.

"I feel you little dude. It's hard to motivate myself to chirp, to walk, and for sure to fly right now. I respect you for even making it to this height," Andy looked out the window, saw the city scape as it swung between the fog and the moonlight.

Andy took a moment to wonder, again, where the Hell he was. He could see the weird half-moon Megabank building in the distance. So he was on the south side of the river, and still in the city. Well the outskirts. The in between. *More in betweens,* Andy shuddered.

Besides lost, Andy was plagued by a lingering sense of regret.

Maybe regret about work and love were buried in there, but the regret he felt deepest tasted like banana. *Shnappsy burps are the worst.*

He gave the bird a little pat on the head, and walked over to the fridge, craving a detox.

Blackberries. Apples. Watermelon. Maybe a fuckin Kiwi! Andy was excited about what he was about to juice, which made him feel like kind of a square.

But he was ready for a cleanse. He was ready for a fresh start. A reset.

He opened the fridge, and much to his chagrin, only one thing awaited him.

Celery. Really, celery?

He checked the cabinets, the freezer, the lazy Susan, even the couch cushions.

Fuck. Just celery huh? That's what I get for wanting a cleanse.

Andy turned on the juicer, not quite knowing what he was doing. The little engine hummed, and he watched the top start to rotate, hum and dance.

He took about four sticks of celery, and sent them down the chute and watched a silly amount of liquid come out. *Mostly water, I guess.*

Andy sniffed the cup.

It smelled like childhood. Parks, field trips. Ants on a log. Minus the ants though. And whatever the peanut butter was supposed to signify in the log metaphor.

Ya, this is what I deserve all right.

Ever so cautious, ever so careful, as if it might taste him back, Andy took a sip.

Celery Juice

The switch to the juicer flipped, all by itself, and the motor again started to hum. Instead of rotating on the interior, however, the outside of the juicer began to shift and change.

It was a little like watching a robot transform into a car. Only it was a juicer, transforming into not a juicer. Andy couldn't quite tell what the goal transformation was.

Compartments opened and closed, revealed gleaming metal pistons and joints. Rods inserted here and there. A bit sexual, and Andy was unsure if he should be turned on or not.

The juicer stretched upwards, and elongated into a humanoid shape. The curved metal melted and rehardened, and formed the first distinct facial feature. A nose. Andy saw bristly little untrimmed wires protrude. Nose hairs to be sure. More wires came out here and there, adding more hair to a more and more Andy-like being. It was small though, not much larger than the juicer. Childlike.

The turbines whirred slower, and the moving parts came into focus as a pair of eyes and a furrowed brow. *It's not a happy little Andybot*, Andy thought to himself.

"Greetings human," the voice was metallic, abrasive, a bit sharp.

"Hello," Andy returned..

"How do you like your deliquesced apium gravieolens?" asked the very robotic robot.

"My what?" Andy looked at his belly button, unsure if he should be insulted.

"Ah, I'm just fucking with you man," said the robot in an altogether different voice, more approximate to what a miniaturized Andy might sound like. "I was asking if you liked your celery juice."

"Oh, haha. Um, I kind of hate it, ya know? But my body is definitely, well, responding?" Andy still tried to convince himself that it was good for him, even as he said this.

"It would seem," replied Andybot, "it's what you deserve."

"Yeah," Andy's voice faltered as he thought of the banana liqueur, "I had it coming."

"We always get what we deserve. Divine justice. It's the only law worth a damn, if you ask me."

Andy hated the law. Cops? Against 'em. Courts? Definitely not for 'em. Anything penal? Not his preference, no thank you. Andy felt his guts wrench when he heard a term like "divine justice." He pictured angels with batons and celestial prisons.

The metal man continued, "God is infallible my friend. If you are born into shit circumstance, sorry little baby, you deserve that. Abused by your coworker? The law has deemed you guilty. Stricken by plague? Hit by a train? Gas line explodes in your face while you're cooking your penne? Judgment has been rendered. Bad things don't happen to good people. Good people happen to bad things."

"Suffering is something that people deserve?" Andy repeated.

"Unequivocally, yes. Sometimes it's some deep deep karma. Past lives shitting on current lives, which will send their own shit further downstream. Other times you can see the cause and effect, like clockwork, within one lifetime. But even if it is ineffable, it is still divine will. Justice has been served, whether you can do the math or not."

"That's fucking terrible," Andy hated it.

"Terrible but true."

"So shit doesn't just happen?"

"Shit does not just happen. Everything happens, as they say, for a reason. But they miss the fact that the reason is themselves."

"We all get what we deserve," Andy kept repeating it, and a familiarity filled him with dread.

"Your end is what you deserve Andy. You asked for this, and God repaid you in kind. Real fair, that God character."

I asked for this? Andy wondered, but wouldn't allow himself to say it aloud.

Andy realized this rhetoric was what Andy always told himself when something went wrong. Rather than allow himself just the slightest bit of grace, Andy always found a way to blame himself.

Even when someone else acted wretched, treated Andy like complete trash, Andy found a way to blame himself.

Andy was to blame, for example, when his ex cheated on him with his roommate. *I wasn't good enough, could never have been good enough for her. I chose the wrong roommate. My abs weren't abby enough. Or maybe I was unsatisfactory at satisfying.*

The feeling was familiar, that beautiful place where self-loathing and inadequacy meet.

"You build your own Hell, Andy," the robots eyes gleamed, sparked deep within.

Andy looked at the celery juice. Regret swam through him, and his heart dropped into his stomach. Andy thought about strawberry juice, pineapple juice. Hell, tomato juice. Andy sipped the celery juiced, felt the grossness wash over him.

He had built his own Hell, and this was what he deserved.

"Remember that Andy, as you come to terms with the End of Days. As you watch people walk away, fall away, that it was you that turned them away. You are your own jury, your own executioner. That's why we call it Judgment Day. The Judgment is from within, not from without."

Judgment day, Andy heard his heart whisper as the robot, whirred and spun, smaller and smaller. Where Andybot's butt had been, there was a chute that shot out the fibrous leftover celery bits.

Yep. *This is what I deserve.*

++

Andy didn't intend to go to Angie's place. His self-loathing was way too high for that. He tried to walk anywhere else, but the fog seemed to siphon him over and over again to the stoop of her apartment.

Andy was afraid to knock, to ring, to go inside. He knew she was going to make him feel terrible. Well, he would make himself feel terrible but she would be his foil. Passive aggressive self-harm.

He again tried to walk through the fog, aimless. The fog though, had very direct aim, and he finally resigned himself to sitting on the stoop of her apartment.

He heard cars in the distance, and the cars became a roar.

He was angry at being angry at himself. *Why am I so intent to hurt myself? And what are my weapons of choice for this perpetual self damnation?*

Andy had a substance abuse problem, for sure.

It's not that he drank every day. That would have maybe been a little bit healthier, to be honest. No, Andy waited until he was at a fever pitch, and then drank enough to make an Irishmen weak in the knees.

Andy had always binged. He remembered being 10 years old, eating nearly two boxes of cereal in a sitting. He knew it was a coping mechanism, a way to have some control of his very out of control life. Dad doesn't want to see you? Eat a box of cereal. Teacher tells you that you're lazy? Eat a box of cereal!

Nowadays, however, he preferred that the grains ferment for a few weeks, and then he would drink his cereal. Lots and lots of cereals.

Angie was different. She liked wine. She liked beer. Hell, she liked gin (Andy loved that about her). Angie, however, had a lot of self-control. *Maybe too much self-control,* Andy mused. She had so much self-control that it made her all the more upset that Andy didn't have any.

She wanted control of his self-control.

Andy believed, however, that it was sort of hard wired at this point. He couldn't reign himself in if he tried. And he had tried. Not terribly hard, mind you, but Andy had tried to be less impulsive. Less inclined to consume his sadness.

Andy heard a flutter above him, and a bushtit made a not so graceful landing next to him.

As shoddy as the bird's landing was, its footing was even less sure than that standing still. It weebled, wobbled, and limped as it hopped towards Andy.

Shit, did I forget the bird in the apartment? And how'd he even get here?

Andy inspected the bedraggled bird, admired all the ways it was more bedraggleder than it was before. Limp wing, lame leg, scales on its scales. A sad little tit.

Andy felt in his pocket for the crumbs of yesterday's snack he knew were probably still there. Andy's pocket were known to hold all sorts of ancient artifacts. There were only a few kernels of amaranth, but the bushtit was appreciative nonetheless. It hopped over to the snack, with a clear intent not to put any weight on its left foot.

"What can I do for you buddy?" Andy hazarded a closer look at the bird's leg, but couldn't see anything wrong. He inspected his fluff, considered the possibility that it was an abdominal or pelvic problem.

"I'm sorry you're hurting buddy. But I don't know what the Hell I'm looking for. I can carry you around with me if you want," the bird cocked its head to the side, considered the proposal.

"Talking to a bird?" Andy jumped at the sound of Angie's voice.

"Oh, yeah. I think he's hurt. Would it be weird if I carried him around with me?"

"Super weird. But sweet too. You can bring him in though, if you're coming up?" Angie motioned with her head towards the stairs.

"I'd love to. I wasn't creeping, by the way. I was just sitting and thinking."

"Right, just sitting and thinking. On *my* doorstep. Whatever, come on," she held open the door. Andy cradled the bushtit, and the last amaranth kernel, and began his slow ascent towards Angie's apartment.

Andy struggled, and Angie turned her head, smiled, and asked him if he needed help.

"I've got it, thanks," whispered Andy over the tiny bird's body.

Andy made straight for Angie's couch, where he set the bushtit on the arm of the chair.

"I couldn't just leave him alone," Andy said, half to himself.

"Did you feel bad leaving *me* alone last night," Angie countered.

"About that. Honestly, I was nervous. I feel like there's a lot unsaid between us, and, I don't know, it feels weird to have sex when we're mad at each other."

"I'm not mad at you. Why do you always think I'm mad? I'm confused and worried, sure."

"Oh, you're not? Well I'm actually not mad at you either!" Andy smiled.

"Clearly," Angie rolled her eyes.

"I'm mad at myself, and I feel like you should be mad at me. I'm broken, and I haven't exactly been coping well with being broken."

"I've noticed, but I don't know if there is a good way to cope with what you've been going through," Angie's eyes were beyond understanding. There was a warmth there that made Andy feel like everything was going to be OK. Like she knew more than even he knew.

With eyes like hers, it was inevitable. Andy cried for the bajillionth time that day.

"I'm sorry. I swear to God I'm so sorry. I'm shitty. I know I'm shitty."

"First of all, stop calling yourself shitty," Angie's voice was stern.

"I feel like I deserve all this pain, all this fucking suffering," Andy spiraled. "And I feel like I can't do anything to fix it."

"You have to stop trying to fix things. And nobody *deserves* pain."

"That's not what the juicer said," Andy whimpered.

"What?" Angie asked, half paying attention as she pulled out a bar of chocolate. "Fuck whoever the Juicer is, Andy. Nobody deserves pain."

Andy eyed "95% Cacao" on the packaging.

"Jesus Angie, you sure do like it dark."

"Mmmhmm," she said as she sucked on a square, "and so do you."

She handed him a piece of chocolate, laced with seduction.

Andy put the chocolate on his tongue, tried to be sensual, but only succeeded at a small gag sound.

Still, Angie smiled.

And her smile was a light. Pure light, as Andy allowed the darkness of the chocolate to swallow him.

95% Cacao

Andy felt the chocolate aphrodisiate him from stem to stern. His blood danced, and so did all his other bodily fluids.

Angie's body pulsed, almost throbbed. She gyrated like a belly dancer, her hips shifted and swayed as her hands caressed her chest. He watched as her breasts swelled into big, voluptuous fruits under her hands. Actual fruits.

Cacao fruits, or nuts, or pods, or whatever you would call them. He recognized them from the back of the chocolate bar, where a Guatemalan guy was expertly removing them from a tree. Andy had read the whole package, a cute little story about how the CEO left behind Wall Street to bring biodynamic ceremonial cacao to rural Ohio soccer moms.

Andy was not aroused by the fruits, as he had been by his split second view of her bare breasts, but they still enticed in their own special way. They looked yummy.

Nothing else had changed about Angie though, which he appreciated. She was sexy enough, just how she was.

She did, however, have a glow about her that regular Angie didn't normally have. Andy would tell her she was glowing, often in fact, but not in the literal sense like this chocolate-chested queen in front of him.

"Do you like?" the Goddess teased, as she swayed her body back and forth.

"Oh ya," Andy said, although the sound was muffled by

involuntary grunts and dry hump rustles from somewhere down below.

"Do you know why I'm here?"

"Ohhhhhh ya," Andy was ready. "I'm ready."

"Good. Now lay back babe," she wiggled. "I'm here to teach you about..."

What what what his libido screamed.

"Impotencccce." she hissed. Serpent.

Andy stared, in shocked silence, "Oh."

"Don't worry honey, I'm not talking about your manhood. Well, not *specifically* about your manhood," Andy withered beneath her appraising gazing.

"You've always been really quite able. Able to do just about anything you put your mind to," Andy felt himself straighten up a bit. "But there comes a time in every person's life, where they are faced with inability. Where they are faced with the realization that they are, genuinely, helpless."

"I don't feel helpless. Hopeless maybe, but not helpless. I don't think."

"Denial is a powerful thing, Andy. Like I said, it might not be now, but you are going to be faced with your own impotency." Andy felt his package shy at the thought. "This impotency requires something of you Andy, and it's something you're going to hate."

"Don't say it."

"You're going to have to ask for help."

Shit.

"You're going to *have* to ask for help. And that takes humility. I'm sorry Andy, I know you pride yourself on being a real independent sort of guy. But you are not stronger than this. Not stronger than time, than pain, than Armageddon. It will bring you to your knees. It will make you weak, and feeble."

Andy already felt weak and feeble, beneath her gaze.

"Humility, however, can act as a spiritual aphrodisiac. It

can be a balm to your impotency. Perhaps not as pleasurable as dark chocolate, but it builds you up from the outside in."

Andy saw himself fail. Saw himself fall. He tried to imagine humility in the face of inability. Could he envision an Armageddon where he could, and would, ask for help? He had always thought that he would face the End of Days alone. He had assumed that he would travel this lonesome highway on, well, his lonesome.

"I don't have to face this alone." Half a question.

"The end doesn't have to be desolation. The people you love, and who love you, want to make this a good end for you. Nobody wants to see you suffer, and they are going to want to help build you back up."

Andy gulped.

"There is no shame in asking for help," she added.

Andy felt shame even entertaining the word help. Sure, the Goddess just suggested that he might actually survive this damned thing if he just had a little humility. To Andy though, eternal damnation was probably a little more likely than groveling.

Andy didn't like to ask his teachers for help, and definitely not his parents. Hell, he never even pushed the little question mark symbol on his online Tax filing service.

He'd always stumbled through life, figured it out on his own. Sure he had slept on a couch or two, but did that really count? It was more just a natural hazard of being a wastoid. It didn't take humility to be too hammered to fit the key in his bike lock.

As his mind inserted the key into the bike lock, he smelled the cacao wafting off the Goddess' breasts.

"I don't know if I know how to ask for help," Andy suggested.

"Well you better figure it out Andy. Otherwise, you're going to have a damn hard time. And you'll leave the people you love ungratified. Unsatisfied. Wanting," she smiled. "They want you whole. I want you whole."

Andy's mouth watered. So did the rest of him.

"And one more thing, Andy."

"Yes?"

"Come here."

++

Angie grabbed Andy, and pulled his body towards hers. He tried to talk, tried to say all the things he wanted to say. He was going to be so damned romantic.

Angie's tongue, however, had other ideas. And that was OK, because parts of Andy's body had ideas of their own.

Time stood still. Andy was used to losing time. He lost time to drugs, alcohol, sleep, and YouTube videos. To have time stand eternal though, in the midst of something so darned nurturing, was a mother fucking godsend to his weak little heart. Angie's body and his were in goddamned cosmic alignment and the stars sang through him.

He felt like all his aches and pains of the last few days fade into Angie's curves. He saw Angels and Demons alike, bow before her holy thighs. Armageddon was made weak before her body.

Angie finished, and so Andy finished too. As she nestled into him, he whispered the sweetest nothings he could imagine into her ear. Nothing came back, and that nothing was punctuated by the sound of her snores.

She was asleep.

Andy wished he could sleep too, but he felt a pull on something other than his crotch.

A chirp from the couch. He would not forget his tiny crippled bird again.

"Chirp chirp?" Andy offered in response.

The bird looked at Andy, and Andy knew it was time to leave.

He walked back over to Angie as he zipped up his pants.

He kissed her on the head, and whispered, "I love you babe. I'll see you tomorrow."

Andy picked up the little bird and walked down the stairs, and out onto the street.

The fog parted. As Andy walked, he turned his eyes skyward and was awestruck by what he saw.

There were stars. Like, real ones. And lots of them.

Living in the heart of the city, Andy had sort of forgotten that the sky was anything more than a weird black outline to the street lamps, billboards and headlights. The stars made him feel puny, teeny weeny, and yet like a baby, they also cradled him ever so gently.

Well bird, at least the End of Days are beautiful, Andy whispered as he and his little friend walked down the street.

Fucking bird doesn't work though, Andy thought to himself, *I think it's about time I gave you a name.*

Andy wracked his brain. He didn't have to wrack too hard, however, because the perfect bushtit name came to him in but a moment.

"I think I'll call you Teat."

Teat chirped happily, and snuggled depeper into Andy's hand.

As Andy swooned at the little bird in his hand, he heard an unmistakable clinking sound. A sound of metal as it moved across glass. A spoon as it glided in circles around an icy sea. A sound he loved. A sound he loathed.

Andy turned the corner, and saw the fountain. Still droopier flower were perched on the far right side. His heart drooped a little itself, at the sight of them.

Time is short, Andy thought to himself.

On the left side of the fountain was a man dressed like every single male coworker he had had over the last twelve years. Vest, not quite long hair, curly mustache, countless tattoos. The uniform was complete. Made all the more complete by the man's cocktail he stirred.

Andy walked up to the guy, and offered some unsolicited advice, "You're stirring with your elbow. You should be stirring with your wrist."

"I'll stir you with my elbow" threatened the man, straightening up.

He strained the cocktail into a rocks glass with a large, hand carved cube.

"Also the color is all wrong. You absolutely added too much bitters."

"You're too much bitters" the man scowled at Andy as he lifted the drink to his lips. He took a sip, and his face contorted as Andy knew it would.

"Let me show you," Andy poured the drink back into the mixing glass, grabbed the bottle of bourbon behind the man and added the most microscopic bit of whiskey to the glass. He gave it a couple quick turns, and returned it to the glass.

"You have an orange?" Andy asked, no expectations that the man would provide one. He did, however, and also produced a peeler and a jar of cherries in the same motion.

"Impressive setup, despite the locale," Andy motioned towards the fountain.

"Ya, I'm heading to a cocktail competition."

Ah cute, Andy thought, as he studied the boy. Young, green, but not broken. *Not yet.*

"Well I'm glad I ran into you then," Andy said as he sprayed the orange's oils over the lip of the glass.

Andy handed the drink to the boy, who tasted it and smiled.

"That's fucking delicious man, thank you. You want a sip?" his eyes shone with pride as he handed it over to Andy.

"Damn right I do," said Andy. He knew, without a doubt, it was going to be a perfect Old Fashioned.

Old Fashioned

Andy turned to face the boy, not bothering to hide the smile on his face.

The boy was oh so young, now that Andy looked closer at him. Sure, he had a mustache, but that didn't mean much. Andy remembered a kid in freshmen year of high school that had a complete frontiersmen caliber beard.

As Andy admired the boy's mustache, all of the boys other facial hair started growing.

Another monkey? Andy thought. *Ho Hum.*

The hair continued to grow, but the boy did not turn terribly apen. Not into a monkey, the boy turned into a man. Andy saw before him a 35 year old man, same boy to be sure. And then that 35 year old man became 40, 50, 60 and well beyond.

His hair grayed. His eyes sprouted crow's feet, which became hawk feet, then eagle feet as his wrinkles wrinkled.

His posture became less and less upright, and Andy soon stood in front of an old man decidedly less tall than the boy he had just met.

His clothes too aged. And not just more worn and torn, but the style changed. From too young to dress so well, to too old to dress so well, in the blink of an eye. Once a caricature of a speakeasy bartender, he was soon too old to be conversant in speaking easy at all. Prohibitively old. Pre-prohibitively old.

"Old Fashioned," Andy chuckled to himself.

"What'd you say!" the old man yelled at Andy.

"I was just admiring that you are an Old Fashioned," Andy yelled right back.

"Damn right I'm Old Fashioned! It's the only right way to be!"

"You're not wrong," said Andy. Andy almost never ordered anything but an Old Fashioned. Even dive bars were subject to Andy's penchant for stirred drinks. He tipped well to justify the nuisance, but they didn't know that until *well* after they had called him a twat.

"Why the Hell would I be wrong?" the old man sneered. "Everything Old Fashioned is superior. The drinks you kids drink are rubbish, ya fancy fucks. Cointreau? Vermouth? Lily little pansies!" Andy laughed. *If Mahattans and Sidecars are newfangled, then maybe he's even older than I thought.*

"And I mean *everything* was better back then boy! No damned cellular phones for one. No damned phones at all. I could disappear when I damn well wanted to. Food trucks? Please. Not unless you count a donkey pullin' a cart o cabbages. And sure as hell no electricity in our homes, let alone in our guitars!"

"And no, if you're wondering. We did not have any pesky Pokemons." The old man saw the disappointment in Andy's eyes, and added, "But we did have our fair share of indentured animals, don't get me wrong."

The old man's eyes glazed as he stared into a distance too distant, "Why, even our Armaggedons were better in the old days."

"Your Armaggedons? Really though?"

"Absolutely! When I was talkin' pansies, I was talkin' you most of all boy! All in touch with yer feelings, finding meaning in chocolate bunnies and noodle shapes. Why, in my day, an Armaggedon was a damned *proper* Armaggedon. Fire and brimstone, demons with whips and Angels with lances of fire. Where is *your* hellfire boy? I promise it's not in a yucca fry, whatever the hell that is."

"I'm kind of happy there's no torture and lava, to be honest. Sounds uncomfortable."

"Pansy!" Andy loved flowers, but this guy seeded some doubts about if he wanted to be one.

"Now St John. Now that was a man with vision! A Goddamned old soul! Cities in the sky, possessed horsemen! You've had two whole days, and not a single Beast with forked tongues. Just juice and dessert! No plagues! No false prophets! It's enough to make an old man weep," he seemed beside himself, a retiree out of time and out of space.

"I'm really sorry sir. I don't really have control over how this plays out. I mean, I'm with you. I totally expected Lambs and Prostitutes and Kings. But all I've gotten are baristas and delicious ethnic cuisine. Well I guess there was the dog queen and the monkey monk. Do they count as beasts? Whatever, it's been hard on my heart! If that's any consolation."

"Hard on your heart. Yer heart? Are you kiddin' me?" His eyes raged.

"Popcorn told me we are all unique. We each experience Armageddon in our own special way!"

"Popcorn is a damn pansy! And you are *not* unique boy! Not if I have anything to say about it. You shall know Armaggedon as all others have known it," Andy watched in horror as flames leapt from the old man's eyes. Not figurative, but actual flames, which singed the old man's eyebrows. His arms gave way to wings, charred and cracked. He hissed, spewed sulfur and smoke.

The sky darkened around Andy, which was impressive because it had already been a real black night. Andy watched the buildings tremble and shake, stood aghast as fire took to anything that would hold it. Asphalt melted, streetlights bowed towards the ground in supplication. The world was reduced to void, except the fountain, except the flowers.

"This will not be different boy. Hear me now, there will be pain. There will be suffering. You shall know wrath for what it is. We shall not spare you. You will be engulfed in eternal darkness. This is Babylon, and the Horsemen do indeed ride. Even you, oh pansy epicurean, shall know famine. Even you, oh hippie-dippie loving heart, shall know war. Even you, oh healthy bike riding hipster, shall know pestilence. And I promise, even you, oh youth eternal, you too shall know *DEATH*."

The sky screamed. What little light there was, bled from the scene, and the never ending black of the midnight sky began to choke Andy's vision.

"Ah yessssss," the words echoed as Andy's eyelids dropped. "Let's do it the Old Fashioned way."

+The 3rd Day+

Andy did actually sleep. It was a sleep as deep as an abyss, a primordial darkness. A dreamless place. A hopeless place.

Andy woke with a start, grabbed at his chest like he half expected his heart to be left behind in the void.

Andy hoped today would be more cheerful. He hoped the buildings would be rebuilt, that the sun would shine with hope and determination. He hoped for the clarity that only morning brings, because its all just allegory, right?

He even hoped to be welcomed to the waking world by the smell of freshly roasted Ethiopian coffee beans. Maybe some well spiced chai, and a pastry. He hoped, even expected these things, although he wasn't quite sure why, because they sure as heck didn't expect him.

The world remained unchanged. Destruction, and most likely death surrounded him. The air was fetid, and hung like a corpse from the gallows.

It would have given Andy the chills, if it wasn't so sweltering. He flapped his hand, but only felt the hot air hit his face with a little more vigor. He stopped.

Andy remembered, and Andy panicked. His brain ran circles as he gently patted his body, as he felt for a downy little ball of tweets he only half remembered.

Chirp! Andy turned his head towards the fountain and

saw Teat above him, the little bird head framed by a sky blaze, celestial fire.

"Thank fucking God," Andy said aloud as he reached for Teat.

"Now why would you want to thank him for *this*?" the voice behind Andy spooked Andy's knee into the fountain.

"Owowowowowwww," Andy howled. His eyes turned to see the Baristo, who stood in front of him with a cute little push cart. It was decorated with faux wood paneling, a hand painted sign, and a pastel umbrella that contrasted so starkly with the apocalyptic scene that Andy's eyes watered.

"What are you doing here?" asked Andy, being genuinely at a loss. He'd never seen a coffee cart in this part of the city, not that he knew what part of the city this was.

"Oh this is just our new cart that we've been experiment- ing with. I do pour overs down at the playscape. Its lovely. And it's *so* nice to get out of that damned shop. Even on a day like today," the Baristo motioned at the forsaken skies.

"*And* I get to bring joy right to your front door! Your weird little fountain shaped door."

Andy was so happy to see Baristo, his eyes started to water again.

"Oh buddy, are you OK? Actually, why am I asking that? You slept outside. You're crying. And it smells like nuclear winter. Of course you're not OK. You need a little huggie?"

Andy nodded, laid his head on the Baristo's shoulder, and cried in earnest.

"Ah Hells mister," they patted Andy on the shoulder. "Well, I've got just the thing you need."

"Oh thank God," Andy said, "Oh thank Goddess. Espresso is *exactly* what I want."

"Not what you want, dude. I got what you need," the Baristo pointed to the bottom of the menu board.

"Bloody Mary," Andy mouthed, not daring to speak aloud.

Andy's stomach clenched. This was the first time he had

felt a genuine aversion to something offered to him in the last few days. Like a big ole fuck no. There was always a bit of wonder, a genuine sense of curiosity. Right now, though, Andy had zero interest in drinking anything remotely like what was being offered.

Despite this, however, Andy knew his preferences didn't matter much. Maybe it was the hangover, maybe it was divine guidance, or maybe it was some good old fashioned masochism. Whatever it was, Andy's mouth said for him, "Sure, might as well."

Andy watched the Baristo grab two bottles. Quick pours, more than a few counts extra. He iced so quickly that Andy almost missed it. Then a quick shake, no flare, just precise in his movements. Too damned precise.

Whoa, Andy thought.

Andy watched in awe as the Baristo methodically put two green olives, two pickled okras, two hellish looking chili peppers, a piece of bacon, three shrimp, and what seemed to be a teeny tiny quiche on the end of a long iron skewer that sizzled as each accoutrement was pierced.

Andy willed himself to take a bite of the quiche first. Maybe the shrimp could be a whimsical sort of experience. Andy knew the angel of olives was more than likely to be bronzed and beautiful.

His salivary glands, however, knew what his mind was still in denial of. There was no other choice.

Andy felt it appropriate to do a little Hail Mary, and as he got to the line "now, and at the hour of our death" felt his stomach lurch yet again.

"Amen," the Baristo finished as Andy took the glass and chug chug chugged.

Bloody Mary

The Baristo turned around, faced a mirror in the background. The scene was dark. The kind of dark that eats other darks for breakfast. Yet the mirror was like any other mirror, a looking glass that reflected the Baristo's lean, stark features.

Baristo turned back towards Andy and gave a flirtatious wink. Then, as they stared into the mirror's eyes, they began a rhythmic chant of, "Bloody Mary. Bloody Mary. Bloody Mary."

The Baristo's eyes blackened like a spotlight fades before a curtain falls. The wind wailed, the dark got darker.

Andy anticipated something medieval. He expected the beanie to turn into an ornate and gilded crown and expected the hoodie to transform into a conservative high collared gown. He imagined someone nearby holding a pike. Andy was uncertain what exactly a pike was, and thought it unlikely to be a fish, although didn't outright deny the possibility.

Andy's preconceived imaginings were one of his favorite parts of the angel revelation process. He loved wading in the whimsy of it all.

The eyes, however, were the only changed feature in the mirror image. Andy thought it ho-hum at first, but the gravity of the gaze was soon all encompassing. Even surrounded by the eternal void of black, they cavernous in their depth. All-consuming, in an eat your soul kind of way.

And they were decidedly fixed on Andy.

As the Baristo turned around, the anti-eyes maintained their gaze. Their dark matter pulled on Andy's, and left him blinkless. For a moment, neither's eyes wavered.

There was an Unholy sound, and the Baristo began to *not* cry blood. No, the eyes were not crying blood, they were gushing blood. A sanguinary flood of biblical proportions. Andy looked at his feet, and gaped as the tide rose. He imagined it would be mere moments before he was afloat in hemoglobin.

"*BLOOOOOOOOOOD.*"

Andy waited a beat, aware that the horror of the moment couldn't possibly have been ruined so easily.

"*BLOOOOOOOOOOD.*"

Nope, too goofy. Andy tried to hold back, but couldn't help it.

"HAHAHAHAHA!"

"What, pray tell, is so funny?" asked the demonic presence, clearly wounded.

"*BLOOOOOOOOOOD,*" Andy replied, and tried to not sound too condescending. "I'm sorry, it was just kind of mindless, ya know? A certain standard has been set by your forebears. I expected something more than *BLOOOOOOOOD.*"

"I was TRYING to be succinct. Sometimes too much can muddy the water, ya know?"

"Okay okay, I'm sorry. So what exactly were you trying to convey with *BLOOOOOOOD,*" Andy couldn't help the mocking tone out of his voice.

"I just feel like you've been fed half-truths, and that the proper gravity of the situation may be lost on you. Like ya, sure, your mind, your emotions and spirit are going to be tortured beyond measure. That's true. Totally true. All of those parts of you, however, are built on a very particular foundation. And that foundation is your body."

Andy felt himself feel himself.

"Your body is going to be visited by all manners of hell.

Armageddon is not so different from you, Andy. It's biological, just like you."

Andy couldn't help but be a little awed by the discrepancy between the hollow, yawning eyes of infinity, still dripping with blood and the matter of fact voice that accompanied it.

"Biological," Andy repeated.

"Visceral. And visceral in a visceral sense. Like, your viscera, your guts shall know what Doom is."

"Oh. Lovely."

"And I'm sorry to say, I'm not here to teach you how to cope with it. Everybody is trying to help you cope. Each has given you a bevy of transformational ways to deal with trauma. They are making you *more* than aware of how your heart shall interpret the maladies of the End of Days. I just feel like someone should be honest about what you are going to cope *WITH*. Your body is going to feel this the most. They talk about the seven levels of Hell, like they get progressively worse. But it wasn't the name calling that tore Jesus asunder. It wasn't his distance from God. Hell, it wasn't even the betrayal of his good buddy Judas. It was the nails and the whips, ya know?"

"Oh awesome, so I should be expecting nails and whips?"

"I think it's pretty clear that we don't know what you should expect. Not really. I've got some bloody good guesses, but there is one thing that I know is absolutely, unequivocally inescapable."

"*BLOOOOOOOOD?*"

"*BLOOOOOOOOD.*"

++

Blood.

It wasn't that Andy had avoided thoughts about what Armageddon would actually look like. He just hadn't been actively thinking about it. He just had other things on his mind.

Like, who could focus on End of Days when they had a little bird to take care of? Who could dwell on Doomsday when their girlfriend kept offering decadent desserts? No one can focus on days ending with bills that need to get paid and you are suddenly without income.

No, Andy hadn't avoided the subject, but now he found that he couldn't sidestep the problem anymore. There comes a time, with all things, where you have to buck up and focus. Get your priorities straight. Focus on the task at hand.

Teat looks hungry. I wonder if that pile of popcorn from a couple days ago is still over there? It would be remiss to not investigate on his buddy's behalf.

Andy walked towards the corner, or what he thought was towards the corner. He cradled Teat close to his own teat. He could clearly feel the little bird's heartbeat, which unnerved him.

It was quick and strong, like a shot of tequila. But it was funky, a little off, also like a shot of tequila.

Andy wondered if birds could have a heart murmur. He

imagined how sad Teat's mother must have been when the doctor revealed that her little fledgling had a congenital heart defect. He felt her pain, considered how sad he would be if he lost his new friend.

And Teat *was*, in fact, Andy's friend. Andy could confide in Teat, without any risk of judgment. And he did so.

"I'm going to tell you something, little buddy. But it's a secret," Andy hesitated. "I'm scared. I know you understand fear, because you're so little and look like you'd be delicious to all manner of beasties."

Teat eyed Andy, suspect, "Not to me! I mean to someone who eats birds. I heard it's a *thing*. But no, for real Teat, I feel like I am starting to see the shape of what is about to happen. Like, in any good horror movie, they only ever show the outline of the monster and that makes it all the scarier. And the specter of the thing has me all panicked like a prom queen."

Teat cooed.

"No Teat, it's not coo at all."

In Andy's musing, he hadn't realized he was at the street corner until he heard the corn pop under his foot. He reached down, picked up a kernel, and held it up to Teat's little beak. The bird happily pecked at it for a minute, then collapsed into a satiated stupor.

At that, Andy took a moment to look around. Across the street, he spotted the girl on the bench.

He walked across the street and looked her up and down. Investigated one of his divine conduits. There had been no real chance to take stock of what she was prior to now. It was like his eyes didn't want to know, but his heart did, so he took this moment to figure it out.

She returned his gaze, taking a particularly long gander at Andy's shoes. Andy looked down and realized that at some point the night prior he had flavored his shoelaces with banana and chocolate. Andy tried to surmount his embarrassment and returned his gaze to the girl's face and studied.

Her eyes mirrored his own. Not only were they cobalt blue, but she had flecks of ochre right where his own were. That shock of blonde hair, however, was not his. Nor was the cute little button nose.

But they were Angie's.

At that, he saw Angie in just about all of her. In her ears, and her well-manicured nails. The way her eyes darted towards his shoes in judgment. The way that she wanted to ask to hold Teat but was going to wait until Andy offered because that was what decorum dictated. And in the way she ate, chewed so darn well, even if Andy wasn't sure what it was she was eating.

He also realized that she was much younger than his initial assessment. She was tiny, and he felt a creep, standing in front of her, not talking, without her parents anywhere nearby.

"Are you alone out here little girl?" *Jesus Christ Andy.*

All the girl did was stare at him in disbelief, as if there was no other way she could be on this desolate plane of existence.

"Right, right. Sorry. Uncool. OK then. What's the snack of the day?"

"Ah you couldn't handle it," she let slip between bites.

Fuck, Andy hated being goaded. Let alone from some twerp. *You went from delicate to dastardly in one fell swoop little girl.*

"Try me."

"Fine," *that was too easy,* "but you have to let me hold your bird."

Andy clutched Teat firmer than he probably should have. He loosened his grip, and looked apologetically at the bird. Teat nodded sagely, and Andy handed over the little bushtit, who peeped in excitement.

"Here you go, but don't say I didn't warn ya," something

about the way she said it gave Andy the heebie-jeebies. Still, Andy put out his hand and accepted the trade..

He couldn't, wouldn't believe his eyes. It was a revolting thing, wrinkled and covered in warts. It was both other-worldly, and horrifyingly familiar.

"What in all the Hells..."

"It's a Ghost Pepper," her smile shocked Andy more than the pepper itself.

She was snacking on ghost peppers.

Andy went to respond, but his body responded for him and his hand pressed the pepper to his pale lips. He clenched his teeth, but his mouth relaxed. He hid his tongue in the back of his mouth, but like some dark serpent, it leapt forward and invited the ghost pepper into its warm embrace.

Ghost Pepper

The wind howled, screamed, wailed, and did all the other imaginable banshee-isms as it whipped about. The sound tore at Andy's ears and he worried they might actually blow off. To be sure, Andy held his ears, which did nothing more than expose his armpits to further assault.

Like dunes dancing in a sandstorm, the buildings were reduced to nothing as they rode the wind. They obscured the red sun with a hue somehow more blood stained. The horizon stretched as all was reduced to none.

Andy watched the wind envelop the little girl. It blew her hair, head, and body away like they were nothing much more than dust. As each part of her was sequentially sent flying, still she remained standing before him.

She was, however, much more see-through than she had been before. If the whole world hadn't just been reduced to nothing, Andy could have seen it through her torso. Instead, prisms of light, consisting entirely of red and darker red, shot needles through the air.

She opened her mouth to speak, and the wind was still. And yet, as soon as her vocal chords struck, it was cacophony all over again. The sound was abusive, so dang loud, yet somehow eerie and cold in the same breath.

Her lips moved and the torrent continued.

"WHAT?" Andy yelled back.

"OH SHIT, SORRY. I USUALLY DEAL WITH FOLKS ALOT OLDER THAN YOU! LEMME TURN DOWN," screamed the specter. "Is that better?"

"So much better!" Andy stuck his finger in his ear hole, checked for blood.

"Let me start again. Hello Andy, my name is Bhut Jolokia. But you can call me ghost."

"Bhut Jolokia sounds way spookier, now that you mention it."

"I know, it's just really hard for people to remember sometimes, let alone pronounce. Anyways, welcome to your third day of torture and suffering at the hands of the specters of oblivion!"

"Ah that's sweet. Thank you! I appreciate that, although I'm going to be honest with you: It's been pretty good up until today. It's been scary and terrible in an existential way, I guess, but everyone has been really nice on the whole."

"Really? What the hell! Who did they send to you? You should have been cowering by the third day, that's kind of the whole point. Show you the hordes of Satan, tempt you with the eternal silence of Abyss, perhaps rake you with Beelzebub's flaming hoes."

"Ya, no flaming hoes sadly. There was a bowl of stew that told me I was going to be forgotten by my loved ones, that was pretty sad. And the Candy Corn goddess was kind of a downer, but really everyone has been super helpful. Helping me prepare to cope, which no doubt will making the actually coping all the easier! Heck, even Bloody Mary gave me some valuable intel, although don't tell her that. I'm sure she wasn't *trying* to be helpful."

"Oh Dark Lord. Freaking amateurs. Sorry, fucking amateurs. I hate when I don't cuss," so did Andy. "Well don't worry, I'm going to be way less helpful. I'm going to be so unhelpful that, fingers upside-down crossed, you won't even make it to your other appointments today. I'll leave you cowering!" Her transparent eyes sparkled with the light of extinguished souls.

She spoke, as if starting all over again, "Hello Andy, I am Bhut Jolokia. I represent the ghosts..."

"I thought Candy corn represented the ghosts," Andy interjected.

"Don't interrupt me!" The wind rose, and Andy bit his tongue, which hurt more than usual considering the capsaicin. "Candy corn is what we would call a friendly ghost. And I promise you Andy, I am no friend of yours. I am a ghost of what you will lose, what has been lost, and what you are losing. And much of that, is your sense of self."

"Ya, I got the feeling I might be losing myself a little bit," Andy felt glum, embodied the whole damn word.

"The End of Days takes everything from you. Your sense of self, your good standing, your love and your free will. All that will be taken from you, but the darkest part of all that, is that you will never forget what you lost. You will be haunted by what you had. You will..."

Andy interrupted again, "Forgive the interruption, but I've noticed a trend with all of this. If this is the End of the World, the Apocalypse, the great Armageddon, why is everyone talking about the afterwards? Like, what does any of this matter if only oblivion comes after this?"

"What nerve! What gall! What idiocy! You are but a bartender! A peon in the cosmic game! You think that your end is *THE* end? Don't be silly. It's just *AN* end. And more than likely, you won't even die," the phantom screamed.

"Really? Oh that's fucking wonderful! Hallelujah! Praises be to the Ghost Pepper!" Andy did a little dance.

"What? No! Stop that! That's not a good thing! This end of yours isn't a good thing! It's terrible, painful, and you're going to lose all that you built! All that you love! You will start from zero!" the winds howled, and the sun flared with rage.

"I can't believe I get to start from zero! That's amazing,

you've given me so much hope! So much more reason to keep going!" His dance continued.

"No hope was given!" The Ghost's face was flat, unmoved, and aggrieved beyond anger. "Listen, I appreciate that you are happy that this isn't the end of it *ALL*. That's not scheduled for another 32.6 billion years, so you can take solace in that, if that's what you're into. But what I'm telling you, if I can be more specific, is that you are apt to lose your lover, your family, your career, your creativity, your hopes and aspirations, your youth, your vigor, your potency!"

Andy didn't dance anymore, "What do you mean, my potency?"

"I mean all of it. Sure, your sexiness, that'll be terrible. But I mean all of your magic. You're an attractive person, someone that has a certain gravitational pull. It's why you can be so successful, so popular, despite being sort of a statistical loser."

"Statistical loser?" Andy bristled.

"By most metrics you have not succeeded. There is no reason you should be as likable as you are. And now reason will reassert itself, because your allure will be gone. We will reduce you to the nothing that you are," she was much more mean spirited all of a sudden. "And the thing about nothing, Andy, is that you will not be able to simply climb a ladder you have already climbed. Wells will be poisoned, bridges shall burn, and you will live on, knowing what you had, knowing what you were, and knowing that you will never have that again. Forever condemned, a ghost."

"Ya no. You're right. You're terrible," Andy whispered.

"Ha! I knew it!" The ghost shone with the light of a thousand dying suns. "Finally, I shall again be in the bad graces of the Evil One! You would not believe what this hot sauce revolution has done for my standing in Hell! All of a sudden, normal ass people enjoy ghost pepper this and ghost pepper that. Fucking brown sugar, pineapple. They even pair me with carrots, for Satan's Sake. How dare those buffoons make me look GOOD! It's a PR nightmare!"

Andy didn't hear Ghost Pepper. He was lost in thoughts of potency. He wasn't exactly sure what it was that made him potent, which scared him all the more. It's one thing to lose what you know you have. It's another to lose your *je ne sais quoi.* Andy was sure, however, that Ghost Pepper was right and he would never forget what he had, once he lost it.

Ghost Pepper still taunted. Ghost Pepper still laughed. Andy, however, turned his back and walked off into the eternal distance. The winds howled, and Ghost Pepper must have blown away, or something. Andy had no idea. He was too focused on his own dissolution. Disillusion.

++

Andy faded back into existence, and to his own dismay, the girl was already at her front door.

Not so much as a goodbye. More like Angie than I thought.

Andy was surprised by his bitter thoughts towards the love of his life, but allowed himself to wallow in his anger for a moment. Teased it out. *It's easy to love seductive Angie, but disappointed Angie?*

Andy's allow the anger to fester for but a moment. He saw the girl turn the doorknob, and realized that she hadn't given him Teat back.

"I'll fucking kill her," Andy soft screamed as he prepared to dart towards the door.

Cheep? Andy looked down at Teat's cute little face. His body relaxed, which was good because it hurt just to stand at ready, to say nothing of get-set or go. Teat pecked at a crumb, unawares of Andy's anguish.

Andy looked closer, curious what Teat was so happy about, and recoiled in horror.

A ghost pepper, lovely.

"You're as demonic as the rest of them!" Andy couldn't even pretend to be mad at him. He picked him up, as well as the ghost pepper and placed them gingerly in his hand.

Remember to wash your hands, remember to wash your hands, remember to wash your hands. Funny how I think that after handling a ghost pepper, but haven't thought to do it for the last day I've been carrying around a dirty ass bird.

Andy walked, and knew full well what he was walking towards. He dreamed of a malt shop. A milkshake would be lovely, absolutely, but he knew he wouldn't be nearly that lucky on a day like today.

Andy looked up at the sun, noted that it looked like suns, the way it doubled behind the haze of roasted flesh and barbequed souls.

"So what do you think about this whole apocalypse thing, huh?" Andy asked the bird. "Sounds to me like I'm going to do something irredeemable and maybe like go to jail or something and then get beat the fuck up in jail every fucking day because why wouldn't I?"

Andy hyperventilated, "Oh shit. Am I going to kill somebody? Think, what's the most irredeemable way to kill somebody, Teat? Drunk driving? Fuck of course it's going to be drunk driving. I know I don't have a car, but what if I steal one to do the damn deed?" Andy felt woozy, and Teat nodded along, made clear he agreed with everything Andy said.

Andy noted some "people" out of the corner of his eye, but was sure they were short a few limbs and eyeballs. Dripped from extra orifices. So he continued to hold eye contact with Teat as the undead passed him by. Teat held the gaze, and Andy found himself caught in a staring contest he couldn't possibly win. Finally, he looked up and found himself next to a diner.

"Nope. Not even today." Andy walked on, and his pelvis grinded and groaned.

He saw a watch store across the street. *Well that's something new.*

Andy approached the window, and appraised a showroom full of clocks tick tick tocking away.

"They all say 7:06" he said aloud.

"Actually, its 6:66," a voice whispered from behind.

"Gahhh!" Andy jump-turned around, and came eye to eye with, well, no one.

Now I'm not even talking to my food. I'm just haunting myself.

The voice in Andy's head wasn't wrong, though. It was in fact, 6:66.

As such, all manner of demons decided it was damn well time to tear at the walls of their prisons. Like flies unzipped, reality busted open, and revealed throbbing horned beasts. Most were fairly cliché. Red skin, tiny mustaches, pokey things.

Others, however, were much more phantasmagoric. Eyeballs within eyeballs within eyeballs, bearing 8 rows of teeth. Devil-sharks, with a myriad of legs, all shapes and sizes. And all of it wreaked like piss and vinegar.

Andy didn't miss a beat. He screamed and sprinted as fast as he could towards the nearest door.

Locked.

Andy sprinted, and his legs and abdomen screamed in agony.

There were ghastly things, brimming over with evil intent. Three headed hell-hounds, sulfurous dragons, and warlocks of every ilk. Andy turned a corner and was confronted by a giant crow, with a smaller bird living inside its gaping beak, and a smaller bird still inside that beak. Not particularly terrifying, kind of novel. Andy felt a tiny shiver run through the palm of his hand, and realized this demon was not designed with Andy in mind.

For Teat, Andy ran again.

God it hurts to run. Andy slowed. *God it hurts to walk.*

Andy was tired of being tired, and so smashed through the next door he came to. An old decrepit diner, unused, the red vinyl booths still whispered of pancakes and sausage.

Andy gagged and charged forward through another door. His mind may have felt unstoppable, but his body knew it was imminently stoppable, so with one final burst Andy flung himself into the last door.

The world around him stilled, and then he himself stilled. Actually, the scene itself demanded that he be still.

Andy was in the midst of a scene both terrifying and real. Decidedly more human than the demonic hellscape he just escaped.

Three young men stood with their backs to Andy. They faced a sheep, hung by its rear legs from the rafters. One of the men rhythmically sharpened an exorbitantly large blade on a whetstone, reciting words in a similarly rhythmic fashion.

One of the men turned towards Andy, at first shocked, but then a knowing smile spread across his face.

"My friend! My guest! Welcome, come in come in!"

Andy was surprised at the invitation, and equally surprised that his feet took a few steps towards the scene.

"On this most auspicious of days, we have a guest my brothers!"

"Auspicious?" Andy said aloud.

"Today is a holy day, my friend! Eid-Al-Adha! The great day of sacrifice."

"I see that," Andy replied, deadpan.

"It is on this day that Ibrahim showed his willingness to sacrifice his son Ismail! And praise be to Allah, a lamb was offered in Ismail's stead! So we show our supreme thanks to our God with a lamb of our own!" The man motioned to the upended animal.

In the heart of the terrible scene, Andy noticed a warmth that was not evident at first glance. Behind the men, in a gentle light, there was a courtyard of candles, smoke and draped tables. People laughed and milled about, and a delectable smell permeated the air.

The man introduced himself as Mahmoud, and shared that Andy had, in fact, broken through his family's front door. Andy didn't hear much, however, as he was caught in the reverie of the beautiful moment, as children smacked each other with sticks in the courtyard beyond.

Andy returned his gaze to the scene in the foreground. The man with the blade walked towards the animal, again, the chill of his recitation cut through the silence. Andy expected a gruesome scene, something akin to a PETA documentary. The man, however, used the blade with precision. There was a moment of struggle, but then a deep and lasting peace took over the room.

The scene propelled itself in fast forward. The blood dripped out, collected beneath the animal and then the sheep was skinned and butchered, quick and precise.

In the background, a fire was ablaze, and steam and smoke filled the air. The different cuts were taken to different corners of the kitchen, and everyone moved with swift and deliberate movements. There was a lot of laughter as the women drank tea, and men mulled over an old book of photographs.

Andy's heart was pulled forward by the moment, carried to a table filled with grape leaves and rice, yogurt and salad, piles of fresh herbs. There was copious amounts of tea poured back and forth, and Andy waited, captivated, as family members came and went. Some came and patted him on the shoulder, like an old friend.

Then Mahmoud walked through a door with a huge covered platter, as he smiled from ear to ear. He looked at Andy, and Andy knew the eyes as those of an old friend. The room turned its gaze towards Andy.

Mahmoud placed the platter in front of Andy, and as he lifted the lid, said, "It is a blessing that you are here with us today. Allah has graced us with your presence. And so, allow me to properly welcome you to my table. This, my friend, is what we call Kalle Pache."

He lifted the lid to the platter, and Andy found himself

face to face with a face. The lamb's head was staring right back at him.

Andy tried to recoil, really he did, but the smell was absolutely wonderful. Warm spices flooded his nostrils, and Andy couldn't have felt more grateful for the moment. He looked up at Mahmoud, and Mahmoud motioned for Andy to help himself.

Andy picked a hefty piece from the lamb's cheek, because he knew he would only have an opportunity like this once.

Andy smiled, and his lips parted. To his own surprise, Andy said "Kheily mamnoon!" and put the cheek in his cheek.

Lamb's Head

Mahmoud's smile was luminous. Andy felt at home, un-like Andy's actual home which was dismal, dark and usually quite unwelcoming these days.

No, Mahmoud's smile was like a warm hug, a jaybird singing, and the smell of fresh cut grass.

This, of course, made it all the more jarring when a glow-ing, disembodied scimitar cut Mahmoud's smiling head off. Well, not disembodied because swords don't typically have bodies. But then, they don't typically go about decapitating of their own volition either.

Andy would have screamed, were he surprised, but it being his second torrent of blood today sort of dulled the effect. Andy was mildly surprised, however, when Mahmoud's head was replaced with a large glowing disc not unlike the sun. It was radiant, blindingly so, and Andy turned his eyes from its brilliance.

The voice that issued forth was similar to Mahmoud's but more mellifluous. Mellifluous in the literal sense, Andy feeling trapped by sticky sweet goodness, imprisoned by ambrosia.

"Andy! I'm sorry you had to see that. It's good for no one's heart to be witness to such a gruesome death. To be honest though, beheading is a pretty normal brand of martyrdom in our tradition. I once saw a guy named Husayn decapitated at

Karbala! What a terrible way to go! But what is one to say in the face of cultural precedent?"

"Still, I'd prefer to avoid it," said Andy, his gaze still averted.

"It seems much less common than it was in my day. Less swords in general, in fact."

"Ya, I think most have been reduced to showpieces in college dorm rooms," Andy said as he turned a blind eye to the battle axe on his own post-university wall.

The Disc sighed.

There was an awkward silence, so Andy filled it, "Why did such a great guy have to lose his life though? Your Husayn buddy, I mean. Not Mahmoud, because surely you didn't kill Mahmoud just to make an entrance. That was just for show, right? He'll be resurrected any moment." The Glowing Disc was silent. "Right?"

"Uh sure ya totally," the Disc shuffled, awkward. It changed the subject, "You said lose his life. Interesting choice of words, lose. I don't see it that way. The nature of sacrifice is not of losing anything. A gift given is never lost."

"I'm not so sure you can give something freely that is as dear to you as your head."

"You think you can't, but that is merely your own attach-ment." the Disc countered.

"How can I not be attached to my head?" Andy fingered his Adam's apple.

"Maybe, in the wake of 'loss' a little bit of unattachment isn't such a bad thing? That Bodhi guy over across the desert, he had it right. Attachment is the root of all suffering. So like a severed head, you should allow yourself to become detached. Sacrifice *yourself.* You're going to lose it all, Andy. What if instead of getting all bent out of shape, you just rolled with it, like a freshly cut cranium? There, you will find peace."

"Peace, huh? Equanimity, right? Ha! Coming from the

Angel who thought to cut Mahmoud's cute little head off for a grand entrance!"

"I never said I was an Angel," the Disc hissed.

"Oh, I just assumed, what with the glowing disc and all," Andy stroked Teat's head, nervous.

"You mean the one that burns your retinas?"

"True. True. That doesn't make it better though. A demon thinks he can teach peace at the Apocalypse? A devil thinks he knows about sacrifice!" Andy shook his head.

"Why is it that only a 'good guy' can teach a valid lesson? Silliness! I know pain, suffering and sacrifice just as much as any of those white feathered fucks. Tell me Andy, is it satiation that teaches you to not eat too much cake? No. It's the Goddamned belly ache."

Andy's stomach grumbled.

"You're about to be shat on Andy. You can choose suffering, or find peace in the poo. It's up to you."

"Doesn't feel like peace is much of an option," Andy looked at Mahmoud's head on the ground.

"Sweet! That's what I like to hear! A proper sacrifice! Suffering it is!" The Disc flared, and its glow was extinguished.

For a moment, Andy saw the outline of Mahmoud's smiling face, burned on his retinas. As that shadow faded, however, all that was left was a stump of a neck, and a cartoonish fountain of blood.

✛✛

There was a scream. More than a scream, it was a room full of screams, but they all coalesced to create one really big scream.

Andy took that as his cue to run.

Fuck it hurts to run.

Andy heard an encouraging chirp from Teat. Andy took that as a sign to run faster, which Andy did, despite the pain.

At the end, I expected pain, but didn't think it'd be in my loins. Wait, are these my loins? By the end of this, Andy was going to make sure he knew what loins were.

Andy turned down the alley, and continued to take erratic turns as to throw his pursuers off his trail. He wound about, winding in a bevy of blindingly badass moves, evading a basilisk here, some ghoulies there.

He found himself, however, right back at the door to Mahmoud's house, having just taken four right turns now that he did the math.

He heard a murderous wail from the adjoining room and sprinted off yet again.

This time, he trusted fear to make him fast enough without bobbing and weaving. He sprinted straight ahead.

He forgot, however, about the circular nature of this hellish neighborhood and found himself, yet again, at Mahmoud's front door.

"Ahh..." Andy began to scream, but was interrupted by, "Psssst! Andy!"

Andy looked across the street and saw Dante looking at him with a mischievous grin from an alleyway.

"Dante, we have to get out of here!"

"You're so right! Hurry, follow me!" Andy sprinted again, barely able to keep up with the surprisingly spry hippie.

Dante darted into an unmarked metal door and Andy hurried in behind him.

A hand grabbed Andy by the shirt and jerk him into a bathroom. Dante eyed Andy, the mischievous look still plastered on his face.

Dante pulled a small bag from his pocket, but Andy was too grateful to care.

"How did you know I was in trouble?"

"What do you mean trouble? I didn't know you were in trouble. I just really wanted some beer, and POOF! There you were! I manifested you bro!" Dante motioned to the little baggie, which now had a car key deep inside. "Snoot?"

Weird, thought Andy. Not because of the drugs, but because Dante didn't have a car to necessitate the key.

"No, thanks man."

Andy wasn't sure if cocaine counted as consumption, but didn't want to risk meeting a cocaine demon. Jaw grinding monsters sounded terrifying right about now. Let alone his heart was already beating a mile a minute, and Andy had promised himself long ago that he wouldn't die in a bathroom stall.

"I will, however, take you up on that beer."

"Suit yourself!" said Dante, as he stashed the baggie.

More erratic than before, Dante burst through the bathroom door into Tiddy's. Andy followed Dante, out into a wildly busy bar area.

It was busier than Andy had ever seen it. That wasn't

saying much, as there was usually only a handful of regulars scattered across the cavernous space.

Today, the bar was packed to the gills with demons of every ilk. Six eyed, tentacled, flaming and spiky. At Tiddy's, at least, they didn't look particularly out of place.

Their tyrannosaur eyes encouraged every move Andy made to be cautious and calculated. He moved in slow motion across the room, sticking to the creatures' peripherals.

"Why is that human acting so fucking weird?" A swamp monster whispered to his friend.

"Does a human need a reason?"

Andy felt a pull towards some sensual succubi as they danced across the room, but convinced his feet to steer clear as he crossed the room at a glacial pace.

Andy sat next to a dead fellow at the bar who had been split right down the middle like a fancy hot dog. The hotdog man turned towards Andy. Ever polite, Andy made eye contact with one eye then leaned over to make contact with the other. He nodded.

On his other side, Dante smiled, with not one but two pitchers of beer.

"Hey Dante, what's with all the demons in the bar tonight?" Andy simply *had* to know if Dante was aware of the lunacy that surrounded him.

"No different than any other night dude. And you're one to talk! You brought a fucking bird into the bar. That's as gnarly as it gets."

Andy looked down at Teat, who returned a loving stare.

I'm grateful for you, little dude, Andy thought.

Dante slid one of the pitchers over to Andy.

"No glasses, dude?" asked Andy.

"And make more work for the lovely bartender?" Dante motioned towards the floating viscera behind the counter, complete with throbbing ectoplasmic spleen.

"No, you're right," Andy said as he grabbed the pitcher.

"To horny demons!" Dante lifted his pitcher.

"To horny demons," Andy laughed. He spotted the succubi, a couple particularly horny demons. Andy held eye contact, lifted the pitcher a foot above his head, and poured the beer straight into his mouth with a wink.

The horny demons howled with glee.

Pitcher of Beer

Andy felt compelled to keep his eyes on the demonesses in the corner but willed himself to look back towards Dante. He would be no woman's feast this night.

Andy didn't know what he had expected when he looked at Dante, but it wasn't this.

Dante's pitcher was there, but Dante was gone. Well not entirely gone. In the pitcher floated Dante's mouth, nose and eyes. Andy had seen some gross shit today, but this was way more grosserer.

Andy was not prepared, however, for the grossest grossness of all. The dismembered eyes started blinking, and then the mouth started moving. The tongue, which wasn't exactly attached to the mouth, squirmed and Andy noticed what must have been a larynx, vibrating at the bottom of the pitcher.

The voice bubbled, not quite drowning.

"I'm so glad we get to hang out! I've heard so much about you, but was worried you'd be above drinking out of a pitcher! Especially now that you've spent so much time with all those Holier than Thou nerds."

"Dante didn't give me much of a choice."

"Yep. Doesn't seem like you have much of that *at all* lately, huh? Well let me introduce myself. I'm A Pitcher of Cheap Ass Beer, but you can call me Binge."

"Binge."

"Yep, that's me. You can think of me as the God of Drowning Your Sorrows."

"You mean Devil."

"Ah tomato potato dude. I would argue that most of your 'Gods' are pretty bad guys when it comes down to it. What with the floods and plagues and all."

"You're not wrong," Andy knew it was true, but still felt a little defeated by the notion of no cosmic good guys.

"True, I'm never wrong. I mean, how could drinking your feelings be wrong? Am I right?"

Andy wasn't sure if he was being facetious or not.

"But really, there's a lot of value in covering it all up. I know, I know! I get a bad rap. Everyone says you gotta feel your feelings man. To binge isn't an appropriate coping mechanism," the mouth said, ever so distinguished. "But then, what *IS* an appropriate coping mechanism? Processing? Coming to terms? What if the terms are fucking terrible! What if what you are expected to cope with is your 'God' abandoning you? Pain? Suffering? Eternal torment? That shit is all borderline fun if you're hammered! Right?"

Andy nodded. This was one angel that actually made a little bit of sense.

"See? I knew it! You're a man of reason! A learn-ed sort of fellow! And this aint your first rodeo, either! I see you! You lost your job? Handle of whiskey. Grandpa died? Cocaine and gin! Disillusioned with capitalism? Kleptomania." Andy looked confused. "Yep, that was me too! Listen, I'm just here to help you navigate this eternal state of unfairness that you find yourself in."

"That's really selfless of you," Andy said, bitter.

"Of course I'm selfless. I'm the definition of ego dissolution. Want to swim in the cosmic sea of euphoria? Why meditate when you can just take a whole lot of substances?

It's direct. I'm all about mainlining, my man," the tongue did a gross little, seductive, waggle after it said mainlining.

"Everybody has been giving you really complicated answers to the end of the world," the pitcher continued. "I'm giving you a really easy one. You're a bartender man, you get it. If everything is falling apart around you, you just drink."

Andy nodded.

"It's only natural with a family like yours! It's what you were born to do!"

Ah, there it was.

Yes, Andy was born into a long lineage of addicts. He was a product of binge eaters, binge drinkers, binge game show watchers, and binge bingers. Andy knew that, he knew that, he knew that. And despite how much he knew that, Andy refused to allow his hand to be forced by something so base as genetics. As fate.

"You had me dude. I was right there with you, until you told me I wasn't choosing to be a shitty drunk. Until you told me that my vices weren't uniquely mine. Not a product of me."

"You're not unique Andy, you're just another addict in a long line of addicts."

"I'm not doomed by those who came before me you shmuck. Maybe I can change. Maybe I can find new ways to cope with pain!" Andy was feeling less and less sure, because he sounded more and more like a disingenuous after-school special.

"Sure Andy, sure you can change. Let's revisit that. Maybe when you're not knee deep in a few pitchers of beer."

"A *FEW* pitchers of beer?"

"Yes, Andy. If nothing else, you're fucking consistent."

Andy heard an audible chug chug chug as he watched the beer flee the pitcher. Andy realized too late, far too late, that the sound came from his own throat.

++

Andy was sloshed. Halfway to horizontal. He stumbled to the kitchen sink, and turned on the water.

He held his finger under the stream, waited for cold water to heal all that ailed him. Or at least to trigger his gag reflex.

Cold water, however, never came. Andy turned the handle to the other side, in hopes of a dyslexic plumber.

Andy waited for a few more seconds, to no avail. Aggrieved, he succumbed to the pressure and bowed his head. He had to win this battle against the beer in his belly.

Damned if I do, damned if I don't, Andy thought as he stuck his mouth under the hot tap water.

Hot Water

A fever pitch. Andy wasn't quite sure what the actual meaning of the phrase was, but he was sure the fairies were in one.

They flew back and forth with a heated sort of energy. Energy that they weren't able to expel, but like a magma, would eventually erupt. And like a volcano, they were looking for someone to rain down upon, to make anew. An offer of fertility, of growth.

When they spotted Andy, they flew to him like flies to a turd.

Despite their chaotic energy, their hurried pattern made his tension melt away. Andy didn't realize he was tense prior to the melting, but he felt muscles loosen that he didn't even know he could tighten. It was the relieved feeling of a long held pee, one held from eyelid to toenail.

A symphony of raspy voices and staccato rhythms danced over Andy's body. Like tiny death metal masseuses, the fairies screamed as they whipped him with flaming flails. It was painful, angry, and ever so righteous. Like a new tattoo, rough sex, or filing taxes.

Sometimes healing is a pillowy cloud. Sometimes it's a cool mountain stream. And sometimes healing is a bone being set. Chock full of adrenaline, and a little bit of anger. Brutal, abusive and painful and shocking enough to fill you with the determination to get better. To be better.

Andy was was steeled in his determination to never feel like this ever again.

The fairies just laughed.

✚✚

Andy was pissed. He was damned tired of being a victim to Armageddon.

No, he would show the next demon what he was made of. He was determined to be the hero of this story. Despite some deeply suppressed fantasies of being a damsel in distress, it was actually no fun being a victim.

Andy set his jaw, and walked straight (or what his drunken brain thought was straight) to the fridge. He was ready to take on whatever little shit dared to stand in his way.

The lone box in the fridge was familiar. Too familiar.

He opened the box, and looked down at the saddest bruschetta he had ever seen. Half limp, half eaten, entirely miserable.

He'd eaten it far too often to have any illusions. He knew it wouldn't feed anything in him, wouldn't satisfy a damn thing. There was a reason, more often than not, he chose a drink (or three) over a shift meal. His work's food sucked.

Forlorn, Andy took a bite.

Shift Meal

"Hello Andrew!"

Leave it to fucking *Dylan* to have the most lackluster entrance a demon could muster. Just a polo shirt, khakis, and a shit eating grin.

"Hi *Dylan.*"

"Listen Andrew, I'm going to skip all the foreplay and get right at it. I feel like we haven't been giving you a proper chance to shine. You are an integral part of the Spoke-Easily team, and we want to help you find your value."

"My value."

"Yes Andrew! I know you have been trading shifts, missing shifts, walking out on shifts. I know you've been drinking a lot on shift. Heck, I even know you've been talking shit about me behind my back. But I *also* know that none of that is your fault! It's ours! We haven't shown you how much we care about you, how much we want you to grow with the company."

"Grow with the company? Are you serious?"

"Serious as Sunday Mass!"

Andy stifled a giggle.

"So Dylan. Since you're *here*, I'm sure you must know that the world is ending," Andy said, almost asking.

"One world is ending Andrew, but another one can begin for you. I didn't tell you *before*, because it wasn't a sure thing, but I got promoted Andrew! We are on the verge of franchising, and I need *you*, yes you, to be the new GM. In fact, there's no one else I would ever dream of for the job."

"Bro. I'm trying to figure out if I even have a place in the world after this one."

"Of course you have a place. You have so much potential, Andrew. We just want to make sure you capitalize on it. When everything seems to be falling apart, you have to take life by the horns. You have so much resolve. We see how *steeled* you are. You're ready to take it all on. We want you to take it all on, with *us*! We're a family here Andrew. We want to support you, because we just want what's best for the family."

"Family," Andy felt it roll around on his tongue little a dirty little worm.

"We can be the best damn speakeasy in the world. You can help us be the trend setters. We can make you an influencer! You can become your very own hashtag! And did I mention we have benefit options?"

"Your benefit options are a fucking scam and you know it Dylan."

"OK, no options. But what would you say to 55 dollars an hour? And Andy, I'm talking hourly. I'm not trying to screw you. I'd never offer you salary, because I know that's not your style. We will just be paying you for the work you *do*, because we know how much you can do. How much you *will* do."

Andy hesitated. Andy was really good at working through his pain. He was really good at ignoring his own needs for the sake of others. Maybe, in the wake of destruction, what he needed was to buckle down. Throw some epic parties, build a whole new beverage and food menu. Maybe do some cool team building. And make bank.

Andy lost himself in a reverie of wholesale accounts, Quickbooks and live music. He could feel the hooks sink in as he thought about his piggy bank growing into a whole hog. He could buy that wheel of Parmesan he'd always dreamed of.

He could take Angie to that omakase joint that only served 12 tables each night.

He could even buy his mom something really nice. Admittedly, Andy wasn't really sure what his mom was into these days, but still! He could get her something expensive because moms *love* expensive stuff.

"Listen Andrew. I told you when I hired you, we want you to be a part of our family. We value family first, and foremost. When you grow, we grow. When you're happy, we're happy. Isn't that what family is all about?" Dylan asked Andy in earnest.

But Andy wasn't quite there. There was something in what Dylan had said.

"I was thinking you could hire the new bar manager," Dylan pried.

Family.

"You could fly in that distiller you love for some staff education. Have him talk about the sustainable wild botanicals on Vancouver Island," Dylan prodded.

Family.

"You've always wanted to put more cheese on the menu. French cheese, Spanish cheese, Greek cheese..." Dylan almost pleaded.

My family. My family. My family.

"You ungrateful little shit," Dylan screamed, "I'm offering you an opportunity to be somebody. To not spend your whole life in the shadow of all your more successful friends. You think you're special? You're only special if we make you special. You were nothing before us, and I promise you will be nothing if you leave. You think I don't have other people that would jump at this opportunity? Don't fucking kid yourself, there are droves and droves. We're a family Andrew, and just like *your* family, we will cut you off. You want this Andrew, or I wouldn't fucking be here. The world is ending, and you're thinking about work. You're just as much of a capitalist fuck as I am."

Andy felt smaller, and smaller still. *My family... My fami... My fam.*

He reached for that light, but still it faded. And Andy was back on that wheel of Parmesan.

Through the haze, Andy saw a calmer, more composed Dylan.

Dylan smiled.

"You don't have to decide now, OK Andrew? You can take a couple days to think about it. You have all the time in the world."

Dylan's last words hung in the air like a guillotine. Andy tried to remember what he was trying to remember. But all that came to mind was that wheel of Parmesan.

All the time in the world. And the wheel of cheese spun round, and round, and round.

++

"Don't you fucking chirp at me."

Andy was more than a little perturbed as he stepped out onto the street.

Why? He thought. *Why in the 7 Hells am I stuck thinking about corporate fealty when there should be more pressing things on my mind?*

Andy used to pride himself on being *thoroughly* anti-capitalist. Andy had been maced outside the treasury, he remembered the feeling of full fat milk being pour all over his face to lessen the hurt, he remembered the glint off the riot police's visors.

Andy knew that corporate interest compromised all meaningful connection with a natural way of living. Andy knew that money turned small business owners into self-righteous fucks. Andy knew the more he worked, the further from himself he felt. Andy knew there were avenues to reciprocity, community, and mutual aid that gave a stiff middle finger to business.

Andy knew all this, and yet also knew he *was* complicit. He liked his handsome living, and if he could make other people happy in the process, all the better! Andy wanted to be successful because he wanted to support his friends and family.

He thought about money, again and again, even as his heart berated him for it.

CHIIIRRRRRRP.

"Oh quiet."

CHIRP.

"No really. Stop."

CHIRP.

"Ok, fine. You're right. I don't have to do anything I don't want to do. But what if I want to do it? I'm tired of struggling, that's for sure. And I'm bored. Maybe moving up the ladder is for the best. Maybe it'll right my wrongs, feed the lonely bits inside my soul. Right Teat?"

Teat stared at Andy.

"Right?"

Teats eyes narrowed.

"Ok. Wrong. You're right. Wrong. Fixating on work is dumb, even when its *not* the end of days. But I finally started to feel comfortable, and now I'm here watching it all slip out of my fingers. It was nice not being worried all the time, and now I have to worry about being broke *and* Armageddon? That's a Hell of a combination."

CHIRRRRRRRP.

"You're right," Andy squeezed the tiny puffball just tight enough. And he was pretty sure the little puffball squeezed right back.

Andy relaxed. Hugs are magic.

"That was nice Teat. Thank you. Maybe all I *ever* need is a good cuddle."

Andy thought about Angie, how she felt against his body. He walked, determined to cuddle her real good, and arrived at her apartment all the quicker.

"You know Teat, I kind of like this whole closed world geography. I can walk any direction, and in not that much time I can be exactly where I'm supposed to be. It's very Tao."

Andy was still blissed out from his avian embrace, and it

had quite the effect on the nearby demonic spawn. No matter how grotesque, no matter how many pentagrams a creature was emblazoned with, they kept their distance. He was untouchable, the power of love shining towards every Baphomet, Beelzebub, and Baphelzebubomet that dared come near.

Andy looked up at Angie's apartment, beamed with pride. He could conquer anything. He had conquered HR. OK, not conquered but he was now steadfast in his resolve to not work any extra hours! Heck, maybe *any* hours, if he was lucky.

Andy's confidence shattered when he saw a shadow behind the curtains. He had seen a lot of shadows in his day, even more so this week, but this was one darned shadowy shadow.

Andy walked up the stairs to Angie's apartment, begged Teat for protection.

Something is wrong.

Tentative, Andy raised his free hand to knock on the door, but it swung open.

Andy gasped.

Angie stood there looking damn fine, and damned near naked. All fear melted away, and Andy stepped into the apartment.

The door shut behind him, and Andy prepared his body for some *sexy* sexy time. His loins hurt, but you know, that was OK. Loins were made to hurt, right?

Andy scanned the room, appraised a box on the counter.

He averted his gaze, not willing to believe what he saw.

He looked around the kitchen, panicked.

Angie said something to him, but he busied himself looking for an apple, or an old pizza crust or a hot kettle. Anything to deter him from the inevitable.

"Andy. *ANDY!*" Angie pinched Andy's weenus, and hard.

"Hey! Careful babe. You know I'm sensitive about my elbows."

"Andy, I asked you like a million times if everything was OK. And clearly its not. And I'm tired of this shit. So I'm going to put down my foot and say if you don't drop this mopey, weird, distant shit, I want you to walk straight the fuck out of here."

Walk straight the fuck out of here, Andy's mind agreed.

Andy turned around to face the door. His 180 degree turn, however, brought him face to face with the box on the counter.

Another 90 degree turn. Counter. Box. Turn. Counter. Box. Turn. Counter. Box.

"What the fuck are you doing? If you want a doughnut, just ask! Why are you acting so weird?"

"I don't want a doughnut!" Andy screamed.

"Then don't have one! Jesus! Why can't you look at me! You came over here, looked at me like I was a very sexy piece of meat, and then immediately started ignoring me as soon as you saw the Hoodoo Doughnuts box. Am I sexy meat, or am I not Andy?"

"You're the sexiest meat I've ever seen," said Andy as he stared at the doughnut box.

Angie opened the box, revealing a maple bacon dough-nut looking equally sexy.

No Andy. Don't. Don't do it. You are strong enough to resist.

Teat started to panic in Andy's hand, as he wiggled and chirped. Frantic, terrified. Knowing.

"Ah, the little guy sounds hungry," said Angie, and she tore a slight corner off the doughnut. She fed it to Teat, whose eyes rolled in the back of his head in a riot of ecstasy and demonic possession.

"Fuck, fine. Jesus get it over with," Andy said as he reached for the doughnut. He wasn't going to let Teat go through this hell alone.

"Wow, don't be so excited about it. Sometimes I wonder if you even appreciate me."

"With all due respect babe. You've sealed my fucking doom," Andy said as he took a bite of the oh so delicious maple bacon doughnut.

Maple Bacon Doughnut

There are a few things Andy would never wish upon his worst enemy. Shingles, working a brunch shift, their loved ones dying before their eyes. And this. Definitely this.

Angie undressed in front of Andy, which should have turned him on real quick like.

The gross little mustache on her face, however, ruined all the theatrics.

Then, to add insult to injury, Angie covered her sweet sweet curves with a bullet proof top and a disgusting blue uniform. Some people might think it sexy, this kind of roleplay, but Andy did not. Not one bit.

Angie's lip was curled up in a knowing grin.

"Well what do we have here?" Angie said, the implication being, she knew exactly what she had here. She motioned towards Andy's hands, and Andy was cuffed.

"Nothing to see here," replied Andy shortly.

"You're damn right there's nothing to see here," Angie spat.

"What's that supposed to mean?"

"Oh, you just strike me as a bit of a nobody. Barely worth my time," she smiled.

"That sounds great. I'd hate to waste your time. So just write me a ticket or whatever it is you need to do and get the fuck on," Andy regretted his choice of words.

"Watch your tongue boy."

Andy glared down at his tongue, his brain admonished his mouth.

"You know why shit like this happens to people like you?"

People like me? Andy thought.

"Because you've got no fucking discipline. You seem to think the rules don't apply to you, but they apply to everyone. That's why you amount to just about jack squat. Because you don't *obey*. This may sound like a joke, like a fucking caricature, but I promise you it most definitely is not."

"So what am I supposed to obey, exactly?"

"The law of the land! And you find yourself in the land of the not quite dead. It's the land of repentance, the land of I'm sorry for my fucking sins. Are you even sorry for your sins? Do you even know what your sins *are* boy?"

Andy felt the anger hit him like a billy club. It was one thing for demons and angels to call him boy. But when a copper calls you "boy," it's a whole different level of demeaning.

"I aint sorry for shit, *PIG*," Andy put some extra emphasis on the P.

"What did you call me?"

"I called you a pig. Discipline? What's disciplined about the end of days? I sure as shit don't see any reason to all this. Looks like chaos, and piggies like you think they can control the chaos, but you fucking breed it."

Andy was on a roll, "You seem to think you know what discipline is, but you've got the meaning backwards *PIG*. You seem to think discipline means to teach, but it means to learn. I'm learning plenty, but that doesn't mean you are teaching me shit. *PIG*."

"Stop calling me that."

"*PIG*."

"Stop it. Don't do this."

"*PIG*."

REEEEEEEEEEEEEEEEEEEE.

The squeal was deafening. Andy covered his ears as Angie's uniform burst at the seams. Angie's flesh bulged, her snout elongated and flattened. Her skin pinkened, and her hair dropped to the ground, only to be replaced by sparse weird little wiry bristle.

REEEEEEEEEEEEEEEEEEE.

As the squeal faded, the pig, now truly of porcine flesh, stared deep into Andy's eyes.

With gravity, the pig bowed to Andy. A deep and genuinely genuine bow.

"My good sir, I thank you for freeing me from my prison," the reverent pig said.

"Your prison?" Andy asked.

"Yes. For too long the mighty doughnut has been usurped by the law. Not a universal law, but a law of men. A law of tyrants. It has been used against the people, a symbol of oppression and not liberation. Today, however, you have freed the true spirit of the doughnut."

"And what exactly is the true spirit of the doughnut?"

"Freedom of course. Where one person sees stricture and a need for discipline, those true of heart see the seed of letting loose. Chains and shackles only serve to break humanity, but the doughnut was birthed to do the opposite. To lift the world of men up! To allow them to choose to eat fat and carbs and not have to fucking worry about it! A doughnut is the heart of healing, and a perfect symbol of unity. Circular. Whole, with a hole. When He spoke of breaking bread, he was most certainly speaking of the doughnut."

A tear came to Andy's eye.

"At the end of days, there are two types of people. There are the prude, those that cling tighter to tightness. They try to keep the world from unraveling, but in the end all they succeed at it knotting it all up. All they succeed at is tying themselves tighter. At times such as these, we are meant to unravel. Anyone who has ever pulled on a thread knows that there is joy in the unspooling. And only when the thread is free from its binding, can a new tapestry begin."

Andy never knew a pig could be so dignified.

"You are the instigator of your own oppression. I want to unfetter you, but the chains are too deeply ingrained. When the time comes, you are going to be strict, you are going to be harsh. You are going to subdue even yourself, and find anger and resentment when you can't be 'disciplined.' You will act as judge and jury, your own executioner. This can't be helped, but I want the essence of the doughnut to stay with you. The great liberator. The tyrants will not fall, but may the heart of rebellion always live within you," the pig again bowed its head solemnly. "Let the doughnut be your guide. Be gentle. Be yielding. Be kind. Be forgiving."

As the pig took a step backwards, Andy reached out, "Please don't leave! I feel like there's so much you have to teach me. To teach everyone," Andy almost cried.

"You already know everything you need to know. Let loose the chains Andy. Each time you bind yourself, let loose the chains."

Andy looked down at handcuffs. Where once had been cold metal, Andy now saw only fried dough and frosting.

Let loose the chains, Andy thought to himself. And he bit through his bindings.

++

Andy wasn't about to run. Not this time. He looked at Angie as tears welled in his eyes.

"Oh babe what's wrong?" she asked.

"I feel like my whole world is unraveling and I can't stop it."

Even though Andy knew that his shitty tapestry needed unraveling, it didn't make it any less scary.

Angie lifted Andy's head, and met his gaze.

"Andy, don't worry about your world unraveling. I'm really fucking good at crochet."

She kissed Andy and he kissed right back. He gripped her tightly, and then realized he needed to loosen up. Her body responded to his gentleness, and she tossed him to the couch.

Maybe there's a little bit of the cop still left in her, Andy thought as his ribs met the wooden frame beneath the cushions. *But I'll gladly help her out of her uniform. Maybe cops and robbers isn't such a bad kink after all.*

The night lasted forever, and so did he.

After he had worn Angie out, he looked out the window to find the moon exactly where he had left it. He traded teat for Teat, and kissed Angie on the head.

"Why are you always leaving?" Angie asked half asleep.

"If I don't leave, how do you expect me to come?" Andy

smiled as he walked towards the door. "Don't worry, I'll be back soon."

Andy opened the door and walked down the stairs to the street below.

On the street corner, he spotted a dog pile of banshees and ogres. They were curled up together, sleeping soundly. No doubt sweet dreams of malevolence everlasting danced through their gross little exposed brains.

The night was peaceful, and Andy's stroll was slow, intentional. He knew where he was headed, and felt emboldened by his conquest of such a Hellish day. Teat dozed in his pocket, and Andy prayed he wouldn't lose the little bird when this was all over.

Prayer, Andy thought. *What's a prayer worth these days? Gods are pettier than men.*

Andy felt his heart being pulled, then his eardrums. A gentle beat, enticing and eerily familiar.

Vermouth? Andy thought. *No, it's something different.*

"ABSINTHE. ABSINTHE. ABSINTHE."

"No fucking way," Andy said aloud.

If vermouth was Andy's wife, then absinthe was his mistress. Andy skipped to the beat, humming and giggling in quick succession.

He turned the corner and beamed at the man in front of him. It looked like the same guy, but a little more, well, French. Andy couldn't explain it if he tried, but he was certain the man was French.

"Bonjour mon ami!" said Andy as he walked up to the man nearly passed out on the fountain. "Did I hear you say you are drinking Absinthe?"

"Oui. Absinthe," said the man shortly, as he regarded Andy skeptically.

"Oh don't worry man, I'm not a cop. I was just eating a cop, but I'm not a cop."

The man scooted his butt away from Andy.

"No no no! Ah whatever, I'm just here because..." Andy forgot why he was there. "I just love you so much right now," Andy could feel tears streaming down his face. He stuck his tongue out and waggled it back and forth in a failed attempt to catch the tears as they cascaded down his cheeks, and giggled all the while.

What am I doing? Andy thought to himself. He felt downright weird, like the hypoxia kind of loopy where body and mind don't want anything to do with each other.

He looked at the flowers on the fountain, hoping they would help bring him back to reality.

Why would the botany of the Apocalypse make me feel less crazy? Andy thought.

And he was right. The flowers did not, in fact, reassure him. They were dancing to the song that the man was no longer singing, swaying and shuffling like a chorus line in a musical. And they were half naked, having lost more than half of their petals now.

Andy turned his gaze to Teat, not wanting to offend the flowers with his ogling. Teat looked up at him and smiled with a mouthful of teeth.

"What the fuck?" Andy said aloud.

"Now it is my turn to say the weird things to you, no?" said a voice to Andy's left.

Andy looked up and saw the man, who had a sickly green tinge to his skin.

"What's. Happening. To. Me." Andy could barely get the words out of his mouth.

"It is, how do you say, time to go down the rabbit hole, no?"

"No."

"No yes? Or no no?" asked the sideways man.

"No no!" screamed Andy.

"Ah, no I am sorry. It is no yes, not, no no," the man was calm. "Now we celebrate l'angel of l'apocalypse! Absinthe!"

"I thought Wormwood was the Angel of the Apocalypse."

"Yes yes. Same same. Except our Angel is a little bit better, because, after all, he is French!"

"Right..."

"Oui. And just be happy I am not a Ukrainian. Because you know his name in Ukraine, no?"

"No. Maybe Wormsynth?" Andy giggled as he imagined a night crawler DJ. Andy looked out of the corner of his eye and was sure he saw a rolling roly-poly with a teeny-tiny glow stick. *Weird.*

"Chernobyl."

The name tore Andy's eyes from the techno bug back to the man in front of him. The man smiled at Andy, which at first seemed malevolent. Andy realized though, that it was just manic. Like a purple cat or something.

"Chernobyl. Ya, no thanks," Andy said as he grabbed the bottle from the man.

"Santé my friend," said the man.

"Santé," replied Andy. He prayed for Wonderland and not Nuclear Holocaust as he took a sip. Then he remembered that whole "off with their heads" business.

Absinthe

Andy looked up and saw a great fire falling from the heavens. It was magnificent, a comet unlike anything he had seen in, at least, the last three days. Vermouth had paled in comparison, had been made literally dull in light of *this* light. This epic celestial phenomenon, complete with the sprays of yellow, green and purple sparks.

The center of the star was shiny, metallic, ribbed and impenetrable. Extra-terrestrial in a very cosmic horror sort of way, certainly not of this planet.

As it laid foot (no, feet) upon the Earth, however, its true nature unfurled. As the flames withered, and the segments uncurled, the form became all the more familiar. Andy was toe to toe to toe to toe to toe with a giant roly-poly.

The six foot tall pill bug showered Andy in Technicolor sparks, as it shook the stardust from its exoskeleton. Andy counted fourteen legs, each adorned with an impressive amount of candy jewelry. The bug wore two pairs of tie-dye sunglasses. One pair covered what Andy presumed were eyes, while the other adorned the tips of its antennae.

"Bonjooooouuuuuuuuuur!" said the bug as it jumped in the air. As it touched upon the ground, it curled into a ball and did a few dizzying laps around the astonished Andy. It uncurled and leapt in front of Andy with all of its arms raised up, waiting for applause.

Andy's clap was slow, still unsure if he was impressed or horrified. Ever since he saw "Honey I Shrunk the Kids" as a child, Andy had been acutely aware of how giant bugs could be simultaneously horrifying and endearing.

"No need to be afraid, mon ami! It is merely I, the harbinger of the end of days!"

"One harbinger has been enough," said Andy. "Anything else on offer, besides harbinging? Something a bit more light-hearted?"

"How about strobe-lighthearted?" The pill bug started did an insect-y click noise that sounded vaguely reminiscent of beatboxing, then proceeded to do a hypnotizing ten limbed robot dance. The night sky flashed as the bug did a fourteen legged moonwalk.

Andy couldn't hold it in any longer. He swiveled his hips, let the rhythm take hold. He giggled as he did the worm, the most apropos dance move he could imagine. As always, he whacked his junk on the floor with a little more force than intended and his breath left him.

Andy didn't care. He hadn't had fun like this in a long time. Hadn't allowed himself.

He was in the middle of some sweet footwork, when Absinthe cut the music.

"Booooo!" Andy yelled.

"I know I know, but we have business to take care of," Absinthe apologized.

Andy was abashed.

"Just kidding!" The lights started flickering again and a dirty little breakdown had Andy going head over heels like a roly-poly. The music cut again.

"But seriously."

The air cannons shot off confetti, and the pill bug spun on its back at maximum velocity. Andy threw his head back, watched the still burning cosmos dance overhead as the bug danced at his feet.

The music stopped. Andy waited. And waited. It didn't return.

Absinthe struggled on its back, trying to get a grip with any of its fourteen feet, to no avail.

"Do you need any help?" asked Andy.

Absinthe responded, a little embarrassed, "Oui. Um, yes please. Merci."

Andy reached out his hand and felt the antennae feel his arm before one of the legs put itself in Andy's hand. Andy shuddered and lifted.

"Who'd have thought?" Andy laughed. "A break dancing bug. I expected a guy in a top hat or a smiling cat or something like that."

"Expectation I am not," the bug said, narrowing its eyes. "Expectation is what got you in this mess in the first place. Reality does only one thing consistently, and that is defy expectation. Little old me, *I* would argue that expectation is the root of most of the world's suffering."

"I can see that," Andy suffered as he waited for the music to come back, as he hoped for it to melt the chilly tone.

"Life is weird. That is why I have avoided it for so long! People buy planners, write on calendars. They expect things to pan out a certain way and then... wham! Off with their heads!"

Andy rubbed his neck, "Rabbit holes are everywhere, and you're going to trip on them no matter how careful your step. It is why dancing is necessary, mon ami! It keeps you on your toes! Keeps you from planning! Puts you in step with the universe, with the pulse of the planet. That is why choreography is very much *not* dancing."

"I have to make some plans, you know? Otherwise how am I going to meal prep? Me with no meal prep is a recipe for potato chip dinners," Andy reflected, however, that potato chip dinners were his favorite kind of dinners.

"Of course. Of course. I know it impossible to live

without at least a *small* modicum of scheduling, but humans put *so* much on the future. It is just amazing how far off you can be! Human logic is powerful, but fails to take into account the Gods' desire to giggle. Absurdity is the very soul of the quantum universe, because shit comes out of nowhere. The best *jokes* come out of nowhere, oh yes, the blind side is the essence of slapstick."

"So my pain is just a Stooges' bit? Apocalypse is for the audience's enjoyment?"

"If it is good comedy, it is for your enjoyment too," Absinthe did jazz-hands, which with ten hands, made Andy mildly catatonic.

"I'm expected to laugh?"

"I, of course, never expect anything. It's against my nature. I will tell you that having a sense of humor might help," the roly-poly smiled, its four mouths curled in a shape which horrified, much more than the intended affect. "And it's only going to get weirder from here, because it's only going to get more real. Imagination isn't the loopy part, we *know* that it's supposed to be cracked. We revel in fantasy because that it defies expectation, just like it promised. No, when you awaken to reality, that's when the really weird shit happens. You are approaching the absurd, where known and the un will intersect."

"So this has been normal by comparison?" Andy was incredulous.

"It has most certainly. I'm not saying it's exactly formulaic, but wrestling your own angels and demons is pretty par for the course. The lessons are much the same. As the last day approaches, as the reality of your new life approaches, you're going to experience some mind boggling oddities. The truth shall set your puny little expectations free, whether you are ready or not! Oh yes, the next two days will be ever so exciting!" Absinthe giggled.

Andy was forlorn again. His mood, a roller coaster of emotions.

Absinthe saw this and offered, "Have you ever seen those crazy yogis who just force laughter until it becomes natural?" Andy nodded. "It's a stupendous act of manipulation. A beautifully profound bit of chicanery. I think we should try it."

"Really though?"

"Like this," the bug opened its grisly little mouth parts, "Hahahahaha!"

"Ha. Ha. Ha. Ha. Ha," Andy said flatly.

"That's it! Keep going! Hahahahaha!"

"Hahahahaha."

"Hahahahaha!"

Andy's situation was ludicrous. The whole damned Armageddon was whack-a-doodle, a cosmic joke he didn't even know the punchline to.

Andy laughed in earnest. His guffaws radiated gratitude. That someone had convinced him to just laugh it off, if even for a moment? So fucking thankful. And that it was a bug? So silly.

Andy saw the lights flicker, as if in response to his laughs, and admired the roly poly as he spun on his back yet again.

Round and round he spun.

The music stopped. Absinthe's spinning stopped. He uncurled, and as he lay on his back, he didn't struggle. He just laid there, let the stars twinkle in his eyes, as he resigned himself to the fate of innumerable roly-polies before him.

His shell paled, turned white as the animating force of the spirit left his body. He was dead, nothing but a husk of his goofball self.

And Andy laughed.

And laughed.

And laughed.

+The 4th Day+

"Anddddddyyyyyyyyyyyyyy..."

Andy rolled over.

"Andyyyyy! Andy! Wake up!"

Andy covered his head with a nonexistent blanket. He grabbed at two Gerber daisy petals, tried to block out the sun. As he lay there though, he felt like a corpse, with the petals payment to cross the river Styx. He shook his head, withdrew his payment.

He had hoped the shaking would have scared off the voice in his head, but again Andy heard the voice plead.

"Please wake up, Andy! I'm so hungry!"

Andy had talked to his stomach before, but it had never talked back. This was new.

Andy berated his stomach, *Quiet you. Can't you go hungry for one fucking minute? Its exhausting.*

"Not in there! Over here!"

Andy opened his eyes but hesitated to look around. He didn't want to know what sort of demon held his name in its mouth. And he *definitely* didn't want to know what it was hungry for. It *did* sound like a child, but everyone knew demonic children were the worst demons of all.

"Oh for fucks sake."

Teat hopped into frame, but he looked *all* wrong. He was a bushtit, to be sure, but he would have a hard time pecking any seed, what with those big pouty lips and pearly white teeth still plastered to his skull.

"Oh Jesus Teat! You're still hideous!"

"Good morning to you too. Sheesh," the birds' lips inverted, a truly horrible frown.

"I'm sorry dude, I just liked you the way you were."

"I wish you'd just like me the way I am. Time changes us all Andy, time changes us all. Hell, come over here to the fountain and take a long hard look at yourself if you think you're so fuckin cute."

Andy always knew Teat was a little shit talker. It just took a more developed larynx to experience it firsthand.

"I'd rather not," Andy didn't feel like staring into the yawning eyes of the demon world this early in the morning.

"So we gonna find some grub or what dude? I'm famished! What's it take to get a pastry round here?" For Teat's sake, Andy wished for an adorable petite croissant.

"Err, I guess we can go to the coffee shop."

"Thatta boy! Chop chop!" Teat audibly clapped his wings, and Andy realized to his continued dismay that Teat had tiny little hands beneath his primary feathers.

Andy pushed himself to the seated position, then struggled to push himself to standing despite using the full support of the fountain. He caught a mere glimpse of his hollow but not quite dead eyes. He averted his gaze however, before he could notice any other gruesome features. His legs trembled as he stood.

Andy tucked the little bird into his palm. Teat whispered something to himself, and as he spoke, Andy felt the tickle of two tiny lips on his fingertips. Andy gagged a little.

As Andy walked, he was all but mindless. He wouldn't allow any of his thoughts to cross the barrier into conscious awareness.

It was a feeling well known to him. He had felt it when his grandfather died. He wouldn't allow himself to come to terms with whatever it was. Andy knew that this denial was the very precipice of understanding. He couldn't avoid the truth much longer, so he allowed himself to float in ignorance for as long as he could sustain it. He blocked it all out. Every bit of it.

The world was different. The fever dream was breaking. Sure there was that eyeball floating in the alley over there, but there were also regular old humans that he shared the sidewalk with now.

They looked dejected, broken by early mornings and wasted weekends. He could see fluorescent bulbs and Bluetooth headsets in their auras, he could taste bureaucracy on their skin. Not quite the walking dead, they oozed a desire to be going anywhere else, their hearts screamed for liberation. And yet the tractor beam held strong, their loneliness bound by the promise of yet another team building exercise. They were stuck.

"You look like that too, you know. The service industry isn't as different as you think it is."Andy tried to ignore Teat. Andy saw the coffee shop ahead, and picked up the pace. Not just running from the truth, he would run towards something!

"Stop!" Teat roared.

Andy stopped as a bus screamed past his eye lashes. Cars crisscrossed in front of him, and the reverie of the empty city was finally and absolutely broken.

'One of the drivers leaned out the window, covered in scales, and hissed with its forked tongue as it drove by.

"This isn't going to be gentle," whispered Teat.

Andy waited for a break in the traffic, and dashed across the street.

I need out of here. I need out of here.

Andy had never felt anxiety in the city before. Not like this. Sure he felt a little more at peace with creation when he was surrounded by moss and dragonflies, but he didn't exactly feel a stranger amongst brownstones and taxis. Being alone for so long (was three days so long?) had clearly taken its toll. He needed space.

Andy opened the door to the coffee shop expecting the hustle of the street. The room was cavernous though. The only other person was Baristo.

"Well hello there," said Baristo, their seductive voice drawing Andy closer.

"Good morning," said Andy, who would not give anything away.

"Is it now?" replied the knowing Baristo with a wink.

People are under the impression that bartenders are therapists, yet seem completely ignorant of the true horrors of humanity a coffee shop employee is privy to. A barista (or baristo) knows depravity like no other.

"I need some real medicine," said Andy with an honesty that surprised himself.

"I know just the thing," said Baristo as they turned their back. When they turned back around, the Baristo was holding a small bamboo whisk, a shallow dish, a bamboo scoop, a small sifter and a black glazed jar with a lid.

"Oooh, a proper ceremony eh?" Andy was intrigued.

"Absolutely. Ritual is everything in matcha, am I right?" Baristo smiled.

"Honestly, I have no idea. Never had the pleasure. I know about it though."

"Whaaaaat? Oh bro, you are in for a treat!"

The Baristo walked over to the sink, and washed their hands like a midwife. The movements were slow, methodical, with a gravity of someone that sought to bring life into the world.

Andy saw the Baristo carefully set the kettle's temperature. They grabbed a small linen cloth, and cleaned each tool as Andy watched the temperature on the kettle climb.

Baristo poured a stream of hot water into shallow dish.

Nice, thought Andy, knowingly. Andy warmed the glass ahead of time when he made a hot toddy.

Andy watched the Baristo lift the lid on the ceramic jar. Every movement was intentional, precise. The small bamboo scoop, something more akin to a tiny backscratcher, was inserted into the jar and Andy strained towards the Baristo's few silent words.

They welcomed the tea onto the scoop. *Cute.*

The tea was vibrant, the green downright nuclear in its luminescence.

Andy heard the door open behind him, but his eyes stayed transfixed on the process. Andy saw a slow stream of water dance across the bowl of powder. The door opened again behind Andy, and he saw Baristo break their gaze with the tea for a moment to acknowledge the waiting customers.

"Ah shit," he heard the Baristo mutter.

They poured the rest of the water, and whisked. Not whisked, beat the tea like a very naughty egg. Brutal.

They poured a bit more water in the cup, and the Baristo pushed the tea across to Andy, chunks and all. Their apology was short, and they welcomed the next customer to the counter without even a suggestion that Andy should pay for the hack job.

Andy could still feel the charge in the air. The room was still humming, but Andy felt like he had might have just been given ceremonial blueballs.

He sighed, and took a sip of the tea, not expecting much.

Matcha

As Baristo talked to the customer that had stepped up behind Andy, they turned their eyes to Andy and bowed in apology. The bow deepened, until their head made full contact with the counter.

Andy waited for the Baristo to rise again, but when they did rise, it was only a couple of inches, and they repeated contact with the counter.

"Don't worry, it's great," offered Andy.

"It was not supposed to be *great*," the grave voice reverberated on the counter below the face. "It was supposed to be sacred."

"Great is its own kind of sacred," said Andy, half believing it.

"The ritual is everything," said the voice, as the Baristo rose to make eye contact with Andy, "because everything is ritual."

The Baristo wore a black kimono, their hair tied back in a tight bun. To say their look was severe was generous. Andy was worried the Baristo, or perhaps Andy, would not survive this disgrace.

"I appreciate the ritual, I do. It's why I love old fashioneds so much, but I don't think it alters the taste at all."

"This is not about taste. The ritual is necessary to appease the Gods."

"I've got no desire to appease any of those shitasses, thank you," Andy knew appeasement was just one step removed from fealty.

"Something of such gravity demands respect Andy. Always. Do not repeat your mistakes."

"*Repeat* my mistakes?" Andy admired the irony of his response.

"Cut the shit. You went into your surgery knowing full well that you were enacting an ancient ritual. You felt the gravity deep in your heart, and yet when it came time to perform the necessary ceremony, you brushed it off. *That* is why you are here."

"Excuse me?" Andy was dead still.

"You had all the tools at your disposal to ensure a positive outcome. The portents were on your side. Yet when the day came, you left the power in the hands of someone else."

"How do you not leave that in someone else's hands? That's what surgery is!" Andy said the words, still not quite knowing what he meant.

"If you had been so wise as to just be humble, to give thanks and ask leniency. To make a fucking offering. You have to make an offering so they don't *take* an offering. Sun Gods don't fuck around Andy. And they certainly don't abide you running away from the ritual."

"I didn't run, I was just laying there." *Huh? Where was I laying? Or was I lying? I'm not a chicken.* Andy hardly recognized his own voice.

"You were high! Willful disassociation is no different than running."

"You're telling me there isn't some aspect of ritual intoxication?" Andy could hear the torment in his own voice, but his mind was completely detached.

"That's not how you did it, and you know it. Even now, you're trying to pull away from the truth. And you don't even have the balls, forgive my choice of words, to ask me to be gentle. So I won't play the part of demure fucking Baristo. I will not speak in metaphor."

"It feels like metaphor."

"It is literal Andy. Every culture that does bloodletting has prescribed fucking methods. You got high with your buddy then laid with a fucking butcher. And you knew it. You made light of yourself, and it was beyond self-deprecation. I can't say for certain, because you won't let anyone in, but I worry you cursed yourself. I worry you did it to yourself."

"I didn't curse myself. *He* did this to me."

"When you are a statistical anomaly, you only have your-self to blame. There is no bad luck."

I don't believe that.

"But I thought shit just happens?" Andy hesitated.

"Yes Andy, shit happens. But this is not that. It's time to take responsibility," the Baristo had the linen cloth, and polished a small paring knife they talked.

"A ritual, is formulaic. You get what you put into it," the Baristo kept their eyes locked on Andy's.

"I first call in the spirits to hold me still. The body wants to run, because it's biological as fuck. The spirits give me bravery by giving me no other option. Then I whisper to the Earth that I humbly ask it to accept my offering. Finally, I ask my body, myself, to allow itself to let the fuck go. To lay it in God's hands."

"Fuck God's hands," said Andy bitingly.

"Don't fuck God's hands, or God's hands will fuck you."

With that, Andy watched the Baristo plunge the knife into their belly. They smiled and fell back into the arms of a waiting Angel. The Angel smiled at Andy, and flew away

And all that was left was a bloody knife.

+ +

Andy's body shook. Green tea always made him shaky, but Andy knew it wasn't just the tea.

He remembered. He remembered being dismembered. Torn asunder. Cut into a thousand little pieces. He remembered his insides as they shamed his outsides. He remembered a table, a blade. A face, a smile, a lie.

He looked at Teat, nestled in his hand, and walked out of the coffee shop without any acknowledgment of anything around him.

The street was quiet, the cars again silent. They idled as they waited for Andy to make the first move. Andy wandered, aimless again.

He walked past the girl on the bench, who called out to him, but he kept walking. He couldn't face her, definitely not *her*, when he felt so weak.

He passed the bench again and again, but refused to stop each time.

On the street corner across from the bench, Teat whispered.

"Talk to her Andy."

He didn't hear the words, but he felt them. He felt her gaze. Felt her love, and yet, Andy was filled with so much shame, and he was worried it would contaminate everything he was close to.

And he was close to her.

He walked across the street. The girl remarked, "You decided to stop."

"I did, but I almost didn't. I feel like maybe I shouldn't have."

"What's that supposed to mean? I'm glad you stopped."

"I'm worried I could hurt you," Andy shuddered at the thought.

"I know you'd never hurt me," Andy wished he could be as certain as she was.

"That was before. I'm not who I used to be. I'm broken, and broken things are sharp."

"I know how to be careful. And so do you."

Andy hesitated.

"I'd love to share something with you," said the girl.

"I'm not hungry," and he wasn't.

"Maybe you will be after I share this," she handed Andy a piece of paper, wadded into a tight little ball.

Andy unfolded the paper, and read the slanted letters.

"THE BEAST IS ALIVE," Andy struggled to read the words aloud, his voice cracking.

"My new chapter read I'm writing. This is just the first installment. It's going to be a whole series of books. Are you already excited for the next one?"

Andy flipped the paper, acknowledged that those four words were the entirety of the work.

So ambiguous, so enticing.

Andy forgot his weight, replaced it with anticipation. Who was the Beast? What was it before it was alive? Andy imagined dead, for some reason, although that's not the ordinary order of things. He imagined himself in the book, and the book inside himself. He let the surgery slip away.

"Of course I'm excited!" he smiled. "When can I expect the next installment?"

"Maybe thirteen or fourteen days," she said, so matter of fact. She seemed younger, yet again. And yet, also, ageless.

"Cool, cool. I can wait," Andy said, despite the anticipation telling him otherwise.

"You ready for something else?" She held out a bag.

"It feels like this is never going to end," Andy resigned himself to bag.

"It only ends when it's over," preschool wisdom is pure.

Andy took a handful of pretzels, hard knots like his stomach. Hard knots like the lump in his throat when he looked at the little girl's face.

She smiled at Andy.

Andy smiled back. *Why knot?* He asked himself, as he tossed a couple in his mouth.

Pretzel Knot

The girl stood up, stretched like a cat. Her back bowed, her arms twisted. Arm over arm, hand over hand, she bent. More contortion than yoga, her knee met her ear, her foot met her face. Her hair weaved itself, braids upon braids.

And still she knotted. Her limbs seemed to stretch and swell and weave, she a fruit of her own loom.

As her neck stretched and nooked itself somewhere between her knee pit and her tailbone, the tailbone calcified with crystalline salt, long and sharp.

She looked at Andy with crossed eyes. She was at once a basilisk and a baked good, serpentine and sumptuous.

Andy tried to speak to her, but his tongue was knots and stumbled.

"Pretzel ssstickssss are knot pretzelsss at all," the child-like Pretzel hissed.

"Oh no? I kind of like them. When I was a kid I would put them sideways in my mouth so I'd have a big wide whale mouth."

"A pretzzzel is not a dessstination. It isss a journey. There are no ssstraight linesss."

"You're telling me."

"You think healing will be ssstraight forward though. But you will double back on yoursssself. You have been through

Hell, you have ssseen pain. You are done with it, you sssay, and but it isss not done with you. It will come back around."

"I feel like I've earned a little bit of fuckin respite."

"The sssurgery wasss not the trial. It wasss merely the fulcrum. The real work isss the aftermath. You will heal, and regresss. Rissse and fall. It isss not eternal, but it isss a long processs. Your heart will sssay I am sssaved, then you will crash again. Do not dessspair."

"I'm pretty sure I can't avoid dessspair," a hiss, like any accent, is contagious.

"Your head. Your heart. They mussst learn everything again. You are ssstarting at sssquare one, and you mussst crawl before you can ssskip. I know you want joy, lightnessss, and levity. I want thisss for you too. It will come back around. It alwaysss comesss back around."

"Recovery sssoundsss sssort of shitty," Andy tried to still the tip of his tongue, but only succeeded in spitting as he hissed.

"It isss. And it isss not jussst your body. You will learn to again be ssspiteful and petty. You will be loathesssome and depresssed. Oh how you will be depresssed. Then you will be in a good placcce. You will find progresss, growth, healing. Then you will ssslip. Then you will ssslide."

"I do love me a good ssslip and ssslide."

"Yesss, but thisss ssslip and ssslide will be on tree rootsss and rocksss and there will be very little water so you will ssstick."

"Well, Hell."

"Sssort of. Yesss. But more like snakkkkesss and laddersss."

"If it's all jussst a knot, can't I jussst cut it? You know, like Alexander did with the Gordian Knot. Repeating passst missstakes is ssso exhausssting. I want to just cut to the chassse," Andy's tongue was getting tired. *How do sssnakes sussstain thisss for ssso long?*

"Cutting isss what got you into thisss in the firssst placcce."

"Well then I can jussst untie the knot."

"But you sssee Andy, thisss knot is baked together. Asss you try to untie the knot, you will tear, you will exposssed. It isss easssier to jussst ssstart from sssscratch."

"Ssstart from sssscratch."

"Yesss. Thisss is a ressset. You are able to begin again. Thisss isss a blesssing."

"Sssomething like that," Andy didn't know if he remembered how to bake in the first place.

"Thisss isss eternity. Cccircles and cccyclesss are necccesssary to sssave oursssselvesss. A good knot isss not much different than infinity. But I promisssse, there issss an end there sssomewhere."

The Pretzel blinked its lazy eyes, and opened its gaping mouth.

It bit down on its tail. Andy recoiled as the pretzel ate itself, one bite at a time.

As it consumed itself, the knot pulled tighter, and tighter, smaller and smaller. With one final nibble, all that was left was a small, lightly salted pretzel and an empty bag.

++

The street was empty yet again. The cars moved on to somewhere else, the girl left nothing but an empty bag that Andy grabbed before the wind could take it. Andy found a trash can, and made to throw it in the trash.

"Whoa whoa whoa," chirped Teat.

"What?" said Andy.

"Salt! Don't be wasting salt! Humans are so quick to waste something that most animals travel miles just to lick off a rock!"

Andy licked his finger, stuck it in the salt in the corner of the bag, and let Teat peck a few crystals with his creepy lips and teeth. Satiated, Teat collapsed again into the nest of Andy's hand.

Andy was ready for a reset. Andy's life had been out of hand for a long time, but its hard to start over when the current has you. Andy had tried to fight the current, but he wasn't a salmon. And now he was taken by the flow of the thing, he found himself thrown from a waterfall, dashed on the rocks below. But on dry land. Maybe.

Andy thought about calling his mom. He always thought about calling his mom. Its hard to ask for help though, especially from your family. Especially from his family.

Like some grand conjuration, Andy's phone rang.

Mom.

Andy didn't hesitate, and answered the phone, "Hi mom."
"Are you OK?"
"Not at all, to be honest."
"I'm coming. Is it OK if I come? I can take work off."
"That would mean a lot."
"OK. I love you. I'll see you soon."

It was short. It was sweet. He didn't have to ask for help, because he really fucking needed it. *That's how help if supposed to work,* Andy thought

Andy looked down at Teat, who smiled up at him with his big buckteeth. He nestled his head back down into his fluffy little body.

Andy felt the nagging hunger again. Spiritual, sure, but mostly digestive. As his perspective widened, as he confronted the idea of recovery, he recognized that despite the impending angels and demons, nutrition was probably really fucking important right now.

He bee-lined to the restaurant, eager to take whatever he got. Maybe even a diner.

A very ordinary, very white bread sandwich shop waited for him, at the end of the block. There was a line out the door. The telltale smell of "fresh baked bread" wafted through the streets. In quotes, because Andy doubted at least one, if not all three of the advertised words.

Andy stood in line, and admired the big signs advertising "New Vegan Turrkee" and "Super Hydroblast Soda is Back for a Limited Time." He looked over the shoulder in front of him, and saw that the woman was looking at the social media page of the sandwich shop she was in fact standing in line for.

That gave Andy a weird sense of vertigo, and he averted his eyes from her screen and looked at the menu up above the sandwich counter. He wanted to be prepared, because he hated to be the guy that took forever to decide between pepperjack or pepperjill. All the while, people would grew progressively more agro in line behind him. *No thank you.*

What's the most bang for my buck? Andy thought to himself. *Club sandwich, of course. Meat on meat on meat, juicy tomatoes (OK, probably mealy), crisp lettuce (soggy more like), and not two but THREE slices of bread. My buck shall bang.*

Andy stepped to the counter and blurted out, "Club Sandwich on wheat, all the everythings, and extra pickle" before the sandwicheer could even open her mouth.

"Frilly toothpick?" she asked.

"It's not a club sandwich without one," Andy said, without missing a beat.

Andy did the electric slide down the counter to the register, grabbing a bag of barbecue chips and a cookie. The bag felt like it had, at the most, eight chips in it. Still, he wasn't willing to pay an additional two bucks for eight more chips.

Andy paid the cashier, and walked over to a seat by the window, to face the dystopian street in front of him. In the background, he could see the sandwich line snaking out across the sidewalk. In the foreground, a huge picture of a well-dressed (see: BORING) business-woman stared right back at him. She smiled, holding a particularly gross looking sandwich. Her eyes seemed to study Andy as he unwrapped his sandwich.

His mind kept reading the word "Muffa-betta!" on the poster. Over and over and over, his thoughts trapped by the advertisement. He took a hesitant sniff of his sandwich.

Mayo. So much mayo. All he could smell was mayo. The bread was profoundly saturated by the mayo.

Not sure if he wanted to be a member of this club, Andy took a bite of his soggy sandwich.

Club Sandwich

The woman on the poster's eyes were hollow. Dead.

But not dead like the undead from yesterday. These eyes were dead like they never had life at all. The kind of dead you see in AI generated people, where they never had the spark of life in the first place. A computer contrivance of what life is supposed to look like.

"Try a Muffa-Betta!" the woman said. "Try a Muffa-Betta! Try a Muffa-betta!" The woman's head twitched and glitched. She bounced as she tried to tear herself from her catch phrase, tried to shake free from her programming. "Muffa, Muffa, Muffa."

With a series of jerky movements, she tore herself from the poster. She shook the paper scraps from her hair, and sat in front of Andy in the booth.

"Whoa. Sorry. It's super easy to manifest in flesh and blood. Child play. But it's not so easy to imbue life into computer generated renderings," she was calm, eyes calculating and cold.

"Uh, no problem. But before you say anything, I have absolutely no intention of every trying anything called a Muffa-betta."

"Good, you don't want to meet that guy anyways. He's a fucking savage," she said, holding up the other half of Andy's club sandwich.

"I'm sure," said Andy. *She better not...*

"Now a club sandwich?" She sniffed the triangle as she thumbed through the layers. "*That's* a sandwich. Not two, but three pieces of bread!" she said with a saccharine smile.

"That's what I said!"

"It's that third piece of bread that really makes it club worthy, am I right?"

"And the frilly toothpick," offered Andy.

"Oh yes, absolutely the toothpick."

"How, exactly, does one become a member of said club?" Andy joked.

"Oh Andy," she said as she brought the sandwich to her lips, "you can't be a member. Not anymore at least."

She took a bite of the sandwich.

Andy reeled at her cannibalism, but was more taken aback by his denial of membership.

"What? Why? What'd I do!?"

"Well Andy, to be honest, you sort of screwed up. You went and got yourself hurt, and now the world has to sort of move on without you."

Andy tried to speak, but she spoke first, "I know it seems unfair, and honestly, it *is* unfair. *You* didn't botch your surgery, but it's what happened. And now everyone is going to have fun without you. That whole 'fear of missing out,' and that fear is founded. It's absolutely justified. You *are* going to miss out, on a lot."

Tears welled up.

"It's not that people will forget about you. Oh some will, sure. But there are those who will remember you, but a you that no longer exists. A phantom. You aren't who you used to be. You aren't jolly old Andy because nobody wants to be with someone in recovery. You're still you, just not in the way they want you to be."

"I'm different now," dawn. Revelation.

"Yes, you're different now. You're not a part of the club.

And you'll realize that really, you never really were a part of the club. Always just a pledge, on the outside looking in."

"I don't want to be a part of their stupid club anyways," Andy hadn't reverted to being a child. It was a statement of fact.

"It's true. You don't. You didn't. It felt like something you wanted, but it's OK to let it go. There is a gravitational pull, a magnetism towards being part of a group, but so much of the social sphere is bullshit." She motioned to a woman in a neighboring booth, "See the woman over there, taking a picture of her sandwich? She's taking a picture of a sandwich, smashing that hashtag so she can feel connected to other people who also eat gross sandwiches."

The woman held up the sandwich to her mouth, and held her phone at arm's length. Andy felt more awkward by the second.

"She wants to belong, which is a totally rational thing. True belonging, though, is something rooted in community. Most modern 'communities' are a fucking sham. Most clubs are a joke, an approximation of true belonging. They are not founded on mutual understanding, however, but instead on a shared experience."

Andy's whole adult life flashed before his eyes, "Like getting wasted."

"Like getting wasted. There's a togetherness there. Drugs, alcohol, music. They create a sense of camaraderie, but not a sense of community. There's a sense of being near, but not close. It's superficial, and you've been plowed to your depths this week. Surface level isn't going to cut it anymore."

"Then where's my community? Where do I find my people?"

"You already found your people. And they already found you."

Andy smiled.

"And what about everyone else? I really do care about them."

"Don't worry about what is left in the wake of your leave. They'll be fine. And maybe one day, when they are ready, they'll come and want to join your club. I'm sorry to be redundant, but you have an opportunity here, to start anew. To build it all from the ground up. True to your values. Your own damned clubhouse Andy, and you can put whatever you want on your sandwich."

"Even a frilly toothpick?"

"Even a frilly toothpick," she said with a smile. Her smile cracked, turned sideways. "And try a Muffa-betta today. Try a Muffa-betta today. Muffa-betta. Mufffaaabbbeeeettaaaaaa."

++

Andy picked up the toothpick that lay on the sandwich wrapper and put it between his teeth. He stared at the woman taking pictures of her sandwich, noticed that she still hadn't taken a bite despite the fact that Andy had finished his entire sandwich. He picked up Teat, who pecked with his chubby little lips at a bread crumb, and walked out the door.

Andy's pocket vibrated, and he pulled out his phone.

"Tiddy's?"

"Tiddy's."

"I'm already here, I'll order for you."

That annoyed Andy. *What makes you think you know what I want, Dante?*

As Andy walked towards the bar, a reel played in his head about how he was going to tell Dante off.

You don't just order for someone Dante. It's fucking rude. What if I've grown? Changed? I'm a different person, with different tastes. Different dreams, desires. I am not my happy hour!

A woman walked by, took a wide circle around Andy.

Definitely talking to myself.

Andy growled audibly as he walked into the bar. He was grumpy, out of sorts. The pain got to Andy, even if he was able to push it to the background. He could only ignore the limp so much.

Andy saw Dante tell the bartender something that made her laugh, and Andy was all the more grumpy for it.

He pulled up a seat next to Dante, ready to verbalize all of his frustrations, all of his pain. Dante smiled and pushed a bucket of peanuts towards Andy.

"I ordered you a water, and peanuts. Hope that's not presumptuous of me."

"Umm thanks" Andy was speechless. *Where's the shnapps? How am I supposed to be mad at nuts?*

"How are you doing? Are you feeling any better? Did you get scheduled for PT yet? How're Angie and Terra? How do you feel about your mom coming?"

Andy answered the questions, and his emotions rose like a tidal wave. His heart smiled at Dante, at his presence, at his prescience and thoughtfulness. But he was still overcome with anxiety and anger.

And pain. So much pain. Some moments were worse than others, and he struggled to grip his mind as it gravitated back in on it. Sometimes it was centralized, but right now it enveloped his whole middle.

Andy grasped for a distraction. A way out, no matter how insignificant.

Like a peanut? Like a peanut.

Peanut

Andy wasn't quite sure what he was looking at. It was like one of those super magnification challenges on a game show. The contestant is shown something ultra zoomed in and they had to guess what it was. They would guess a vegetable, or a flower and the grand reveal would be a beetle's butt hole.

This was kind of waffle-like. Definitely porous. Porous like human skin, and equally grimy and oily. Andy felt vaguely nauseous looking at it, and hoped it would back the fuck up.

Like a rocket leaving orbit, with a broader perspective of the Earth below, Andy was relieved to see the porous skin waffle get further away.

As it receded and came into focus, Andy felt silly that he hadn't suspected a peanut. He gave himself a little grace though, because even if he had expected a peanut, he probably wouldn't have guessed it would be so darned dapper. Although again, he should have seen it coming.

The monocled peanut smiled at Andy, and tipped his top hat in his direction.

"Good day!" said the legume.

"And also to you!" Andy returned the peanut's haughty tone.

"You look well, all things considered m'boy!"

"Um, thank you, Mr. Peanut sir." Andy didn't feel thankful.

"To note, I'm *a* Mr. Peanut. Not *the* Mr. Peanut," Andy was crestfallen.

"But *truly* though Andy! You've been through quite the ordeal! And all the more so, after the last few days. You're doing great, considering a body can only take so much and you've been putting yours through its paces!"

"Ya, you're not wrong. I'm feeling a bit run down, that's for sure. But at least I've been eating well!" Andy hesitated, "For me at least..."

"I don't know if I'd say well. A nibble here, a nibble there, washed down with a healthy dose of alcohol. Not the makings of a healthy man Andy."

"Oh I'm resilient, don't you worry about me," said Andy flexing his, admittedly, flabby biceps. "And isn't there some adage from somewhere that says the dose makes the poison?"

"Well for one, you're terrible at dosage. It's why your bosses make you use a jigger when you make cocktails. You can't eyeball for shit."

Andy tried to eyeball his eyeball, to confirm if there was something wrong with his guesstimater. He only succeeded in making himself dizzy.

"And further, there *are* toxins in this world Andy. Things that you, in particular, would do well to avoid. Just look at me!" Sir Peanut pointed to his gross wafflesome body.

"Sure you're gross, but I wouldn't say toxically so."

"Andy! Peanuts are, more often than not, one of the most contaminated plants on the planet. We are incredibly susceptible to mold, which begets aflotoxin. Aflo-*TOXIN*. I think the name says it all. And look at this beautiful skin of mine! See how sexy and porous it is?"

Andy gagged a little when he considered the sexiness of pores. He tried to suppress a flashback to one of the acne treatment commercials about dirt, oil and clogs, to no effect.

"While it makes me damn good looking, it also makes me very susceptible to all sorts of toxins. Not just aflotoxin, but pesticides too! Did you know that peanuts are one of the most sprayed crops on the planet? Along with cotton of course. And guess what they rotate peanut crops with?"

"Cotton?" Andy said sheepishly.

"Cotton. I'm just swimming in bad shit for you. Hell, Pythagoras even said you shouldn't eat legumes at all!"

"The triangle guy?"

"The triangle guy! He said that legumes are imbued with the souls of humans. Or fetuses. Or something like that." Andy looked at the talking Peanut, full of spirit, and thought the triangle guy might have been on to something.

"Although... some say he meant the breath of life leaves you every time you fart," Sir Peanut muttered.

"So avoid the dust on crops, lest I crop dust everyone around me."

"And yourself in the process! You can't tell me you really like basking in your own nasty," Mr. Peanut turned his nubby little nose upwards, and looked down it.

"I don't know, I think it makes me endearing."

"There is nothing endearing about hurting yourself Andy." And there it was.

Andy tried to justify, "But don't peanuts have like... good fats and vitamin E and stuff?"

"Of course Andy. Of course. But context is everything. Organic peanuts, grown in dry soil."

Andy picked at the metaphor, "So, organic peanuts are maybe like, I don't know, just stopping at one glass of wine? And dry soil would be drinking it with a healthy well balanced meal?"

"You're getting the idea."

"Oh my God that's so boring!" Andy knew he had self-destructive habits, but they were sort of what made Andy, well, Andy.

"There's nothing boring about it. You've just been conditioned to only be responsive to the extremities of life for the last 20 years or so. Maybe what you need is to just, as they say 'pump the brakes.'"

"Ugggh," Andy felt the familiar specter of self-loathing creep up on him.

"Listen Andy, I know what you're thinking. But stop it. No one is saying you are the reason this happened to you," Mr. Peanut *did* know what he was thinking. "It was just shit luck. Truly." Andy allowed himself an iota of relief.

"It was out of your hands, but recovery is not. Your recovery is contingent on you dropping some of your more toxic traits. That is where your agency lies. Not in the past, but in the future. Old habits served you when you needed them, in whatever capacity. I promise you though, they no longer serve you."

"I should have known there would be two meanings for the *recovery* everyone's been getting on about."

"Well now you know. You also know what is toxic, Andy. To quote the Bard, 'With a taste, of a poison paradise. I'm addicted to you.' You're not too high Andy, you can come back down."

"Shakespeare said all that?"

"Nope, different Spear."

Mr. Peanut shimmied, shook his nuts inside of himself. He danced backwards out of the spotlight.

Maybe, Andy thought, *being porous is sexy after all.*

+ +

Andy came back to himself in the bar. That was something new. Not groggy, still vertical, not to arise from a couch. Just salt on his lips (kind of sexy) and a bit parched.

He thanked Dante, then told him all about his recovery and his family. He told him when he was going to start PT. He told him about his mom, his therapist, and his petty (and not so petty) grievances with the healthcare system.

He enjoyed the conversation, and walked out of the bar feeling like it was the first time he and Dante had spent actual, quality time together since they had been coworkers.

Andy smiled as he walked out on the street. It was a dismal fucking street, to be sure. He couldn't see the demons, but he could sure smell them, and the potential for jump scares still lurked on every corner. Despite all that, however, his step had pep as he walked to his apartment.

Teat was also in a particularly good mood, singing a little song about some "fine little bushtits, seated in a row." Further pep was added, and his step faltered. Pain. Again.

He noted the bench in front of the apartment. Empty. He opened the front door.

He walked up the stairs one at a time, *worked* up the stairs one at a time.

Belabored by the sheer enormity of the task, his mood

plummeted. Even as he reached the landing of the second floor, his heart remained grounded. No elation in elevation.

As he stumbled in the front door, Andy's eyes sprinted to the kitchen, and his feet were quick to follow. He went to the fridge to grab a soda water.

Bubbles will lift me up.

Empty fridge.

Bare cupboards.

I really need to do a real shop one of these days.

The last little bit of joy squealed out of him like an untied balloon. Andy was used to waves of depression, but this came upon him like a tsunami. He hurt, he was lonely. He looked around the apartment and didn't see any sign of his roommates.

Fuck sobriety, Andy thought as he opened the freezer, hoping.

No booze. Just ice.

He laid his head in the freezer, his face pointed at an over turned ice tray.

He felt the heat of the day, the weight of forever

The cool felt good, though. There was that, at least.

Andy stuck out his tongue, a desperate act. It flailed around, looking for companionship. No longer alone, it greeted an ice cube.

Ice

There was a tiny mountain, covered in fluffy white pow pow.

The faeries were dressed in adorably tiny beanies, snow pants, and shells. They had tiny gloves, and tiny scarves wrapped between their tiny wings.

A few, faces gripped by determination, loaded ice cubes into an industrial snow-cone machine. It launched the powder high up the tiny mountain. At the base, a bunch of faeries, who waited in line for the ski lift, let out a roar.

Ice cube trays slowed at the bottom, picked up the waiting fairings. They were then taken back up and over a mountain. Below, the mountain shined with thawed and refrozen ice cream.

A slalom course careened through ancient, freezer-burned broccoli florets. The majority of the faeries, however, waited in line for the big air. It launched off a huge ice kicker, a spot where the ice machine had leaked after being unplugged months earlier.

Andy watched the fairies shred on tiny snowboards made of fish sticks. He smiled as one of the faeries caught some serious air and stomped the landing.

"Chill!" hooted the other faeries, enthralled in the competition.

Andy stared, longingly, as a couple fairies lit up a tiny joint which looked not unlike rice from a frozen dinner.

"Chill," said one as they let a cloud escape from their nostrils.

"Chill," said another as they watched someone face plant on the big air. Andy laughed along with the faeries, smiled at the faeries in hopes of a drag. They did not oblige, merely returned focus to the competition.

Andy went red in the face.

"Chill," said one of the fairies, as they blew a cloud in Andy's face.

"Chill," agreed another as they returned their eyes to the big air competition in progress.

Andy laid his head back down on the freezer, and felt the cool bring him back down to Earth.

"Chill," Andy whispered to himself as the snow blanketed his face.

+ +

"You sure are chill," Teat said as he stared into Andy's eyes. His voice was calm, but his eyes were not.

"Not me though! I'm *hungry*. You can eat all the damned ice cubes you want, but I need some real ass sustenance. Was there anything in the freezer, or were you just frosting your tips?" Andy shrugged, "Come on boy! Chop chop!"

Andy went deep inside, replayed the scene in his head.

Mmmmm, snowboards, Andy thought.

Andy pulled the loose fish sticks out of the freezer. In all, including the pieces which had to be pried from the bottom of the freezer, there were fifteen and a half sticks. Dang near the whole box, upended.

Terra sure does love to play in the freezer, Andy mused.

Andy walked to a closed cabinet, rummaged around for a circular pan.

Hell, Andy realized he could have had a solid 45 seconds of preheat time, if he had the presence of mind to turn on the oven *before* he walked over to the cabinet. *Time is hungry.*

He walked back, turned the oven to 450 and threw the pan of fish sticks into the oven with little ceremony. *Too much walking.*

"And now we wait," Teat muttered as his beady little eyes stared at the impenetrable darkness of the smoke stained oven window.

And they waited. Andy tried to play a party game with Teat, to fill a little time.

"20 questions?"

"Absolutely not."

"Why not?"

"That's a question. And I said NO."

"What? Really?

"That's three questions."

"What's your problem? Are you just hungry, or is something bothering you?"

"I'm not sure if that counts as five or six. But please just stop while you're ahead."

"Fine, I give up."

"Big Bird."

"What?"

"I was thinking of Big Bird."

"Oh fuck off," Andy muttered.

"I'm sorry. I'm just really in my head, ya know?" said Teat. Andy watched the bird's little lips flap, tried to take it seriously.

"Like, I'm not sure if I'm ever going to fly again. Like sure, I can hop around a bit, but fly? Not so sure. And I'm so fucking dooooowwwwn about that. But then, I think about my cousin Garvey. Fuckin hell of a guy, that Garvey. Great family man, killer forager, and can totally shred the thermals. But he just lost his wife. To a fucking cat. And now he has to raise his three little chicks on his own. His nest is totally falling apart, but he has to feed his kids, ya know? *And* he has carpal tunnel," Andy nodded. "So I'm like, what the fuck right do I have to be sad? This aint suffering. Garvey knows suffering."

"But you aren't Garvey," Andy said. "Angie always says you can't equate suffering. Your sadness, your pain, your hardships are your own. They aren't invalidated because someone else is having a 'harder' time. You gotta be more gentle on yourself."

The room started to smell decidedly toasted, so Andy walked over to the oven, flipped the fish sticks, and put them back in the oven. He walked back over and sat on the couch next to Teat. *Too much walking.*

"I know the feeling though," said Andy. "Like, do I even have a right to call this an End of Days? Like, what is my trauma in the face of war? What is my pain in the face of genocide or abuse? Fucking nothing."

"And yet everything," offered Teat. They both sat in silence for about six minutes longer.

BUZZZZZZZZZZZZZZZZZZZZZZZ.

Andy put one stick on Teat's plate, and fourteen on his own.

"You've got to be kidding me," complained Teat.

"You're actually significantly less than 1/15th my size. I'm being generous."

"If I finish it, can I have another?" Teat puffed. *Too damned cute for his own good.*

"For you Teat, anything," Andy smiled and took his first bite.

Fish Sticks

Andy watched Teat peck at the fish stick. He didn't seem to get anywhere, and Andy thought he should maybe cut it into little pieces.

As Andy reached over with his fork, Teat began to swell. A swollen Teat.

First, the feathers became hair. The effect wasn't unlike a kiwi bird, but with a creepier vibe. More akin to a mouse with a beak.

The beaked mouse began to puff aloud, as it was filled with more and more air. It grew at a quicker clip, until it was as tall as Andy but not nearly as good looking. Until, then, it *was* as good looking as Andy.

Teat had become Andy. Looked just like him, except his shoulder was swollen and he definitely buckeled more swashes. Teat had an eye patch, big ole hoop earrings, and a lumpy shoulder that wiggled beneath his coat. He removed his coat, only to reveal Teat reborn as a fleshy parrot growth on his very own shoulder.

"Teat. You're me!"

"Of course I'm ye, ye scallywag! Ye *just* come to that conclusion?"

It *was* self-evident, now that Andy thought about it, but instead of respond, Andy just nodded.

"Aye, I'm ye. And ye know why I'm ye?"

"Because you're a figment of my imagination, a manifestation of all the ways I can cope with a singular trauma?"

"Kind o' sort o'. But no, I be ye, because ye are the best teacher of ye."

"And what are you here to teach me?"

"That yarrrr what ye eat."

"I yarrrr what I eat," Andy squinted one eye as he said it.

"Aye. The grub ye eat defines ye. But also everythin' yer very soul consumes be ye as well. Ye embody that which surrounds ye," Teat's motioned his hooked arm towards the everything that surrounded Andy. "Ye see, we be manifestations o' all that bullshite we allow into our bodies. The shanties ye listen te, the crew ye keep, and absolutely the grub ye eat."

"Thar's mighty powers in each 'n' every aspect o' reality. That's the gist o' what this week was about. Ye have surrounded yeself with shite fer too damn long, ye damn near became shite. If ye be conscious of what ye consume though, ye might just become a shark."

"You eat sharks?" Andy had mixed feelings about that. He was all for embodying such a mighty beast, but he was also pretty sure it wasn't quite ecologically sound to eat apex predators in the first place.

"O' course I eat sharks! What did ye reckon I eat? Flax muffins 'n' chia seeds? I aim te be mighty! I aim te be a scoundrel! And so I eat leviathans and demand me acquaintances carry a cutlass! But ye know what? I could make grub like chia seeds work fer me! I could reckon that seeds is plants, and plants is growth, and growth is power. Power enough fer the Raramuri to run fer feckin leagues and leagues!"

Andy was surprised a pirate parrot knew anything about central Mexican tribal endurance athletes, let alone their eating habits.

"And thar's the trick Andy. Thar's the trick, because ye can put yer intention into and onto what yer about te eat!

It's all about contextualizin it before ye let it deep in te yer heart."

"Oh ya? So I can make eating sugary cereal an act of magical manifestation?"

"Ab-se-feckin-loot-ly. Ye can spin yer own luck into them charms. It's all 'bout intention."

"It's all about intention."

"Aye. Fish sticks can be chopped bits o' bottom feeders. They can make ye lowly, 'n' poor, 'n' make ye look sideways at everythin,'" Teat rolled his eyes to the side.

"Or they can make ye swim against the tide. They can help ye become one with the waves. They can teach ye to be a proper crew, swimmin' in a school. They can be much more than the summa thar parts."

"Because yarr what you eat," Andy repeated, a halfhearted pirate indeed.

"Aye. So be wary where ye dare te harvest ye energies. And make sure ye put good magic in t' each and every inter- action Andy, as it'll feed yer very soul. Dun be bingin' on self loathin' er pity, lest ye want to be loathesome and pitiful."

Andy stared into the pirate's eyes, catching the gleam of the sun in his hair. He heard the cry of a seagull, lone but not quite forelorn. He smelled the bladderwrack and rotting sea lions, and felt a deep longing for some grog (although Andy was sure he didn't know quite what grog was).

Andy smiled at the pirate. Teat and his pirate body smiled a toothy grin back, as did the enormous shark lurking behind, as it bit the pirate in half. There was blood, but it was quick. The pirate was cleaved in two before he could even began to imagine his life was over. The smile was still plas- tered on his face. The water darkened, and small fish came to feed on the bits.

Amidst gore and seawater, the shark turned its head to face Andy. It wore a patch, spoke in Teat's voice.

"Aye Andy," bellowed the shark, "Yarr what ye eat."

++

Andy heard the gentle click of a peg leg on the deck. He looked up, noted that the peg leg was, in fact, Angie as she closed the door to Terra's room.

Terra's room.

She smiled at Andy and walked towards the kitchen. She opened the fridge, which brimmed over with food, and pulled out a small white box.

As she sat down on the couch next to Andy, she was quick to speak first.

"I hope you had a good day to yourself. How are you feeling?"

"I feel OK. Pain has been up and down, and my low points were definitely less low than they have been."

"Well that's good. What'd you do anyways? We've been gone all day and it doesn't look like you've been here at all." Andy laughed, aware that she meant the house still looked clean, unlived in.

"I've just been out walking. Got some food, hit the coffee shop. Trying to get more comfortable being in public, so I'm forcing myself to be social. And by social, I mean awkwardly talking to the Baristo, or making small talk with some other random folk out in the world," Andy admitted.

Andy really did try to maintain his composure in public, but after months of not really going out in the world, being seen by just about anyone gave him the most wrenching anxiety he could imagine.

"I know it's awkward, but I'm super proud of you for getting out there. And I'm proud of you for applying for jobs. I know its super nerve wracking but I really appreciate it," she smiled at Andy as she opened the box.

I really appreciate you, Andy thought to himself. He wasn't sure why he didn't say it aloud, but it was likely because he said it so damned often, he felt like it was losing its value. So he just smiled at her and allowed his eyes to drop to the immaculate tiramisu in the to-go container.

"Nice, did you and Terra go to the Trattoria?"

"Ya. Terra was terrifyingly starving and ate all of her food, *and* what was left of mine. So there was nothing to bring home to you. Sorry."

"Don't apologize," said Andy, and he meant it. "All I need is a bite of that glorious little nugget."

"Then open up," she said as Andy laid back on her lap. He was trying to be sexy, but the pain in his abdomen made it more than a little bit awkward to lower himself down. And then the angle for her to get the fork to him was all askew. Hardly sexy.

After a moment of fumbling, though, she found his mouth. God, how she found his mouth.

Tiramisu

As Andy laid in Angie's lap, he felt the curves and curls of her outfit gather beneath him. A gown grew where he lay.

For once, he felt himself change with her. His beard and hair grew, and his jeans and shirt seemed to knit themselves into one tiny little cloth over his loins. He felt sure, absolutely, that they *were* his loins.

He looked himself over, and at his wife's Holy visage. Together, they were a facsimile of Michaelangelo's Pieta, the Virgin cradling her Son. Angie was cold, like marble, and looked at him with tears behind her eyes.

"Yes, like the Mother and the Child," she whispered to Andy.

"Only not her child, because I'm your husband and that's *creepy*."

"Whatever you say Andy," she said softly. "The archetype is the Mother, no matter the relationship. Whether your wife, your mother, or your neighbor, we are here to carry your weight for you."

"I feel like I should carry my own weight, thank you," said Andy, feigning both pride and power.

"You don't begrudge espresso to help you find a little levity. You allow lady fingers to lighten your load," Andy went in for the joke, but was stilled by the Mother's finger on his lips. "You allow all of Tiramisu to lift you up. Tiramisu *means* pick me up, and it does just that. You let a fucking dessert raise you up, so why do you begrudge *us* the opportunity to do the same?"

"I just..."

"You just nothing. Healing is a helping hand. Healing is humility Andy. You can't do this all by yourself," she said, soft yet stern.

"The worst moment in my life was when you had to help me get my pants on last week," Andy said, tears on his cheek.

"Why? What was so embarrassing?"

"It wasn't that you did it. It's that I *couldn't* do it. I was literally unable. I reached and reached, and I couldn't grab my fucking underwear. It's just weak. I'm just weak," Andy didn't even try to hold back the tears now.

"It's not weak to need help Andy. It's weak to not accept it. It's weak to choose suffering when you can heal and you can grow, with just a *little* helping hand. And not from just anyone Andy! From the love of your fucking life. She's... *I'm* here to help you, because I want to. Because I need to. It's in my very nature to help you. To heal you. I've done it time and time again, and it's not different now that you are hurt. I don't see why this would make it any different."

"It's different because I don't know if it's going to work. I always had so much faith in my body, in your hands. But this feels different. This *looks* different. I'm broken."

"*Nothing* is broken beyond repair."

"You don't know that! What's the point of picking something up if it's just a bunch of shattered pieces? Remnants in fact, because I'm not even sure where half of me went! I'm not the fucking same person I was!" There was anger now, along with the sadness and fear.

"Good."

"Excuse me?"

"I said good. I'm glad you're not the same person you were."

"It was fucking stolen from me!"

"I reiterate, *good*. Listen Andy, I didn't wish this upon you. I never would. I never could. But there's a blessing here. Maybe when we pick you up, maybe when we put you back together, we can leave some stuff behind? Maybe all that was stolen were some dead leaves and branches. Maybe this was a proper little pruning, and suddenly your heart will get the sunshine it has been missing for so long, because you were carrying too much damn foliage. Maybe, just maybe, you were broken so you could be made whole again."

"It hurts,"Andy's tears streamed across the Mother's legs.

"Of course it does, but I'm here to carry that weight for you. Your mother wants to carry some of that weight for you. Hell, even your child is here to carry some of that weight for you."

"That's just terrible."

"Is it? She wants to do it. She loves helping you. She gets this beautiful little glint in her eyes when she can do something for *you* for once. She's got the Mother in her too, you know."

"I know," Andy whispered.

"It's absolutely an uphill battle Andy. Its heavy, but unlike Sisyphus you don't have to bear the weight alone," she lifted Andy to look in his eyes. "Are you willing to take a helping hand? Accept a little pick me up?"

"As long as it tastes like tiramisu, I think I can handle that."

"Sometimes it'll taste like dessert, other times like the desert. A mouthful of sand. It will, nonetheless, still give you the momentum you need."

"A mouthful of sand..."

"Burning. Choking. But maybe necessary."

"Cool. Great. Awesome."

"But we can start right here. With mascarpone and espresso," she picked Andy up and held out a finger covered in dessert. "One pant leg at a time."

"One pant leg at a time," Andy said as he licked the tiramisu from her cold marble finger.

++

Andy looked Angie in the eyes and started bawling. Again.

"Oh babe, I'm so sorry," she whispered as he cried. She cradled him in her arms and rocked him back and forth.

"Thank you for being here," he said over the hush of his tears.

"Where else would I be?"

"Anywhere else," Andy was embarrassed. He tried not to be, but every time he cried (which was all the time lately) he felt a great and heavy shame.

"I'm going to go for a walk," he said, not looking Angie in the eyes.

"You don't have to, but OK. Please be safe. And bring your phone," she said as she handed him his bag.

He couldn't carry anything in his pockets these days. He gently put his phone inside the bag. He avoided disturbing the bushtit that was asleep, curled in his right mitten, and gently slung the bag over his shoulder.

"I will. I love you," he said, not waiting for an answer as he walked out the front door.

The street was silent. Gone were the zombies and the demons. Wraiths no longer hid behind each and every hedge, but Andy was pretty sure they'd taken up residence *somewhere* nearby.

"Should've seen it coming dude," Andy heard from his bag.

"Huh?" said Andy as he lifted Teat from the bag.

"The demons were inside you *all along*. That's a trite ass lesson, if I've ever heard one. I feel like we could've guessed that, what, four days ago? The real monsters lurk inside your heart? Boo! Cliche!"

"Oh there's still demons in the world Teat. How else do you explain the shit-ass surgeon that started this whole fucking nightmare?"

"Yeah, I guess you're right. Ineptitude is pretty much evil incarnate on this plane."

"Ha," Andy *tried* to laugh as he imagined a demon realm of ignoramuses and dunces with doctoral degrees. That definitely tracked as Hell in his book, but he couldn't find the humor in it quite yet.

Andy had no illusions about the rest of his night, and walked straight towards the fountain. No romantic walk, just pure purpose.

There were no songs on the wind tonight.

No chipper mood on the face of the man at the fountain.

Just a sad, forlorn vase full of flowers, barely holding on.

"Getting pretty close to the end, aren't we buddy?" the man said, as he appraised Andy's limp without a bit of modesty. Andy was used to people gawking at this point, but it still made his blood boil a little bit.

"Let's just get this over with. What you got for me?"

"It's not *from* me, but it's definitely for you," said the man.

"Huh?"

The man handed over a clear rocks glass, filled with opaque greyish liquid.

He didn't need to say anything, but he did anyways, "Vodka Squirt."

"He's here," Andy whispered to Teat, tucked neatly in his pocket.

He's here, Andy thought as he took a deep breath and sipped.

Vodka Squirt

And he was.

He came in a puff of smoke. Not spiritual, not other-worldly. Just a cheap ass cigarette.

Andy's grandfather stood, smoked, smiled.

"I..." Andy began.

"I know Andy. But I didn't miss you. I was with you the whole time," his grandfather said, a gentle barb.

"That's bullshit," Andy wouldn't allow himself to believe that. "You left me a long long time ago."

CRACK. The sound was audible, but Andy couldn't figure out where it came from.

"Every time you see a can of Squirt, every time you smell a cigarette, every time you eat a cashew for God's sake. You conjure me Andy, each and every time."

"I mean yes, I can smell you. I can hear you. But that doesn't mean I feel you. It doesn't mean I feel any of your warmth, any of your love."

CRACK.

"That's you keeping it out. You have a tool, a talisman. You have the ability to conjure spirits, and embody those spirits but you choose to lock it out."

CRACK. This time, Andy could see a tiny crack in his grandfather's face. He could see the mask, breaking.

"Fucking demon! Don't you dare use my grandfather

against me!" Andy put his hands up like he was going to box, like he could fight what was coming.

"You lock it out, because you are afraid of what it would mean to take control. To try and actively heal. Integration my boy. Integration is allowing others to infiltrate your heart. Integration is allowing the outside in."

CRAAACKKK. The face flaked like porcelain, like dry clay. The eyes beneath looked like his grandfather's eyes. The nose beneath looked like his grandfather's nose.

"Do you know what a sacrament is Andy? A sacrament is an embodiment. It's a physical manifestation of something inside you, that was there all along. And each and every time you deny that little piece of you, each time you don't participate in the sacrament, you take a step away from that Holy Communion."

"Holy communion. Now I fucking *know* you aren't my grandfather."

CRAAAAAACK. The last of the porcelain fell, and the face was whole again. The face looking back at Andy was his grandfather's face, to be sure. But it was also his grandmother's face. And his father's and his mother's.

The face was his.

"Who are you?" Andy asked, breathless.

"I could ask you the same thing."

Andy was silent.

"I'll tell you who you are Andy. You are each and every interaction you've ever had. Everyone you've ever met. You are an amalgamation, a great chimera of experience. This week has been a week of sacrament, a week of eating divine principles embodied."

"That feeling, when you drink a vodka Squirt, when you feel your grandfather speaking through you: that *is* your grandfather speaking through you. You are your associations. That is what this week has been all about. It's about recognizing yourself in the each and every. It's about allowing the world around you to conjure huge spiritual principles inside you. Allowing something as mundane as popcorn to conjure something as magic as chaos. Allowing something as brutal as a botched vasectomy *heal you*. Its letting the outside in."

Andy studied his face, looking for doubt. But there was no doubt.

"Squirt is artificial flavor, brominated vegetable oil, and corn syrup. It is as much a perversion as you could possibly imagine. And yet... *and yet* it can conjure some of the most profound love you have ever felt. It can conjure your dreams, your past, your comfort. It can conjure things you thought were lost. It can unlock something in you that you didn't *know* there was a key for. If fucking *SQUIRT* can do that, then anything can do that. Let the world show you who you are."

"It was me all along."

"Of course it was you all along Andy. It's *all* you. You show empathy, love, and respect because you *hope* that there is something outside you. But experientially, it's all you. You can't possibly experience the world as anyone but yourself. Thus, you create your world around you. Every interaction, every single thing holds you within it. The world molded, by you. And you molded by it. That is why this is *your* Armageddon Andy. This is your awakening, your eye opening moment. It is your face to face with God. And look at your God, Andy. Look at this experience of the divine. What do you see?"

"Me."

"You. It was you all along. It's not a fucking platitude. It's not some mystical mumbo jumbo. There are infinities within you. Everything that can, and will be experienced, is inside you. You are looking for validation outside yourself. You are looking for healing outside yourself. You are looking for love outside yourself. *That* is why you feel alone when you drink vodka and Squirt. Not because your grandfather isn't with you, but because you are looking the wrong direction."

The other Andy stared deeply into Andy's eyes. They were harsh eyes, but deep and forgiving.

"So what do I do now?" asked Andy.

"You're asking yourself that. You're always asking yourself that. You have to come to terms with this. You're going to hear time and time again that your healing is within you. You went through Hell Andy, and mother fuckers are going to try and tell you that you are the only one holding you back. And they are right. But not in the way they mean, and not in the way you think I mean."

"Then what do you mean?"

"You've been running from these things for too long. From the pain, the sorrow, the shame and the anger. You run from them because you think they are outside of you. But they aren't. They are the bones of this experience. This path of healing, this path of loss. It's all within you. And it's making you stronger. When you curl in a ball crying. When you are crippled with anxiety. When you are alone. Most of all when you are alone, you are getting stronger. More whole. Because you are allowing something in, something that you thought was other. You are becoming more whole."

The other Andy walked closer to him. He was close as a breath, as a whisper.

"I wish I could have been your grandfather Andy. But all I can offer you, is what he made you. And he made you a really beautiful man. Every time you plant a seed. Every time you savor your first sip of coffee. Every time you hug your mother. Every single time, you are allowing his love to flow through you."

The other Andy nodded. It was a subtle thing, hardly worth noticing. But it was familiar, and warm, and in that moment, Andy felt his grandfather's arms wrap around him.

+The 5th Day+

The morning was slow. All mornings were slow for Andy these days.

Gravity had become a demon, an enemy that lurked in the shadows, waited for his feet to touch the ground. So he laid for as long as he could, as to not tempt the demon from its cave.

Terra walked into the room and climbed into bed.

"Be careful," Andy said, his voice tipped in anger and fear. Andy didn't want to flinch, but his body reacted without any input from his heart.

"Oops sorry daddy," Terra said gently. "Do you want to read this book to me?"

Terra held out a chapter book Andy didn't recognize. There were mice, turtles and squirrels eating cupcakes. *Perfect*, thought Andy.

"I'd love to," said Andy as he opened the book. Angie walked into the room.

"I thought we were going to the coffee shop Terra," she said.

"Oh yeah! Daddy, we are going to get pastries and I want you to come with."

Ugghh.

"Seriously though Andy, it'll be good to get you out. You haven't been out since we went on that walk in the woods."

The walk in the woods. Andy shuddered thinking about the pain, the humiliation. Andy had made it maybe 30 feet from the car when his body rebelled. His stomach, his crotch, his legs, his back. Everything, in unison, said *"FUCK YOU ANDY"* and sent him back to the car, crying.

"You can stay in the car," Angie offered.

"OK," Andy said as he stumbled out of the bedroom. "Do you want anything mom?"

Andy's mom was in the kitchen, cutting something, cooking something. Andy's brain didn't have much interest in details.

"Get me a vanilla latte please! I'm making something *yummmyyyyyy,*" she added. Andy's mom wasn't much of a cook. It wasn't that she was bad, she was actually quite good in fact. She just didn't really *do it.* But when she did, it was a bit of an event.

"Awesome, we'll see you soon," said Andy, as he shut the door behind him.

Andy always insisted on driving, because he hated to feel cramped. Cramped meant cramping, and Andy was pretty sure he was just one giant walking cramp these days.

The drive was short. Too short for Andy to build any sort of courage. Gone was the city, replaced by the solace of the country. But with that solace came empty roads and fast cars. Fast cars, the enemy of wasting time, they hampered Andy's ability to fight his anxiety. Too efficient for their own good.

Andy wanted to go in, really he did. It was one of the few places in town that reminded him of the city. In a small town, a small *rural* town, a coffee shop this hip and delicious was the ultimate novelty. And the Baristo really was a sweetheart, a kindred spirit to be certain.

And yet, Andy couldn't convince himself to get out of the seat. He hated the way it felt to walk, and he could only imagine what it looked like. *Whatever* it looked like, he didn't want people to see it. Definitely not people he liked and respected.

"Can you just get me a..." Andy wanted to say cappuccino. Cortado. Latte. Fuck, a drip coffee. "...golden milk."

"A golden milk? Really?" Angie was incredulous.

"I'm trying to be good."

"OK. We'll be right back. Come on Terra."

Andy watched their slow entrance into the cafe. Terra bounced off light poles, danced with her reflection. Andy smiled.

Andy eyed the leather chair, the huge ficus plant, and the round stone coffee table. He imagined the hipstery lifestyle magazine that sat on the table, and fantasized getting comfy and reading.

Truly, Andy wished he could go in. But he couldn't. Not yet.

He watched the Baristo bow, the ever gracious service industry homie. He saw himself in them, and Andy knew the feeling was mutual. Andy watched Angie motion to the car, and Andy hazarded an awkward wave. Baristo smiled, and Andy immediately felt a deep pang of regret that he didn't even remember Baristo's name. After a few quick, efficient moves, Angie's hands were full.

Angie opened the door, and Terra came running, danish in hand.

"Mommy got you *your* drink!" she said, as if to say, *no you may not have a bite of my danish.*

"Here you go babe," Angie said as she slid into the seat next to Andy. She handed him the golden milk, and Andy sniffed it hesitantly.

"I'm sure it's good," Angie said reassuringly, "everything they make is good."

"Yeah," said Andy, resigned to his fate. He looked up, and gave the Baristo a smile and wave as he took a sip and threw the car in reverse.

Golden Milk

As Andy threw the car in reverse, Andy himself was thrown in reverse.

His body passed through the driver's seat, and he flew into the backseat next to Terra's car-seat.

Terra wasn't there of course, just some nebulous spooky shadowy blob. Angie was gone too. But in the driver's seat, Andy could see the Baristo's telltale beanie.

The Baristo turned their head, not trusting the rear view mirror (like any good driver wouldn't.)

Andy wasn't surprised to see the Baristo had Andy's face. He did, however, feel a tangible sadness. His mind wouldn't even *pretend* that these spirits were anything other than the Self anymore.

"How's the Golden Milk?" Baristo asked.

"Turmeric-y."

"I bet. But you love turmeric, right?"

"Yeah, but not like this," said Andy dejectedly, "Not like this. But you know..."

"Inflammation," they said at the same time.

"Yeah yeah yeah," said the Baristo. "A martyr for the cause. All for the sake of healing, right?"

"Yep."

"Do you even know what inflammation *is*?" asked the Baristo, pointedly.

"The increase in the price of goods, at the same time as the purchasing power of money drops?"

"Ha. Inflation. Try again."

"OK fine. Big puffy redness."

"Yes. But more to our point, inflammation is a defense mechanism," said the Baristo. "It's your body, your immune system, sending a huge amount of resources to help itself heal."

"I must be in dire need of help and healing, because Jesus Christ I'm inflamed all the fuck over."

"Indeed. Your tenderness is literally your body's way of coping with a really traumatic experience. Your sensitivity is your healing."

"That can't be fucking true. I mean yes, with my body, but don't try and tell me my sensitivity has some sort of deeper significance. Being an overly emotional, hyper touchy wiener can't possibly be helping me. It's just hurting."

"It hurts, sure, but its insulating you. That emotional and spiritual puffiness is a much needed cushion. The betrayal you feel, from the doctor, from your peers, from your work and from your family is fucking real. And the most natural thing in the world is for you to demand some space. Your inflammation is giving you what you wouldn't willingly ask for yourself."

"But turmeric isn't inflammatory, it's anti-inflammatory," Andy said the unspoken.

"Yep. Hey, don't look at me. I mean, I *am* you. What do *you* think I'm going to say?" nudged the Baristo.

"If inflammation is distance, then my spiritual turmeric must be closeness. Like, closeness to other people? Again with the closeness?" Andy barfed a little bit in his mouth.

"Again."

"I'm not ready," wailed Andy.

"Of course you're not. It's fucking scary to let people back in. It's scary to go out in public, to be seen. Its scary to tell your story, to be vulnerable to people that weren't there for the whole damned thing. The thing that is scaring you the most about that though, is that people won't see you the same."

"You're right," Andy agreed, hesitantly.

"And so are you. People won't see the old you, because he fucking died. He was literally thrown into oblivion by what you went through. And that's a beautiful fucking thing."

"That's what you all keep saying, but it doesn't feel very beautiful."

"We repeat ourselves to make it unavoidably obvious," Andy winced.

"And change is hard, to be sure. I won't deny that. But you have been given a divine *out*. You have an *excuse* to change, and no one can hold it against you. Trauma is the ultimate 'get out of jail free' card. You are, in essence, being given an ultimatum to start over." Andy sighed.

"But don't get me wrong, it's not as easy as all that. Your brain and your body are going to take a long fucking time to catch up. You'll think you can do this. You'll assume you should that. You'll confuse past habits for current desires. All of this, because your former self is so ingrained into your very essence. You *will* be tricked into thinking you're that *old* you. But let him the fuck go."

"But he was so cute, and nice, and charming."

"So are you."

"No I'm not. I'm crotchety and bitter and can't be on my feet for long without getting really freakin pissy. Who would want to spend time with *that*?" asked Andy, as he looked at his legs with deep, abiding spite.

"That's OK. Do me a favor Andy. Think about Angie. What is the first thing you loved about her?"

"Her butt." *No question.*

"After that," urged the Baristo.

"Oh. That. We were talking about Edgar Allen Poe.

About Rilke. And she told me *they* were proof positive that it wasn't a bad thing to be sad. That it's good to mourn, to feel the weight of loss, the weight of emptiness. That there's beauty in the broken bits."

"She's fucking wise," said Baristo.

"Yes. Yes she is," confirmed Andy.

"So let them in. Let in the people who want to be close. Distance was good, but closeness is better. They're telling you they want to be close to you. Let them see the new you. The crippled you. The broken you. The sad you."

"Fuck."

"I know. It sucks. But it's OK if things suck. Its OK if things are hard. And its OK for people to see that. Its valid, its genuine. And if they love you, truly, they want to see all of you."

"All of me," repeated Andy as the face began to fade from the rear-view. Andy looked into his own eyes, watched them flee. But then, just like that, the Baristo was back again.

"Oh, Andy. One more thing. Something that you might appreciate," the Baristo's grin was contagious.

"Yes?"

"Coffee is full of anti-oxidants."

"And?"

"Anti-oxidants are anti-inflammatory."

Andy looked down at the Golden Milk, then back up at the rear view mirror. The reflection smiled, and nodded.

"Thank you," Andy whispered, a tear in his eye.

$$++$$

"Will you drive babe? I'm going to sit in back with Terra," Andy smiled to his daughter in the rear view. He put the car back into park.

"Sure," said Angie. Rather than get out of the car, she simply slid over the center console into the driver's seat, as Andy took the long slow walk to the backseat.

"How ya doing buddy?" Andy asked Terra as he plunked in the seat next to her.

"Good," she said, a bit guilty. "I didn't save you any danish. I forgot."

"Ah, its OK babe. I'm guessing it was yummy?"

"So yummy."

Angie took the long way home, as if she sensed Andy's need for fresh air. Air was fresh *everywhere* around here, and just a cracked window fed his soul.

Andy missed hiking, he missed biking. He missed what his life had been not too long ago.

So much can change in just a couple weeks, Andy thought.

Andy had left the city a long time ago. It wasn't that it was a bad place, but it was bad for him. A place of habits and harm. He wanted space. So here they were, in the land of space eternal. His family given room to grow.

Still, his mind wandered the old haunts as they drove. His dreams meandered the old alleys. His end of days, bejeweled with reminders of home. He scanned the landscape, admired the pine trees, even as he searched for the landscape for ethnic food and punk rockers in vain.

The plateau spread out in front of the car, gulches and arroyos dotted the landscape as the car climbed well above the town below. This was about as roundabout a way home as could be managed, and Andy was grateful to Angie for her thoughtfulness.

"Holy cow! You won't imagine it! I found you something daddy," said Terra. *Most adorable voice ever.*

Andy looked in Terra's hand. Two crusty old stickers, and one equally crusty dinosaur fruit snack.

"Oooooh," said Andy, not entirely disingenuous. Sure it was ancient and covered in God knows what, but that felt authentically prehistoric. And Andy could never turn down a fruit snack.

"What kind is it?" he asked.

"Yellow. Lemon I think," she replied.

"I actually meant what kind of dinosaur."

"I think an Ankylosaurus. See," she pointed at the snack's club tail.

"Good identification babe," said Andy as he grabbed it out of her hand. "Lemon you say?"

"Lemon!"

"Alright, here comes the Allosaurus. *Grrrrraarrrrrrrggggh-hhh.*"

The fearsome carnivore hardly stalked its prey at all. The Ankylosaurus was petrified, un-moving beneath the gaping, salivating jaws. The Allosaurus let out one final roar, and the Ankylosaurus could do nothing but weep tiny, lemon flavored tears. If it could have, it most certainly *would have* screamed.

Dinosaur Fruitsnack

Andy looked at his daughter.

The moment she was born, he knew there was nothing in this world he could ever love more. He knew he would do anything for her, without question. His heart swelled every time he looked at her.

Even now, as her face elongated and became ever so scaly. Even as her car seat fused to her back, hardening into a shell of interlocking plates. Even as her tailbone elongated, into first a vestigial tail, then widening to a small tree trunk. Even as she grew spikes, and her tail sprouted what looked like a medieval weapon of war. Even then, he loved her most of all.

"Daddy," oh how he loved her little voice.

"Daddy," the dinosaur roared.

Andy was so lost in his love, that he wasn't exactly responsive to the 24 foot long dinosaur that had destroyed his family vehicle.

"Oh, yes sweetie?" said Andy, coming back to his senses.

"Daddy! This is likely to be the easiest lesson. Maybe that is because my brain is the size of a couple walnuts," Andy gaped at the giant creature, marveling that it could somehow be propelled by a brain smaller than his fist. "Or maybe it's because the simple lessons are the most important ones."

"I'm OK with simple. My brain is fried. Anti-depressants,

thick curtains, and way too much Netflix have reduced me to not much more than a single celled organism."

"Good. Then listen carefully. I know life is hard right now. But don't forget to have fun."

"Have fun?"

"Fruit snacks aren't worth much, tangibly. Even a child can easily crush an entire box in a sitting. They have negligible nutrients, are mostly sugar and color," Andy nodded, a bit sad. "But I'll be damned if they aren't super fun to eat."

Andy smiled.

"You know how some people think dinosaurs aren't real?" The Ankylosaurus continued, "I weep for them. Not because they are ignorant, but because they lack imagination. They lack the *whimsy* to imagine a world with giant birdy-lizardy things wandering giant horsetails and terrifying tar pits. Dinosaurs are just fun, even just in your head."

"And terrifying, which is its own kind of fun," suggested Andy. "I mean, just the thought of a creature having to eat 550 pounds of gingko leaves a day to survive is *freaky*. To say nothing of Mr, or Mrs, Tyrant o' Saur tearing *whole limbs* off of said giant."

"I know, right? Fantastical! There's a reason kids eat up anything dinosaur, and that's because it requires some amazingly vibrant imaginings to even suggest such a thing. To re-imagine a world as lush as a dinosaur's, all from just looking at a few bones, is pure magic."

Andy thought back to his own childhood. He would use his pointer fingers as triceratops horns, then chase girls he thought were cute across the playground. He remembered the awe, the true wonder he felt when he saw his first dinosaur skeleton. He remembered dinosaur cartoons, and the omnipresent dream of being a paleontologist so he could live in that world forever.

"Fun, whimsy and imagination are absolutely requisite to healing. To happiness. I know you really really like reading non-fiction books about identifying indigenous plants. That's great. That's neat. But there is a reason you want to read books about elves, dragons, Neanderthal sorcerers and warrior monks. You need some fun in your life."

"Are you saying pain and suffering aren't fun? How dare you!" said Andy, trying to lighten *himself* up.

"Seriously Andy. It's terrible what you are going through. But you know what else is terrible? Dinosaurs. Literally, the name means terrible lizards. So if it's going to be terrible, at least make it 35 feet of terror. Might as well be a fun tyrant."

"Yeah," said Andy, imagining himself imagining.

"And you have the greatest teacher in the world, just screaming for a chance to teach you how to have fun again. The greatest gift a child can give you is levity. She's showing you that life isn't just a series of traumas and mistakes. It's a divine comedy. And giggles and smiles are absolutely what you need right now."

Andy smiled at the giant lizard. He hadn't realized his daughter's voice had never left it. Seven metric tons of the cutest darn voice Andy had ever heard.

"I'm sorry I've been so grumpy," Andy told the dinosaur, with tears in his eyes. "I'm trying to get back to where I was, I swear."

"I don't want you back where you were daddy," said the dinosaur. "I want you right where you are. I want you here."

"I'm here baby. I'm here."

++

Andy rested his head on Terra's shoulder. Her itty bitty shoulder slumped as she dozed.

She never napped, unless they were driving. And it was early, so she must not have slept well. He wished her sweet dreams, as he listened to the sound of her breath.

She was truly angelic, well above any of the shmucks Andy had met over the last five days. True divinity.

Andy caught Angie's eyes in the rear view mirror and smiled. She hugged the curves, ever so gentle. She had nowhere else to be, and Andy could tell that she too was grateful for the quiet. He didn't know what she was thinking. He didn't want to know.

Andy worried she hated who he was, who he had become. And he said that out loud. A lot. His confidence was dashed, his heart was splintered. He had promised to help her, forever and always. And now he just felt a hindrance.

She pulled onto their block, onto their driveway, and into the garage.

Terra woke up, not with a start, but definitely with a little bit extra. She unclipped her seatbelt and ran into the house, curious what grandma could be cooking. She always woke up ravenous, proof positive she was absolutely Andy's child.

Andy walked into the house, and was struck with a wave of nausea. He smelled pancakes. And he smelled sausage.

He panicked, just a little. And then, the nausea was gone. Like it was never there.

Anywhere else, in any other context, the telltale diner smell would send him running. But seeing his mom behind the stove, making him breakfast, alleviated any and all symptoms. It was his childhood, all over again.

Andy realized something in that moment. Diners didn't make him nauseous because he hated pancakes and sausage. He hated pancakes and sausage, because he missed his fucking mom.

For years he had missed her, but he would only ever admit it late at night to his wife, when he was particularly annoyed at his mom for not calling. He missed her presence, missed her advice. Just plain missed her.

But then, he was crippled by the surgery, and she was the first person to reach out.

Of course she was. How could she not be? She's my fucking mom, thought Andy. But still, it felt really good when she had offered to come help take care of him.

"It smells good momma," Andy said, and Angie shot him a look of disbelief.

He laid down at the couch, despairing at the idea of sitting at the kitchen table. The thought of a wooden chair on his bruised testicles made Andy's whole body tense.

He tried his damnedest to not let his body tense up. Every time Terra ran near him, every time he sat down on the toilet, every time he even imagined sitting at the kitchen table, he tensed up. And it only made the pain worse. His body just wanted to relax, but it was so overworked, overtaxed, overwhelmed that it couldn't. It was stuck in this feedback loop that made his days last forever.

"Will you eat at the table?" his mom asked.

"Abso-fucking-lutely not." *No way.*

She sighed, and made him a plate. She walked over to the couch, and set the plate on the arm rest.

"How are you feeling?"

"Like hell," he said, trying to not be short with his mother but absolutely failing.

"That's good! Better!"

"What?" he said, incredulous.

"When I asked yesterday, you started bawling. Progress is progress!" she smiled.

"Yeah, I guess so," he smirked.

Andy grabbed his fork, and methodically alternated pancake and sausage pieces into a towering bite. He scraped as much syrup off the plate onto the bite, and smiled. "Thank you for being here mommy."

"Of course. You're my baby!"

Andy smiled, and put way too much food into his mouth.

Pancakes and Sausage

He knew the booth like the back of its hand. He recognized the tear in the vinyl, and fingered the gap in the wood. He removed the wrapper from his straw, and shoved it into the gap, like he always did.

His hands were smaller than he remembered. No hand tattoos. No wedding rings. Just tiny hands, not much bigger than Terra's.

He looked up at his mom. She was mid-20s, hair a riot of curls that only the 80s thought were appropriate. She had her overalls on. Her only overalls, the overalls she wore every day. The overalls that were in every single photo. The overalls Andy hoped she still owned.

He could smell the orange juice and the 2% milk. *Kind of gross*, Andy thought, *reminiscing on the smell of orange juice and milk*. But he did.

The diner looked like all the other ones just like it. A now defunct chain, they were ubiquitous at one point and Andy remembered going to this particular one at least once a week. He always eyeballed the pies. It was not their dessert spot, however, it was their breakfast spot, and he doubted he and his mom had ever even *tried* the pies.

"I'm so sorry bubba," his mom said gently.

Andy looked up, and started to cry.

"Thank you," he said.

"For what?" she asked.

"Being sorry."

"How could I not be? No one deserves this sort of pain," her eyes dripped with pity.

"Thank you," he whimpered again.

"You know Andy, there's not very much room for empathy in this world."

"That's a pretty harsh thing to say," Andy said, a little resentful.

"It's true though. You've been wronged, left and right. I can see that, Angie can see that. But most people are so wrapped in their shit, they honestly have no idea how incredibly traumatic this has been for you. They have no concept that your life is forever changed. That you are not the same person, and that you are hurting. Not even the people you thought you were close to."

"That I *thought* I was close to..." Andy bristled.

"Yes, thought. This trauma is a giant sieve Andy. A spiritual filter, and a whole lot of people are going to end up going down the drain," Andy's lower lip stuck itself out. "And that doesn't make them bad people. It just means they aren't *your* people."

"You see them?" his mom pointed to the booth in the corner, where Angie, Terra, and Andy's real mom sat. "Those are your people. Your coworkers? Your customers? They aren't your people. You might spend 40 hours a week with them, talk to them pretty much non-stop for four to eight hours a day sometimes. But that doesn't make them yours."

Andy was speechless.

"Like I said, I'm not saying they are bad people. In fact, most of them are really quite good people. But we only have so much room in our heads and our hearts for people. Everyone's got their own shit going on Andy. It's not that they don't wish you well, but energy is a limited resource, and we *all* have to ration it." It was so matter of fact, it stung.

"I just thought..." Andy had heard this so many times this week, in so many ways, but it still made him feel very alone.

"You thought you were the center of everyone's universe, because you are the center of your universe. I'm not saying this to be cruel, but to give you some context as to why people act the way they do."

Andy started to cry, but then his mom reached out her hand, "But I'm your person Bubba. That beautiful wife and that baby girl, they are your people. You have people that care so much about you that will reach out time and time again."

"And the part that's really going to fuck with you Andy, is the people you never expected reaching out," Andy could already think of a couple people. "And do you know what that means Andy? That you were their people, but they weren't yours. That you were the one that didn't have room in your heart for them."

"Oi..." Andy felt like a shithead.

"But you are being given an opportunity to open up your heart a little wider. To reapportion *your* resources."

"I don't have much to give."

"You don't need to do anything, other than be thankful. You don't even *have* to do that. But honestly, just be grateful that people care, even if they aren't the people you expected, or even wanted. There are people that are actually alone in this world Andy. You aren't alone."

Andy looked over at his family, "I'm absolutely thankful for them. Beyond anything I could ever express."

"They know that."

"I hope so."

"They do. But do you know how you can show them? Come back to them. Try, one day at a time, to come back to the people you love. It's a long road to walk Andy, but just knowing that you are making the effort is going to put their hearts at ease. They are worried about you."

"I am too," said Andy.

"You're going to be fine Bubba. You're already better. And actually *better*. Every moment, we get better, because this life is all about pulling back the curtain on our true selves. Even in our darkest times. That's what apocalypse is. I'm sure you know what the word means, right?"

Andy did, "Uncovering. It's called Revelations for a reason, I suppose. End of Days show us what we really are?"

"Exactly. And do you know what you are Andy?" she smiled.

"What?"

"Loved, Andy. You. Are. Loved."

++

They didn't even talk about it. They just sort of did it.

The hot spring was a 30 minute drive south. They hadn't been in a couple months, which for card carrying members was *way* too long.

They packed the car after breakfast. Towels, swim suits, snacks. The excitement was palpable. Terra was giddy.

The drive was hypnotic. The hills were dusted in snow, and Andy sat in the backseat with Terra and they watched the storm clouds descend towards the valley. Hot springs *always* got Andy jazzed but soaking on a cold winter day was a different kind of healing altogether.

As they pulled into the parking lot, Andy watched a flock of bushtits coast through a gap in the juniper, landing on a naked apple tree that was hanging over one of the rock lined pools. He stepped out of the car, and heard them chirping to each other, their whispers punctuated by tiny steam clouds.

He reached his hand into his pocket, searched for something he couldn't quite remember.

Andy dressed alone, leaving Terra and Angie to meet him at the pool. He made quick work of the process, hoping to avoid being caught in the dressing room looking decrepit.

Andy wore nothing more than a towel and trunks, and stepped out onto the mass of flagstones leading to the pool.

His body tensed. The cold poked and prodded and doubled him over.

The walk was so far, the trunks not supportive enough.

He limped, hobbled, nearly crawled his way to the pool where Terra and Angie were already sitting. Angie looked at Andy apologetically, but spared him any questions. He lowered himself into the pool, and felt his muscles release. As he came to a seat next to his family, he released a breath that he didn't know he held.

Angie offered no words, but caressed his hair as he lay his head back into the hot water. He tried to smile, but realized it a bit too strenuous for him at the moment. He floated for a moment, *tried* to keep himself afloat, but even that was too much for him, his core severely depleted.

Andy sat back up, and gave Terra a devious smile. He dipped his face into the water, allowing just a bit to pass past his lips.

"Terra," Angie was quick to say, "we don't drink the water in the pool. Even at a hot spring."

Terra obliged, but Andy was far past the point of no return. He swallowed.

Spring Water

Andy lay back, allowed himself to float again. This time was different.

As he bobbed back and forth, he floated upwards. Pulled, perhaps by his chest, but more likely by his crotch. He made a squeal, but allowed himself to succumb to a weightlessness that was punctuated by a sure tightness in the groin.

Andy was amongst the clouds, bushtits dancing back and forth on the thermals. A fairy, a regal sort, sat upon a throne of clouds. The throne wept, water cascading down its sides, and imbued the scene with a bit of emotion, though Andy wasn't quite sure what the emotion was supposed to be.

"Holy water," said the queen.

"The holiest," offered Andy as he floated on the dream. "But I still hurt."

"People sometimes think the Holy is supposed to wash away all pain and suffering, but that's not it at all."

Andy admitted, "I expected this to be a panacea for sure. I thought I could just be magically healed."

"Healing is never magic Andy," she said gently. "Healing is work. Healing is an action word. A verb. It's a process. To just give you health, to just return you to a state of equilibrium would be the least Holy thing I could offer you. It would negate your ability to heal yourself, negate your process."

"Fuck a process, I just don't want to hurt."

"Then it has to hurt. Maybe if you crawled to these springs, praying every few feet on a 100 mile journey. Maybe *then* the spirits would have seen it fit to heal you right up, to bless you with a miracle. But then, you would have *already* put in the work."

"I find it completely fucking maddening that the spirit of a mother fucking hot springs, bastion of relaxation, is offering me a prescription to work harder."

"I sure am. Mineral springs are one of the oldest forms of therapy available. But you know what therapy is? Work. Just wait Andy, just wait. Physical therapy is fucking *hard*. Talk therapy? *Painful*. It's all up hill from here baby."

"And so what then? What is the promise for all that work? To get back to where I was?"

"You keep saying back to where you were. There is no back to where you were. That's gone. Your path has branched, diverged. You're on a whole new path. So I guess *that* is what your struggle, your pain and your process can offer you. A new path."

"Hot springs are the beautiful end result of an underground current working its damnedest, through bedrock. To find a new way to the surface. Through limestone and mud, years and years of sediment. The water takes the earth with it, trace minerals, microscopic crystals, and comes out the other side full of life and full of love. Full of magic. It can only become wholly itself by pushing through some really adverse fucking conditions. Then, and *only* then, can it heal not just itself but the world around it."

"Hustle and grind?"

"Absolutely not. Take your time, be patient with yourself."

As she said this, the waters on the throne began to calcify around her. Slowly, the water built itself higher and higher, crystallizing around her torso, her neck, and face. Her lips remained, and beckoned Andy closer

"Take it slow. Healing comes at a geologic pace."

Her lips sealed, and Andy felt his body calcify around him. He felt his weight, the gravity of himself. And he fell.

+ +

Andy came back to his body and so did his pain. He whispered to Angie, and they got out of the pool.

They went to the indoor pool, and he watched as Terra and Angie splashed around. Andy laid on a beach chair, wrapped in blankets, hoping to absorb whatever rays of sun managed to negotiate their way between the clouds.

Andy pulled out his phone, noted a missed text.

Andy felt alienated from just about everyone. In the wake of so much trauma, he didn't even want to hang out with anyone. Genuinely, zero fucking interest.

But Dante had reached out from the very beginning. When he was delirious with pain, when he was half in this world and half in the next, Dante checked on him, time and again.

It was amazing, how something so little could mean so much. So Andy made it a point to talk to him. He didn't really talk to anyone, unless you counted sending memes to people on social media. Dante though, he would talk to. Share his struggles with.

"You wanna come hang out, smoke some pot or something?" read the text.

Andy hadn't been out of the house, socially, in an eternity.

"I'm not really smoking right now. Trying to be a good boy," he wrote back.

"I'm down to just sit around and sip something. Maybe I'll make you something fancy," Dante responded.

Andy mulled it over as they drove home. Wondered if he was ready.

Andy was scared to ask Angie if it was OK. Deep down, there was this heavy dose of doubt that said, "If you're good enough to go to a friend's house, then you're good enough to do everything else."

Totally not logical, but he had some deep pangs of guilt at not working, about not starting physical therapy. Guilty about not being more engaged with Terra, about not doing *anything* he could deem productive.

He was also just scared to admit that he needed to get out of the fucking house.

"Um... b-babe," Andy stuttered. "Is it OK if I go over to Dante's house before dinner?"

Angie looked shocked, but at the same time relieved, "If you're up for it, I don't see why not. You're not going to drink are you?"

"Honestly babe, I don't know if I'm ever going to drink again," he said it, and for the first time in his life it felt like he meant it. Sure the cocktail of drugs he was on was a manifest hindrance, but his heart didn't really feel up to it anymore either. And that was saying a lot, because Andy had struggled with the sauce for a long time.

"And I'm not going to smoke either. Just need some buddy time."

"Deal," said Angie.

"Hey Terra," said Andy, "I'm going to go see Dante. I'll be back for dinner though."

"Will you do night night?"

"Sure babe, I'll do night night."

Andy dropped the duo off at home, walked them in to tell his mom that he was going out.

"Have fun sweetie," his mom said.

Andy walked out to the car, and when he opened the car door, there was a small bird sitting on the passenger seat.

"Hey buddy, how are *you* doing?" asked Teat.

"Teat! Where the hell you been? I'm doing shitty by the way! Terrible! Terrified? Why? Scared to be social. Like super scared."

"Whoa whoa. Slow down buddy boy. I'll be with you, if you want," the sweet little bird responded.

"That'd be great," said Andy as he tucked him into his coat pocket.

The drive was short, and the lack of prep time made any all the more nervous. Andy hesitated as he walked towards the towering stairs of Dante's apartment.

Dante was on the deck at the top, smoking a cigarette.

"Hey bud, it's good to see you," he hollered down. "Do you need some help up?"

"Nah man. I think it'd honestly just make it harder," Andy took the steps one at a time.

Winded, he arrived on the landing to Dante's fanfare. Whoops and cheers, a little mocking but also super heartening. He smiled and hugged the hairy dude.

They walked in, straight to the kitchen counter.

"You want some juice? Beer? I got this barrel aged sour that's dope," offered Dante.

"Ah no beer man. I'm on so many God forsaken pharmaceuticals," Andy secretly really wanted a beer. "What's that in the pitcher though?" Andy motioned to a creepy creamy carafe.

"Oh that," Dante seemed embarrassed, "that's just some almond & walnut milk that I made. I'm sick of buying so much damn milk at the store."

"That's fucking awesome. I haven't had homemade almond milk in forever. Can I get a glug?"

"Uh, sure man" Dante poured them each a tiny glass.

"Cheers my dude, its good to see you. Upright and every-thing!"

"It's good to be seen," said Andy, as he took a sip.

Nut Milk

Andy laid on the table, all but alone, despite the nurse in the corner.

The doctor walked into the room, yet the room stayed silent.

Andy offered to break the silence, "How ya doing doc?"

"Shitty," he sneered. "That's why I'm taking it out on you." The doctor motioned to Andy's soon to be modified genitals.

What the fuck, Andy thought to himself.

The surgery began without much ceremony.

Next to Andy was a tray, replete with a medieval collection of tools. There was a tiny welder, Andy was sure there was a technical name for the little bitty torch, but the doctor wasn't about to offer anything helpful. There were also a couple scalpels, a multi-needled doohickey and lots of those blue surgery napkins which obscured Andy's view of the procedure.

The doctor took the doohickey, said a succinct "local anesthetic" and promptly lit Andy's crotch up with the needles. Andy felt numb, actually and metaphorically.

The doctor grabbed the scalpel, made an incision, which Andy could feel vaguely.

Then there was a tug. And another tug. Andy was sure the doctor was looking to remove the entirety of his tubes. His whole pipeworks shuddered deep in his body.

"Oooh," Andy moaned.

"Oh shit, you shouldn't be feeling it that much," said the doctor. He grabbed the doohickey and gave Andy more than a few additional blasts from the anesthetic. It did not have the intended effect. The pain was more now. And more. And more.

The doctor grabbed the tiny torch, sent it behind the curtain of napkins, towards Andy's junk. A hiss, and moments later a jet of blood rocketed skyward.

"The fun part," said the doctor as he laughed.

One side done, Andy prepared for the worst. But the second side came and went, unimaginably uneventful in comparison to the first. So much so, that Andy felt like he had imagined the hazards of the first go round. It was a blur, and Andy was blurred by it.

The doctor stood up, removed his gloves. He avoided Andy's gaze, whether that was intentional or just his nature, was hard for Andy to ascertain.

"Go home, rest for 48 hours. After that, you'll get progressively better. Make a follow up at the desk."

And that was that. There was a maze of florescent lights, a short drive home, and sleep. Lots of sleep.

The next day was fine. Super sore, but fine. Nothing more than expected, and definitely not less than expected.

At the 48 hour mark, Andy decided it was time to stop being a lazy shmuck. He walked around, hung out in the kitchen, and checked the oil in the car. As the day wore on though, he felt increasingly sore.

He inspected the handy work, looking at his black and purple nuts.

Well, he thought, *it certainly LOOKS like I won't be able to have another kid.*

The next day, they were still purple. And sore. Well, more sore. In fact, the soreness had graduated to hurt. And they were bigger. Were they bigger? He had to ask.

"Babe!" he called to Angie. "Does this look OK?"

"I don't really know what OK is supposed to look like, Andy. The doctor said there would be swelling and soreness, right?"

"Ya, but I feel like this is more than that. Could you maybe call the doctor?" Andy didn't have it in him to talk to anyone right now.

"Sure babe."

Minutes later: "The office says the doctor is on *vacation*? Are you fucking kidding me? That's not OK! And they had *nothing* for me, so I'm going to call some other urologists."

Even more minutes later, "I can't get hold of anyone. It's like this whole fuckin' area is on vacation. I know it's right after Christmas, but come on!"

"OK," Andy grumbled. "I'm going to lie down."

Andy slept, fitfully. He dreamed of the surgery, the pain, and fire. Brimstone. Hellish.

He awoke covered in sweat, terrified to look at himself. He braved an inspection and yelled to Angie. She winced.

"I'm going to try calling again."

She called. Andy lay in the bath, looking at how swollen he looked. How foreign he looked.

"She pretty much said, 'Fuck off, I can't help you, go to the hospital.' So I think we have to take you to the ER."

"Fuuuuuuck," Andy moaned.

The ER was a blur. Too fast, too much information for a brain too addled with pain. Angie didn't come in. They didn't want Terra to see this, and they didn't have anyone who could watch her. So Andy was alone.

The staff looked. They grimaced. They asked questions. They gave him narcotics.

The on staff MD told Andy he had a hematoma. Told Andy it would likely relieve itself on its own.

They sent Andy home.

Andy laid awake, throbbing, screaming, and crying. He

lost touch with reality, came back, and was lost again. He was delusional, he rode a wave something like a high, but that was in actuality a lowly sort of low.

The next morning, he was bigger. And not in a sexy way. And he hurt, even more. And not in a sexy way.

He called his mom. He didn't know what she said. Angie talked to her, he didn't know what she said. He just laid there, and wept. Heavy, deep, fitful sobs.

"I have to take you back to the ER babe."

The ER was much the same. Apologetic eyes, reiterations of "hematoma" and "here have some pain meds." Angie was tired of platitudes and lazy medicine.

"Jesus Christ, can't you just take the hematoma out?"

"Oh," said the doctor, "maybe?" It was the most concomitant response imaginable. "I can ask the surgeon if he can do it."

More waiting. Eternities past, universes were born and extinguished in the in between.

Swells of pain sent Andy skyward, and he felt for Angie's hand. She held it, squeezed it. He whispered he loved her, but couldn't hear his own words. Terra said something funny. Andy's head laughed but his body refused.

"Alright," said the doctor, "the surgeon talked to your doctor, and we got the go ahead."

"Of course the fucking surgeon can get hold of the fucking doctor," growled Angie. The doctor nodded apologetically, left them alone.

The surgery came and went like a dream. Ketamine, and not the fun and transcendent experience Andy had imagined, or hoped for. Dark. Impenetrable.

He woke up the next morning, sore. Still he throbbed, but there was light between the pain.

He studied himself, the bloody gauze, the gaunt flesh. He looked up, searched for Angie, but found no one but a shadow.

"Hello Andy," said the shadow.

"Why in the flying *fuck* did you think I should relive that?" Andy was aghast.

"Stars are born, and stars will die. Empires will rise and crumble. And still, Andy, you will relive it. Again and again. Probably forever."

"Fuck me! Why?"

"People talk about the effects of trauma. The PTSD. The irrational fears, the anger, the jump scares. The symbolism that surrounds and abounds. They talk about everything that suggests the trauma, but never talk about the real effect, which is the trauma itself. The *trauma* is the true specter."

"The trauma is the trauma. Self-evident, bordering on reductive," Andy said, ever more smug.

"It is, and that's what makes it so damned dangerous. When we focus on externalities, at the residuals from the surgery, we forget that it wasn't just your heart, soul, ego, and path that were fractured. Your body was fractured most of all. Your nerves are shot, your muscles are atrophied. You are hurt in the most visceral of ways, and that is *really* important for you not to forget."

"How could I?" Andy dreamed of a day that he could actually forget his physical anguish.

"Oh you will, time and again. You will feel yourself lost, afloat without a boat. Drifting. And that is when you will remind yourself, 'My boat was capsized.' Your body is the ground level, Andy. And everything builds itself upon it. It's all the harder to reach spiritual highs when your body is in the gutter."

"So then what do I do?"

"Therapy dude. Physical therapy. You need to take care of this mortal coil. It seems trite, but it's absolutely necessary for you to pay attention to what your body is telling you. Rest when it needs rest, stretch, eat healthy, avoid shit that is going to aggravate you. I'm sorry if I sound like a doctor, but I am."

"No you aren't... you're nuts and water."

"Yeah, but I'm also the divine embodiment of requisite self-healing. The spirit of slowing the fuck down. I'm the angel of pain, and coping. Your coming aversion to medicine is to be expected, but don't let that be an aversion to healing. You have to heal yourself."

"Ah come on now... you're telling me I can't get a little help? I can't do this on my own."

"Of course you can ask for help, but no one knows your body like you do. No one can implicitly know what you need except yourself."

"Ya, I suppose that makes sense. Hey... can I say something?"

"Absolutely," said the spirit, expectantly.

"Nut milk? Seriously? Fucking gross."

"Like I was saying Andy... sometimes metaphor isn't necessary. Sometimes it's OK for pain and suffering to be really damn literal."

The doctor walked out of the room, and left Andy to lay with himself, on the cold metal table.

＋＋

The pain was all Andy could stomach, as he walked down Dante's stairs towards his car. He was barely present. His eyes scanned the dark street for his dark car, but all he saw was more darkness.

He finally reached the car, opened the door, and threw himself onto the seat with a groan.

Andy groaned a lot these days. Not as sexy as he hoped, he just sounded like he was 75. Not just 75, but thoroughly abused over eight decades. Like an old coal miner with a prostate problem.

Andy supposed, he *did* have a prostate problem. Or round bout those parts. Andy was sobered by how the surgery revealed his ignorance of the male anatomy.

He reached into his pocket, fished for his keys. All he found was Teat.

"Hey buddy, how ya feeling?" chirped the bird.

"God I'm tired of that question," Andy sighed.

"Sorry," said Teat, as he feathered over Andy's keys.

"I just hate myself," he whispered towards Teat, but *to* himself.

"You shouldn't," offered Teat.

"Ya ya I know," said Andy as he tried to pull his sweater over his head. Tried, because Andy was brand new to his body. He had to relearn how to use every muscle. How to do the most basic fucking thing.

I don't want to go home, thought Andy. *But I'm damned hungry.*

The window was open in the car, and Andy smelled the air. Rain.

No, not rain, thought Andy. *Cognac.*

No, not cognac. Armagnac.

Leave it to Andy be able to differentiate styles of brandy quicker than he could distinguish alcohol from natural phenomenon like rain.

"That's my cue," said Teat, as he flew out the window.

Andy marveled as Teat flew. He flew through the air, and as he glided, the rain glanced off his feathers. *Not rain*, Andy reminded himself, *eau de vie.*

What a beautiful Armageddon, Andy thought. *Birds soaring through booze.* Teat looped between street lights, smiled as his wings became soaked in the spirit.

He flew faster, and faster. Impossibly fast.

There was levity there, but also a grim determination, as Teat picked up speed.

With horror, Andy watched as Teat hit some maximum velocity and burst into flames. The bushtit comet flew across the street and crashed next to Andy in the passenger seat.

Andy sat, stunned, staring at the sizzling little bird.

He saw Teat's beak move up and down, but Andy couldn't make out any words.

As Andy leaned closer to listen, he couldn't help but sniff.

Teat said what Andy couldn't, "I smell delicious."

Andy refused to speak.

"You know what you have to do," said Teat.

Andy wanted to restrain himself. He wanted to cradle his friend.

He wanted to mourn, but his lips mouthed "thank you."

Andy lifted Teat to his mouth. The charred Teat sat

upright, "Jesus man, cover yourself up when you do this. Can you imagine what someone would *think* if they saw you eat a tiny flambéed bird in your car?"

Andy grabbed his sweater from behind his back, and draped it overhead. With as much solemnity as he could muster, Andy took a bite of his dear friend, Teat.

Ortolan

The beast was an abomination.

What was cute about the tiny bird, was made monstrous when scaled to pachyderm proportions. Beady eyes, sharp beak, feathers bristling. Teat was something of a gryphon, and as he beat his wings, Andy lost his footing and fell to his knees before the great tit.

"Do you know why I asked you to cover yourself when you ate my flesh Andy?"

"So people wouldn't judge me."

"Sure. People. Why not? But mostly, God. The ritual of eating songbirds beneath a napkin is deeply rooted in European culture, but just as deeply rooted is the sense of shame surrounding it. The shame is forgotten in the preparation, in the context of catching and preparing the bird. It has become just another vestige of cultural heritage, I suppose. But in the consummation of the act, there is great shame."

"Good! Don't they like, force feed endangered birds and then blind them? Sounds pretty shameful to me."

"Yes. Its, admittedly, quite brutal. But do you know what the *actual* shame is Andy? Shame is the realization that things are not the way they are meant to be. That, perhaps, the act is a perversion of what is good. What is right. It is diverting the eyes from the way things are, towards the way things *should* be. And 'shoulds' are oh so dangerous Andy, because they are entirely imaginary. *That* is shame."

Andy opened his mouth, to speak for the birds, but Teat continued, "One of the great injustices of a tragedy, is that it acts as a paradigm shift. The world as it was, ceases to be, and a new world, often perpendicular to the other, takes its place. It is in these times that we are most gripped by a sense of the way things ought to be," Andy nodded.

"But that is purely mental gymnastics. That is denial. A fallacy. Expectations gripped by a fantasy. It blinds to the way things actually *are*."

Teat could see the glazed over look in Andy's eyes, "You feel so much shame, so much self-hate for what has happened to you. You feel like if you had done something differently, you would be in a different place. Regrets permeate your soul right now, and with that comes a sense of shame that you disrupted the natural order of things. That you disappointed your family, your friends, yourself, your *God*. And so you are condemned to a present not your own."

"Not only that, but you also feel shame for *what* happened to you. It's shameful enough to be hurt. But you are hurt in your 'private parts.' The parts we should never make public. And lo and behold, you exude an 'I'm broken in my naughty bits' air about yourself. The embarrassment is rife."

"You are contained, and in your containment, you hide from yourself. You hide from yourself, not because something like this shouldn't or couldn't happen to you. No, you hide because something like this *did* happen to you. It disrupts your personal narrative, your personal mythology, your personal spirituality to be broken in such a way, because what you are seems inconsistent to what you were."

"It's not fair," was all Andy could muster.

"Again, fairness is a reflection on the way things *ought* to be. Which is fiction. This is the way things are. You can't cover this up, because this is central to your story. This is your tragedy, your trauma, and your hell. Denial only feeds the flames, gives the act more shame, more gravity. You don't need any more gravity, you've been grounded to the point that you can barely walk. You need levity. You need light."

"How am I supposed to find levity in this?"

"I cannot give you levity, but I can give you less weight by showing you your shame. Not what you are shameful of, but to show you the shame itself. To show you the burden you have given to yourself, simply by denying the truth. Denying that this could, and *did* happen to you."

Andy felt a weight ease off his chest.

"I care less about you eating a bird than about the napkin. I care about covering it up. I want for you one thing, and that is acceptance. Acceptance of what was, what is, and what will come to be. Shed a little light on it."

Teat lifted his wings, and the sun shone through the feathers. The not so little bird beat his wings, and floated above Andy for a moment. With an ear piercing chirp, he flew off. Eventually, he met the sun, and was lost in its glow.

Andy allowed his fear to fly with Teat. A veil, lifted, and Andy saw his pain for what it was. His own.

✚✚

Andy pulled into the driveway, noted the sole light on in the living room.

Mom and Terra must be asleep, he thought, as he opened the front door with care.

Angie was sitting on the couch. She smiled at Andy, as he shut the door behind him. He walked over to the couch, and nestled in next to her.

"How was your time?" she asked.

"It was nice. Good for my heart," said Andy. And he meant it.

"I'm glad babe. I saved some dinner for you, it's on the stove."

"Thanks. I ate a little at Dante's, so maybe I'll save it for lunch tomorrow," Andy knew he would never eat the leftovers, but thought it the polite thing to say.

"We don't have any dessert and it makes me kind of sad," said Angie, a not so subtle hint.

"Give me a second," said Andy. He walked into the kitchen, rummaged through the entire pantry.

He checked for chocolate chips, to no avail.

Hot chocolate, he thought, but they were out of cocoa powder.

He even checked where they hid the surplus of Terra's Halloween candy, only to return empty handed.

No chocolate whatsoever. No candies. No baked goods. *No granola bars for God's sake.*

"I'm going to have to improvise babe," offered Andy.

"Okay," she hesitated, maybe a teensy bit afraid of what was in store for her.

Jesus, there's not even flour.

Rice. Rice? Rice. Andy thought.

Milk, sugar, pistachios, cardamom. The ingredients leapt to his fingertips as if they had been waiting for him.

Andy babied the pudding, cooking it as slow as Angie's sighs from the living room would abide. It was a slow process, but a beautiful one. He watched it come together, slow but sure. He smiled. He'd missed this.

Still warm, he walked two small bowls towards the couch. He noticed a few dried roses from the garden on the window sill. He delicately plucked a few petals, adding just enough romance to be presentable after nearly thirty minutes in the kitchen.

He handed Angie her dish.

"Spoon?" she prodded at the pudding with her finger.

"Shit sorry," Andy ran to the kitchen and back, and marveled that he was sort of quick about it.

"Thanks babe, this looks lovely," her praise not lost on him. He hadn't cooked much of anything lately, and her appreciation was genuine and warmed his heart like the bowl warmed his hands.

"I love you," he said, as he spooned the pudding into his mouth.

Shir Birinj

Angie was always Persian. At least a little bit. Well removed by time and space, yet now she held herself like a proper Scheherazade. Properly Persian.

She sat in front of a long pool, a full moon illuminating her delicate features. Her cheeks and eyebrows were strong, her smile shined more than her silks and jewels could hope to. There was more detail, to be sure, but he couldn't steal his eyes back from hers.

She sat on a cushion, and so did Andy.

A very comfy cushion, admired Andy.

A chorus of birds, not one of them a tit, sang from the lemon trees.

"I'm sorry we didn't have any chocolate," Andy said, even as he reveled in how damn *good* his rice pudding came out.

"You're right. It's not chocolate. It doesn't have that *power* that chocolate has over me. But it has everything else," she seemed to whisper to the pudding. "There is so much more to love. I'm sorry for that human inclination to fixate Andy. To focus, to swim in expectation."

Dripping with sincerity, she continued "Tunnel vision is inevitable. The mind is only able to exercise its breadth in spurts. Time and again, you see the grandeur that the universe has to offer. You become a cosmic soul, swimming in a sea of eternity. Your deep and abiding desire to see beyond your confines, to grow into infinity. You want to grow into the world around you, but your humanity brings you back to your pain, to your suffering, again and again. It shrinks you."

"I just want to be able to appreciate things beyond this mortal fucking coil. I use coil literally, although probably not etymologically. I feel curled in on myself, a giant fucking fetus. Focused, fixated on my broken body. I just want to hear the birds chirping and not think they are talking about my nuts."

"They must inform each other, Andy. You are trying to embrace the entirety, while avoiding the inevitable interpenetration of infinity with your very singular pain. You cannot divorce yourself from it, but it can become a part of your symphony. It can become a part of everything else, it can be entire."

"That's sounds like some esoteric mumbo jumbo," Andy said, an accusation to be sure.

"Look at this Shir Birinj, Andy. It is a beautiful amalgamation, a Holy sum of its parts. Were you to remove any part of it, it would cease to be itself. The quality of the rice, the slow warming of the milk. The cardamom, the sugar and the pistachio all built a delicate balance of texture and taste. Even the garnish, the extra bits. Those rose petals are absolutely requisite to the beauty of the pudding." She smiled.

Andy looked at the pudding, "Are you saying my trauma and pain are just a garnish?"

"Everything is just a garnish. Nothing is more or less, in the recipe of the soul. All is one, and we are nothing if not the sum of our parts. When you fixate on not fixating, focus on not focusing, you are in fact just looking deeper into your trauma's eyes. When you allow your pain to be, allow your hurt to inform each and every moment, it asserts less and less control of you."

"It reminds me of getting a tattoo for some reason," reflected Andy. "When you try to ignore the pain, it reasserts itself again and again. But if you just look at it, take it at face value, and allow it to become part of the process, it hurts a lot less. It just blends into it."

"Exactly. Pain is part of the process, part of the pattern. Life is suffering, and life is also beautiful. So suffering must, inevitably, become a part of that beauty."

Andy didn't like that one bit, "I don't like that one bit. Well I do, but it just sounds, well, hard."

"It's not hard, it's just being gentle with yourself. Gentle with the notion that you are going to get tunnel vision. And remembering, inevitably, that its also beautiful to just admire the inside of the tunnel."

"I do love me a good cave. Stalactites and guano and all that good shit."

"Exactly Andy. Guano is good shit," she motioned to the garden around her. "And as we both know, cave shit makes the best kind of fertilizer."

"Growth," was all Andy could say in response.

"You aren't growing. You are growth itself. You, reaching towards the light. Above," she motioned towards the moon, "is the ineffable. And below, is the mundane. The visceral."

"Your experience, your pain, is the bridge in between. Every experience, every struggle... each and every time you marry Heaven and Earth. Eternity wanted to experience pain, wanted to shine its heavenly light upon loss and trauma. And so, here you are. It's all part of your process, all part of your becoming."

Andy looked at the moon, felt Her touch on his skin. And his skin responded with sharpness.

There was peace.

And then there was pain.

But in the pain, again, there was peace.

✚✚

Andy tucked Angie in. He rubbed her head, as he would rub his own. He eased her tension, and he eased his own. She smiled, drifted off to somewhere Andy dared not follow.

No, there was one last thing.

He cracked the door to Terra's room, smiled at her porcelain face. Untouched by time, unbroken. And yet, he knew she would feel pain as deeply as he.

She would know loss as she found distance from whatever angelic realm she had so recently arrived from.

And she would be better for it.

He left her to her dreams, and promised to find her there.

Through the garage, he approached the backyard. His hand felt the cold of the knob, and he took courage in the feeling.

The blue moon stilled the night, and stale snow crunched beneath his feet. He walked behind the shed, the alley between his neighbor's yard and his own.

There was a voice on the wind. It sang a song of loss and death. It was hollow. Not empty, but cavernous, waiting to be fill and be filled.

The voice was his own.

"Wormwood wormwood wormwood," he chanted. "Wormwood wormwood wormwood."

The journey was short, but the cold made the moments stretch. Made his steps a stutter.

He arrived at the chipped birdbath, the water shallow and frozen. The pump seized by the cold.

One one side of the fountain was the flower bed. Dead, a husk of itself. The wind would shake the last petals to the ground before his eyes, he was sure.

On the other side of the fountain, stood a small bush. He had planted it years earlier. It was dead too, probably. This year, everything died. But the foliage was still soft, and it bowed in the wind.

"Hello wormwood," he said, as he let his fingers dance on the leaves.

"Hello Andy," the bush spoke. "Hungry?"

"I thought you'd never ask."

He plucked a single leaf, gave it a little spank to wake it up. So pungent, the bitterness shrill above the frigid night's air. Not a moment to lose, and yet lost to the moment, he tossed the leaf on his tongue.

Wormwood

He heard first, the crack. The crackle. As if the fabric of the universe itself tore into myriad. He saw the tear, the fissure.

No. Not a fissure, but a wisp. A tendril of smoke.

And then, the bush was ablaze. Fully alight, it lit up the night.

Burning bush, nice, thought Andy.

The flames leapt, danced and fed themselves.

And as they grew, they took the shape of a man. An older man, bent by time. Bent by time, and bent by something else, that made him favor one leg.

His face was lined, his hair was gray.

Not much grayer than it is now, Andy thought.

Andy stood before himself, older and perhaps wiser.

"Was I ever so young?" asked Wormwood.

"I think you look great, all things considered."

"I could say the same of you," appraised the older Andy.

"Ah you sweet thing. It's OK, I know what I look like," Andy's self-consciousness showing.

"Battle hardened, but still yourself. Always still yourself," Andy saw a tear in Wormwood's eyes. "I'm glad you chose me as the last."

"You mean Wormwood?"

"No. That you chose me, that you chose *you*. That you

chose yourself. You've been so wrapped up in analogy, so wrapped up in metaphor, that I thought that we'd never get a chance to get some me time."

"Oh, well. I'm glad you're glad," said Andy.

"Do you know what a wormhole is Andy?"

"A tunnel connecting two separate points in space-time?"

"Sure." Andy felt proud. "But no." Andy felt less proud.

"They aren't separate points Andy. They are a continuum. They are not distinct from one another. That's why travel between the two is so damned dilated. Because they are one and the same."

"I feel like quite a few theoretical physicists would take issue with that," warned Andy.

"One and the same. That is Apocalypse for you Andy. That is your *revelation*. Your grand unveiling that you knew from the get go. That the beginning, Andy, *IS* the end."

"Please don't tell me this is some fucking karmic loop of joy, swollen nuts, and rebirth. I was born of the testes and to the testes I shall return," Andy felt sick.

"Not exactly, but rapture and suffering are intimately tied together. And they will visit you again and again and again, forever more."

"What a terrible moral."

"Is it though?" asked elder Andy. "Would you take it all back? Would you free yourself from the karmic cycle? Would you choose ascension? Would you choose absolution?"

Andy swam in his pain. He felt his anger swell, his frustration and sadness clashing in his heart. He felt hopeless, broken, torn away from himself. He felt alone, forgotten. As bitter as wormwood.

Then he saw his mom's face. Caring, doting. She dried his tears, and he saw his mother born again.

He saw Dante, and the Baristo. They became more real in the moments after his death. Once just shadows, he was supported by each of their weight, and he felt the Earth support him through their hands.

He saw Angie's face. The surgery had been to bring her piece of mind, and yet through all of this, she had been the one to bring him piece of mind. A partner, sharing in his pain and his joy. Sacrificing for his rebirth, with every hour she was awake. He loved her again. Over and over again. A love, brand new, yet as old as time. Eternal.

And then he thought of Terra. The extra time with her. The extended story times, the early morning giggles. Even when it was punctuated with irritability and being in constant fear of her flailing limbs, he savored every moment with her. He watched her grow, bathing in the beauty of more time spent.

When Andy saw himself in the mirror, he had nothing but hate. But when Andy saw himself in her, he had nothing but love. She softened him, blessed him with each and every moment. She gave him meaning in the midst of the mire. She reminded him *why*, again and again.

Because Terra gave him beauty. And because Terra gave him love.

"And so Andy, would you take it all back?"

And Terra gave him light.

Most of all, she gave him light. Bright. Maybe blinding.

+++

Fluorescent light. Bright. Maybe blinding.

Andy laid on the table, all but alone, despite the nurse in the corner.

The doctor walked into the room, yet the room remained silent.

Andy offered to break the silence, "How ya doing doc?"

"Shitty," he sneered. "That's why I'm taking it out on you."

Somewhere, not so far, Terra laughed.

And Andy smiled.

Nickolas Paullus is a daddio first and foremost. He lives in Colorado with his lovely wife, kiddo and a gaggle of creatures. He walks, gardens, cooks, and plays. He likes writing quite a bit. He finds it cathartic, magical, and oh so mystical. So he'll probably keep doing it.

Wormwood is his first novel, and unlikely to be his last.

Inquiries, Outquiries, and general "Hey how ya doins" can be directed to

nick.aaron.paul@gmail
nickaaronpaul.com
@nick.aaron.paul (Instagram)

www.ingramcontent.com/pod-product-compliance
Lightning Source LLC
Chambersburg PA
CBHW022112310726
48972CB00007B/2009